In 1939, the world tumbles toward war and

the lives of two young men will be forever changed.

James Brennan grew up in the poorest of Dublin's tenements, turning adversity to advantage wherever he could. But he's nearly a man now—with a good education at that—and wants more from life than what awaits as a day laborer, or following his father into the factory.

Otto Werner is the privileged son of a German diplomat stationed in Dublin. Otto is destined for great things in the new Europe sure to arise after Germany's victory in the war. But he's a lonely young man, living in Ireland with only his father for company, cut off from friends and family back home.

The two teens meet by chance, and each sees in the other a means to advance his own interests. But they become friends, and then—surprisingly, dar_____ As the globe spirals deeper into ch_____ oung men deepens; but their _____ for-bidden love.

As war comes closer and c_____e, everything they believe—about themselves, about each other, about the world around them—will be shattered. Will their love for each other survive the pull toward destruction in a world gone mad?

DUBLIN BAY

Tides of Change, Book One

John Patrick

A NineStar Press Publication

www.ninestarpress.com

Dublin Bay

ISBN: 978-1-64890-411-0

First Edition, October, 2021

Also available in eBook, ISBN: 978-1-64890-410-3

CONTENT WARNING:

This book contains depictions of war, bombings, concentration camps, and mention of past trauma and sexual assault.

Chapter One

SEPTEMBER 1939

I was standing ankle-deep in the murky shallows of Dublin Bay when I first saw Otto Werner. The tide was receding and I was following its path, scraping mussels off the rocks of the break-water with my dull knife. My feet pulled out of the thick mud with a suctioning plop each step I took.

Otto stood at the far end of the pier above me, enduring the attentions of a woman—his mother, I guessed—as she fussed over him, tucking back his hair, straightening his tie, smoothing his lapels. He was nearly as tall as she was.

Just for a moment, a shaft of sunlight broke through the clouds and spotlighted him, a golden youth descended from heaven.

He looked dressed for Mass, or a wake.

My vantage point was limited by the height of the piled rocks, and I needed a better look. I wedged my wooden bucket into a wide opening between boulders and pulled myself up, slipping on seaweed and scraping my side.

The woman released him, smoothed the front of her coat, then placed one hand on top of his head, as if in benediction.

Her other hand gripped her hat as a sudden gust threatened to lift it.

A man who had to be his father stood behind him, looking impatient. The man and his son were both tall, lean figures, with shockingly bright blond hair, although the youth would need to grow several more inches if he was to reach his father's height. They wore hats of an unusual style. The man carried himself with authority and stood as if on parade. The son was gangly but tried to mirror his father's pose now that he'd been released from his mother's arms.

The *Cambria* mailboat was docked farther down, at the end of the pier, and when I pulled my eyes away from the youth, I noticed dozens of people waiting to board, along with stacked piles of trunks and packages staged for loading. All of the passengers were dressed in finery.

It was an odd time for so many people to be traveling to Wales, less than two weeks after the declaration of war.

I climbed down and stepped back into the shallows to continue my work, moving deeper into the bay as I filled my bucket. The top of the breakwater was just above my head, and all sound from the shore was washed out by the waves breaking against the rocks ahead of me. The sun was suddenly bright again, and the harbor waters shifted from deep purple to green and silver.

Once I'd filled my bucket with mussels, I added seawater and fixed the wooden lid to the top. I made my way back to dry land, green strands of rockweed clinging to my calves below my rolled-up trousers. Small cuts covered my fingers, and sandy grit smeared my face from when I'd leveraged myself up for a closer look at the people on the dock.

As I stepped from the narrow strip of stones above the tide line onto the pier itself, I saw the *Cambria* pulling away, steam whistling in a high shriek as the screws churned the water. Terns dove into the frothy mix.

The man and his son were still standing on the dock.

I put my bucket down and stretched my shoulders, then picked it up and walked to the harbormaster's station at the front of the pier. My dad's cousin, Eamon, worked for the harbormaster, and he was leaning against the side of the building next to my bicycle, finishing the black bread and cheese I'd given him when I arrived. He waved forward the group of children waiting their turn at the rocks, and they raced toward the sand with their jumble of buckets and rakes.

Eamon eyed my haul. "Good take, Jimmy?" he asked between mouthfuls.

"Yes, and there'll be plenty left for that gang too." I nodded to the children disappearing down the mudflat.

"Good. I don't mind holding them off for you, but they need to get theirs too."

I righted my bike, and Eamon helped me fit the weighty bucket into the square metal cage above my rear tire. "What's with the mailboat?" I asked.

"That's the Germans. We got word yesterday of some sort of deal to get them home. The ones who wanted to leave, anyway. Makes no sense to me. I'd rather sit the fighting out right here if I was them."

I looked to my right, down the length of the dock, and saw the man and his son heading our way. It was obvious they were German now that I knew—sharp-angled faces and oddly cut clothes. Their hats made me think of the Alps. The son glanced back, once, at the *Cambria* as it made its way through the breakwater and into the bay.

I turned back to Eamon. "Who do you think will win?"

"I don't know. Plenty wouldn't mind seeing the Germans give the English a good thrashing, that's for sure," he replied.

I thought of my older brother, Liam, who'd been spending a lot of time with his IRA pals before he joined the Irish Defense Force. There was no love lost between him and the English. My dad didn't offer an opinion. "Keep your head down and tend to your own," he'd say. "We'll have enough on our plates with our own Emergency." But then, he was often half lost in drink and spared little time thinking beyond the next glass.

"Right. We'll just keep our heads down," I told Eamon, echoing my father.

The man and his son had stopped at the street, beside a fancy black car with a small German flag on its antenna. The youth kept pointing at me as he spoke with his father. I supposed I looked a proper mess.

I'd just gotten my bicycle rolling, not an easy task with thirty pounds of mussels on the back, when the man called out to me.

"Boy. Stop a moment." I barely avoided toppling over as I brought myself to an abrupt halt next to them. I stood on my toes, straddling the bike to keep it steady.

"Those are mussels, yes? Are they for sale?" he asked.

I didn't say anything. They weren't for sale; they were destined for our stewpot at home. Meat of any sort had become quite dear since the Emergency was announced, with rumors of rationing ahead. Most families like mine had resorted to scavenging what they could. And anyway, mussels were working-people food, so why would this German gentleman be interested?

He must have read the suspicion in my eyes. "My son and I are celebrating our first night as bachelors." He glanced at the young man next to him. "Isn't that right, Otto?" Otto. A harsh, foreign-sounding name. Otto remained silent, studying me.

The man turned back to me and continued. "We had them once from a street vendor in France, and Otto loved them, but his mother wouldn't permit them in the house. She said they were too common." He seemed to realize that was a mistake, and he looked aside. "That is... I mean, Otto and I both liked them."

When I didn't respond, he asked, "How much do want for the whole bucket?"

I still hadn't answered his question if they were for sale. The son—Otto—was staring at me. I had strands of seaweed wrapped around my legs, and my gritty hair was plastered to the side of my face. I was puzzling through the man's accent, somehow crisply British yet guttural at the same time. I returned Otto's stare, wondering if he would sound the same.

His piercing blue eyes didn't leave mine as he took a step toward me and held out his hand. "I'm Otto," he said.

Both of my hands had scrapes and cuts and were covered in sand and drying mud. There was no clean surface for me to wipe them.

"Otto..." his father began, before trailing off uncomfortably.

What else could I do? I extended my hand and, as lightly as I could without offending, closed it around his. "Jimmy," I replied. Then, for some reason, I added, "James."

"Hello, James. Would you sell your mussels to us? My father and I wouldn't know where to buy them at the market." His English was much better than his father's but sounded more forced, perhaps because he spoke slowly, as if he wanted to be certain of each word before letting it out.

What was it about this strange, foreign youth that fascinated me? He looked to be about my age, sixteen or so. He was a good four inches taller though, and his skin was a smooth, rich cream, without scars or scrapes or sand or mud. He'd removed his hat and his blond curls shifted about in the wind.

His father spoke again and offered a ridiculous price for the bucket. We could buy a real Sunday roast with that, even carrots and potatoes, and have some to spare.

I schooled my expression. "Oh, sure, that's a fair price for the lot of 'em," I offered as casually as I could.

The man seemed relieved. "Good," he said and glanced at his son, as if seeking to confirm he'd done the right thing.

Otto's wide smile was a surprise. It transformed him somehow.

Something ticked over deep inside me.

Mr. Werner—Otto had made the introductions—said they lived in Beggars Bush and provided the number for their town house. He asked if I'd be able to deliver the mussels right away. I said yes, but I wasn't sure. I didn't know the neighborhood and would most likely have been chased out had I ever dared enter in the first place.

Otto sensed my discomfort and came to my rescue, the first of many times he would do so. "Father, you go on ahead.

It's less than two miles. I'll walk with James and show him the way."

Mr. Werner looked uncertain. I tried to appear disinterested, though for reasons I didn't understand—not then, anyway—I wanted to spend more time with Otto. Mr. Werner looked at my bike and the basket cage with the bucket and decided on the path of least resistance. This is something I would come to learn he did all the time.

"All right." He gave Otto a stern look. "But straight home, yes?"

"Yes, Father, of course."

Chapter Two

SEPTEMBER 1939

My heavily weighted bike was difficult to maneuver, so we walked slowly. It was a busy Saturday afternoon, warm for September, so we avoided the main shopping districts and instead hugged the curve of Dublin Bay, walking all the way up Strand Road and only cutting over once we reached Saint Mary's.

Otto was lonely.

That was clear to me even then, when I first met him. There were no other German children in Dublin near his age, and his mother and sister had gone home. Otto was left with just his father for company, but Mr. Werner's work at the German legation took more and more of his time now that the war had started.

"We're not that important," he declared at one point, after I'd asked about the car. I'd never been in a car and was curious what it felt like to ride in one. "We don't usually get to use it. It's just that the legation was taking people to the dock, and the driver offered to take us home."

"Will they be back? Your mother and sister, I mean?"

"When the war's over, yes."

We walked in silence for several blocks after that. I imagined we were both thinking about what the war might bring. I didn't know any English people, or even other Irish from up north, so Otto was the first person I met whose country was actually "at war."

"Did you want to stay here with your father, or did you want to go home?"

He looked at me and raised an eyebrow, as if surprised by the question. The sun had disappeared again, and a light mist filled the air, scented with the low tide of the bay. Drops of water clung to the tips of his pale eyebrows. "Oh, stay here, of course," he replied. "It's my duty. My father says I must learn English and your culture. The Reich will need young people like me in the future."

"But we're not English," I said.

He didn't respond to that. Instead, he asked me about myself.

"I live in Saint Agatha's Parish, in the North Strand." I looked at the stately buildings gracing the neighborhood around us and didn't mention that my entire family lived in three rooms carved out of a decrepit mansion a hundred years old, or that there was no indoor toilet or running water.

"I just finished my secondary education at the O'Connell School," I added and waited for his reaction. It was a good school, and I was proud of my accomplishment. I hoped to find a respectable, middle-class job. But I'd had no luck so far. Everyone who talked to me about a job saw only a poor boy from the tenements.

Otto hadn't heard of Saint Agatha's, the North Strand, or the O'Connell School. We lived in different worlds.

As we walked deeper into the city, away from the bay, we attracted more and more attention. I stopped. "Hold my bike steady for a second." He did, and I bent over to brush the dried strands of seaweed from my calves, then rolled down my trouser legs. There was nothing I could do about the sand clogs I was wearing; I hadn't brought my shoes. I scrubbed my hands through my hair, releasing a cloud of grit. I had wavy black hair with tinges of red, and after combing my fingers through it, I thought it felt more or less in place.

Otto looked at me critically.

"Better," he said. He reached into his waistcoat and pulled out a white handkerchief. "Here, you can clean your face and hands."

I opened the lid of my bucket and dipped the cloth into the seawater. I wiped much of the dried mud off my face and hands, then stuffed the cloth in my pocket. "I'll get this cleaned and return it to you."

"No, please. Keep it."

We reached Otto's building—a long terrace of granite apartments trimmed in marble. His door was in the middle of the block, beyond a small courtyard. I looked around for a place to put my bike.

"We're going to continue around the block to the back entrance."

Of course. A separate entrance for servants and boys carrying mussels. I was glad I hadn't come alone.

We made our way down the long block of flats, around a corner, and halfway down the back alley. "This is it," Otto said, pushing open a low iron gate and stepping into a small back garden. He held the gate open for me, and I rolled my bike through.

There was a coal truck farther down the alley, and a dairy cart just entering behind it. "This way." Otto approached the back door. I recognized the leafy tops of carrots and turnips in the garden around us, but otherwise the various patches of green meant nothing to me. The door opened into a wood-framed shed that had been built onto the back of the stone building. "You can bring your bike in here."

I had to first remove the bucket, as entering the room required stepping over a stone threshold, and maneuvering my bike over the ledge with the unbalanced weight on the back would have been tricky. Once we were inside, with the bucket settled on the floor and my bicycle propped against the wall, Otto closed the outside door and crossed the narrow width of the room to an interior door. He opened it and stepped through, then held it for me. "Come in, please." He extended his arm into the space.

I picked up the mussels and made my way through the shed, walking past gardening tools and stacked wooden crates, many labeled in German. When I stepped through the door, I found myself in a kitchen and washroom. There was a four-burner oven that had to be gas fed, as there was no space for wood or coal. Two washbasins stood side by side against one wall, and a large bathing tub filled a corner. Cabinets and cupboards lined the walls.

I'd never seen such a fine thing.

Across the room, up two steps, was another closed door. Otto walked toward it. "Come through. We'll go find Father."

"I can't go in there!" I replied in a slightly panicked tone. Even if I were clean, it wouldn't have been appropriate.

Otto looked startled at first, then seemed to realize what he had suggested. "Right. Well"—he looked around the room—"at least tell me how I'm supposed to cook these."

"What? *You're* going to cook them?"

"Well, yes. My mother and sister do all the cooking, normally. But they've gone home now. My father would eat at the pub all the time, but I don't like going there too much." He ran a hand through his hair and looked down at the floor. "I think we make people uncomfortable."

I looked around the kitchen, as if an answer might magically appear. I knew nothing of cooking. There was an old masonry fireplace in one of my family's three rooms, and when there was fuel of some sort, there was usually a stewpot hanging there. But that was the extent of what I knew about preparing food. And there hadn't been fuel for some time now.

"I don't know," I told him. "You just dump them into the pot with whatever's stewing." At least, that's what my mother was going to do with them. "What do you have? Potatoes or onions? Cabbage, maybe?"

Otto looked alarmed. "No. We have none of that. That's not the way they made it in France. It just came in a bowl, in some sort of a broth. With bread too." He looked at the table where a leftover heel of bread sat, probably from the family's morning breakfast. "I didn't plan this very well, did I? Father won't be happy."

He dug into his pocket and pulled out a few coins. "Here," he said, handing them to me. I looked at them in my palm, more money than I'd ever held before. "This is what my father promised you for the mussels." He paused a moment. "It's more than it should be, isn't it?"

"Maybe just a little," I allowed.

He smiled again. "Don't worry. It's okay; I just need to know how things work if I'm going to be managing the household."

I pocketed the money, and we both stood looking at each other. Was Otto also thinking of a way to keep our meeting going? I thought he was.

A plan began to take shape in my mind.

"Listen," I said to him. "Put the mussels in the sink and cover them with cold water. That will pull out the sand. My mother's a great cook. She'll know what to do. I can ask her." That was a lie, nothing more than a delaying tactic. "And then I can come back to help you, maybe?"

Otto reached forward and, for the second time, grasped my hand, using both of his. "Oh, James, that would be wonderful. I can't thank you enough. I want my father to be able to trust me."

I doubted my mother knew anything about making mussels in this French way, but it was a start, and gave me an excuse to come back. Otto placed the stopper in the sink and turned the faucet. Water began pouring out. I'd heard of this but had never seen it. It was like a small indoor pump, but without a handle. What a marvel!

I carried the bucket to the sink and carefully tilted it so the mussels slid into the water.

"Let these sit for a couple of hours. I'll be back, and we'll get you all sorted."

★

The North Strand was a different world than Beggars Bush, but only a couple of miles separated them, and I was home in no time.

At first glance, the buildings on my street looked even more grand than the one Otto lived in. A hundred years ago, each of these buildings had housed a wealthy family and their servants, but over the last decades they'd been chopped into smaller and smaller living quarters. My family's building housed nearly a dozen families, some crammed into just one room. There was one privy out back for everyone, along with a water pump and a shed where a few pigs were kept.

I dashed through the front door and scrambled up three flights, lifting my bike over the heads of a group of boys playing on the second landing. The hallway was dark, and I stumbled to the end where our flat was, praying I didn't step in anything on the way. I pushed open the door. "Ma," I called.

She came around the corner, a short woman with sharp eyes in a dirt-smudged face. Her hands were blackened, and she wiped them on a cloth tied to her waist as she came into the room. "I managed a little coal to heat the stewpot—" She looked up at me. "Jimmy, where are the mussels?"

I ignored her and went to the table, pushed aside a pile of sewing, and withdrew the coins from my pocket. "Look!" I exclaimed, placing them on the table.

Her eyes widened as she came closer. She reached forward and fingered the coins apart, counting. "Where did you get this?" I tried to ignore the note of fear and suspicion in her voice. I didn't blame her. Seeing the coins together like this on our table made it so real.

"I sold the mussels." Even as I said it, I realized that would only increase her concern. No one would pay that much money for a bucket of mussels.

"This is more money than your father earns in a week at the foundry. Don't you lie to me, James Brennan." She gave me *the stare*.

"I'm not lying," I insisted. "There were a bunch of Germans at the dock, leaving on the mailboat. Eamon said there was some deal worked out to get them home. Anyway, this one guy stayed, and he said his kid wanted mussels. And he offered to buy my bucket from me, and this is what he offered."

Even then I felt a twinge of...something...referring to Otto as "his kid." Some deep instinct urged me to hide him.

"But..." My mother looked at the coins again. "That's more than enough for all the mussels in Dublin Bay."

"I know, but there's more. He needs me to cook them for him. He wants to have what he had in France once." I felt a little bit bad about the deception. Cooking the mussels had been my idea, not Mr. Werner's. And the money was still outrageous, even with the work of cooking them.

And, well, it wasn't a *lie*, not exactly. The lies would come later, piles and piles of them.

"Can you tell me how to make French mussels? So I can go back and finish the job?"

My mother was a shrewd woman, and although she still looked at me suspiciously, I could see her calculating. "Why doesn't his wife cook them?" she asked.

"She went back to Germany because of the war. Just this morning. Right before he bought the mussels from me. He hasn't…figured things out yet, I think." *And Otto needs me to do this for him*, I didn't say out loud.

"I have no idea what French mussels are," my mother said. I was about to protest—surely she could tell me *something*—but she continued. "Annabelle is in the basement with the laundry. Go down and tell her to come up. Give yourself a wash when you're down there, then come back." She picked up the coins and put them in her apron pocket.

I didn't know what her plan was, but I didn't stay to ask. I ran down to the basement, where there were a few shared washing tubs and a large stove for heating water. Annabelle was a year older than me and took on whatever jobs she could— mostly laundry and sewing. There were several women working in the basement, laughing with one another as they scrubbed against washboards in the tubs. I gave Bella her instructions, then poured a large bucket of water into a basin. "Hey," protested Clara. She was one of four daughters who lived in the room below ours.

"I'll replace it as soon as I'm finished and fill another for you as well," I told her, stripping off my shirt and trousers, leaving me in just my drawers. I grabbed a rag and began to scrub myself clean.

One of the older ladies gave me a once-over and said, "He makes a fine lad to look at, Clara."

They all laughed at that, and I sped through my washing, dunking my entire head under at the end and giving it a good scrub.

When I was done, I put my shirt back on but left my gritty trousers on top of Bella's laundry pile and ran to the rear yard, where I filled two buckets and returned to deliver them to Clara, who offered me a pretty smile and blushed.

Upstairs, my mom was laying out a clean white apron on the bed, and she told me to put my Sunday trousers on. "I sent Annabelle up to Mrs. Gleason. She worked in that fancy restaurant kitchen. If anyone knows how to make French mussels, it'll be her." She handed me a few of the coins I'd received from Otto. "You're going to take your sister back to those Germans, and she's going to cook their meal. And make sure she does a good job. If the man's foolish enough to pay this kind of money for mussels, he might be foolish enough to pay more for the service.

"Use this to buy whatever your sister tells you she needs, and get a stewing chicken and turnips for us on your way back. A real chicken tonight, Jimmy! Such luck."

Chapter Three

SEPTEMBER 1939

Bella and I made our way across the city, stopping at a nicer market square than the one serving our neighborhood. Thankfully, Mrs. Gleason knew about French mussels and told Bella what she'd need, along with the substitutions we could use if we had to. Butter was the only easy one. After that there was something called garlic, and if we couldn't find garlic, we could use something called shallots. If desperate, we could use leeks. "Just the white parts," Mrs. Gleason cautioned.

Then there was the cooking wine. Cooking wine! Whoever heard of such a thing? Sherry would work if we couldn't find the cooking wine and, if desperate, Guinness.

And it didn't stop at that. There were herbs too—parsley or basil. "But don't get clever," Mrs. Gleason warned. "Better nothing if you can't find those." Finally, she told us a good bakery should have a long loaf of French bread, which we would toast and serve with lots of butter.

We spent nearly an hour at the market, going from stall to stall, but in the end, we emerged with butter, leeks, Guinness, a big round loaf of Irish black bread, and no herbs. We decided we would just make do.

By the time we got to Otto's, I'd convinced myself our inadequate supplies would be a disaster. At the alley gate, Bella stopped and carefully removed the white apron she'd folded under her coat, slipped it on, and tied it neatly in the back. She twirled once in front of me and laughed. "What do you think, Jimmy? I make a likely cook, don't I?"

Before I could I respond, the door opened, and Otto stepped out to greet us. He must have been waiting at the kitchen window.

"You came back," he exclaimed, relief clear in his voice.

"Of course we did. Told you we would, didn't I?" Bella and I stepped through the gate, and my sister immediately proved how clever she could be at subterfuge. "Oh, lovely!" she said, scanning across the herb garden. "That's parsley, isn't it?" She glanced up at Otto as she asked the question, not giving away the fact that she had no idea what parsley might look like.

"Yes," Otto replied. "My mother did have parsley here." He walked over to a patch of tiny flat-leaved greens. "They're getting old now, in September."

"Would you mind terribly if we used some? I wasn't able to find any at the market, and parsley finishes off a dish of French mussels nicely." Bella smiled up at him.

"Please do," he replied. "Miss—?"

"Otto, this is my sister, Annabelle Brennan. She's going to cook your dinner this evening."

★

After the introductions were made, we went into the kitchen. Bella tried for a look of professional detachment, but she couldn't help gaping as she looked about the space, her eyes sparkling.

"There should be snipping shears right in that drawer, Annabelle," Otto told my sister, indicating the top drawer on a blue-painted cabinet between the stove and the washbasins. "Help yourself to whatever you'd like from the garden. Anything you don't find useful will all just go to waste at this point." He turned back to me. "I'm afraid it'll be pub dinners for my father and me from here on in." He grimaced. "How long will it be before the mussels are ready? I'd like to tell him when to expect dinner."

"I'll need an hour," said Bella.

"Perfect. I'll leave you to it, then." He headed to the door and opened it. "I'm so glad you came back," he called over his shoulder.

Once Otto had shut the door behind him, Bella turned to me, grinning. "Oh, Jimmy," she exclaimed, beginning to turn in a circle with her arms held wide. "What a space. We could *live* here! Running water, and a bathing tub, and…is that a *gas* oven?" She hurried over to it. "How does it work?"

"I think you just turn the knob and put a match to that hole down there, and the flame lights. I imagine those burners on the top work the same way."

Bella noticed the tall and narrow wooden cabinet with thick double doors in the far corner. "What's in there?" she asked me.

"Go see for yourself," I told her, folding my arms against my chest and leaning back against the counter, smiling in anticipation. I wanted to see her reaction.

She opened the door on the right side of the cabinet and immediately slammed it shut when she felt the cold air. She whipped around to face me. "An icebox," she whispered in awe.

I'd looked inside when I was here earlier. There was a bottle of milk on the bottom shelf and just a sliver of ice left in the box on top. It had been mostly emptied, probably by Otto's mother before she left. It was clear no one expected the Werner men to do any shopping and cooking, and if Mr. Werner had any plans beyond eating at the pub, he hadn't shared them with Otto.

"It's the future, Jimmy! We're looking at the future."

"Somebody's future, that's for sure."

The meal turned out to be a success.

Bella shared with me all of Mrs. Gleason's instructions, and between the two of us we managed to sauté the leeks without burning them, reduce the Guinness by half, and steam the mussels in the fragrant broth. I sliced and toasted the black bread in the oven, and when Otto came back, he showed Bella how to plate it. She finished it off by sprinkling the chopped parsley over the dish and placing a thick slab of butter on a small plate.

It looked and smelled extraordinary.

"Do you know how to serve?" Otto asked my sister. I couldn't take offense at his question. Neither of us had ever stepped foot in a real dining room before, and Otto must have sensed we were unfamiliar with the finer points of domestic service.

"What? Good heavens, no! I've never done such a thing." She looked at me in panic. "You didn't tell me I'd have to go in there."

"I didn't know," I responded and turned to Otto. "Is this necessary? Bella thought she was just cooking."

"I have a plan," Otto said mysteriously. "It will be easy, Annabelle. Here's what we'll do." Otto took both bowls of mussels and put them on a large serving tray. He took another tray from inside the blue cabinet and placed two small plates, two empty bowls, and the butter on it. As he did so, he instructed my sister on a series of rules for serving at table. Where to put the plates and bowls, how to arrange the utensils and glasses. I could see Bella becoming overwhelmed.

So could Otto. "Never mind," he said. "Just do your best. Give me a couple of minutes to make sure we're both seated, then come in with the platter of mussels and put it on the sideboard—"

"The what?" Bella interrupted.

"The sideboard. It's the narrow table against the far wall. Just walk around the table, to your left…" At my sister's panicked look, he trailed off. "It doesn't matter," he said. "Just make sure you put my father's food in front of him first, then serve me. You can do that, right?"

"Yes…" Bella replied, sounding uncertain.

"And put the empty bowls next to our plates for the shells. The butter and the basket of bread go in the middle between us. That's it." He beamed at Bella. She nodded uncertainly.

"But why are you asking her to do all this?" I asked.

Otto turned back to me. "We can't eat every meal at the pub. I'm going to try to convince my father to have you come back and do this again."

Bella and I looked at each other and tried to conceal our excitement. "I can help you carry, Bella," I said.

"No," Otto said. "You need to stay out of sight." At my frown, he continued, "I told him I found an experienced cook to come today." Bella blanched at that. "It'll be okay," Otto said to her. "He's not fussy, and he'll be thrilled to be served at table. I just don't want him to know yet that you're James's sister."

"You're going by James now?" Bella asked me.

"Let's stay focused on what's important here," I responded, hoping my blush didn't show. "All right, off you go. I'll listen at the door, and when I hear you and your father, I'll send in Annabelle."

Otto gave us a nod and headed into the dining room. Bella was taking deep breaths, and I leaned against the door, listening. After a moment, I heard them settle into place, so I picked up the tray with the mussels and held it out for my sister, who steadied herself and took it from me; then I went and opened the door for her. "Remember," I whispered, "put the tray down on the sideboard first, then bowls in front of Mr. Werner, then Otto. And straight back. You can do this!"

"Thank you, *James*," she said, cocking an eyebrow before disappearing into the dining room.

I busied myself fussing over the next tray, but Otto had already arranged everything on it. Bella came back in and took the tray from my hands and then swept out the room. She was gone longer this time, and I heard Mr. Werner's voice at one point. Then, more loudly from Otto as Bella was coming back into the kitchen, "Thank you, Annabelle. We'll call for you if we need anything else."

Bella collapsed into the chair by the table, shaking with nerves. We both started giggling. When we got that out of our systems, I asked, "How did it go? What did he say?"

"He asked how a filthy, potato-grubbing peasant had gotten into his house." My eyes widened in shock, even though I quickly realized she was kidding.

"Bella..."

"He said, 'This smells wonderful, miss. I'm glad my son brought you in to cook for us.' They have strange accents, don't they, the both of them?"

"I suspect your German would sound worse," I replied. "What did you say? Did you thank him?"

"Well, Otto didn't tell me anything about talking, did he? So I just smiled, and...I think I might have tried to curtsy."

"Jesus! You weren't carrying anything when you tried that, were you?"

"Language, *James*," she admonished me. "Well, I didn't fall over, but I'm afraid I might have looked less than gracious— more like a girl with bad monthlies." This comment got us laughing again. I didn't realize how much tension we'd built up.

"What next, though?" she asked. "Otto didn't say anything about clearing or cleaning up."

"Let's clean up these pots at least, quietly so we don't disturb the Werners." We did, and before long, the door opened, and Otto stepped through, a huge smile on his face. My stomach made a strange little flip to see it.

"That was perfect," he said excitedly. "I asked my father if he'd have you back to make Sunday dinner for us this weekend, and he agreed!" I squeezed Bella's hand. He turned to me. "And if you can gather mussels for us again on Sunday, James, he'd like that too." Bella's clasp tightened in mine. "Since he was so pleased with dinner, I didn't mind telling him that Annabelle was your sister. He'll be in to arrange things. In the meantime, Annabelle, you can come in and clear the plates."

Bella hurried back into the dining room, leaving Otto and me alone. "I hope you don't mind," he said. "I had the impression that you might appreciate the work. There's no obligation, of course, if you'd prefer she not do this."

"Oh, but I *do* appreciate it. Annabelle is always looking for work."

"And I'll be happy to see you back with her too, James," Otto added. It could have been his language skills that made that sound...odd, somehow. But whatever it was, it reflected my own feelings.

Bella came back carrying a tray with empty bowls and plates; then she returned to the dining room, holding the door for Mr. Werner as he came into the kitchen.

"Well," he said to me, "I'd hardly recognize you without half of Dublin Bay stuck to you."

"Yes, sir. Harvesting mussels is a dirty business for sure."

"Father, I don't think you were properly introduced at the dock. This is James Brennan. You've met his sister, Annabelle."

"Yes," he said and did not offer to shake my hand. "You're a fortunate young man to have a sister who knows how to cook, Brennan. She did a very competent job."

"Thank you, sir," I replied as Bella made her way back into the kitchen with the bowls of shells.

"I understand she would be available to do this again on Sunday? Those damn closing hours at the pub on Sunday afternoons are very inconvenient."

Otto cast a quick apologetic glance at Annabelle for his father's use of language.

"Yes, sir, she's an excellent cook and in high demand." I briefly wondered if two lies in one statement was better or worse than two separate lies.

Mr. Werner nodded. "My wife took care of all these things. Otto has convinced me we'll need more support than I was considering. I'll confess I don't know the prevailing wages for a cook's services…?"

I saw Bella freeze at the sink. Why hadn't we discussed this? I had no idea what a cook earned either, but I knew it was a prized job, as much for the food scraps as the coins. I began spluttering when Otto spoke up.

"Father, she spent nearly as much time here cooking, serving, and cleaning as her brother did collecting our food. It's women's work, and easier, but I would think half of what you'd paid for James's services would be appropriate?"

It was my turn to freeze. Did Otto know what he was suggesting? That was more than Bella would earn during a *month* of sewing and laundry. I felt myself beginning to panic—I *liked* Otto and didn't want to take unfair advantage. At least not *too* unfair. I was about to suggest something more reasonable when Mr. Werner agreed.

"Quite right, son. Give the young man the coins for his sister's service."

With that, Mr. Werner nodded to me and retreated back into the house. Otto took the coins out of his pocket and placed them carefully in my palm, letting his fingertips rest for a moment on my calloused palm. "I know. It's a lot. It's okay," he whispered so quietly that I didn't think Bella heard over her washing.

★

After confirming with Otto that his offer to take whatever greens we'd like from the garden was serious, we collected parsnips and carrots, then headed home, stopping at the nicer market again for a stewing chicken. I also bought a few pounds of beef bones and onions. It was traditional in our building that when someone came upon good fortune, there would be a communal stewpot in the basement.

Tomorrow, even the poorest of us would have a rich bowl of beef broth and vegetables.

My mother was thrilled with Bella's success and the fact that she'd been invited back on Sunday. I gave her the change from our shopping, as well as the pay I received for Bella's work. We'd never had so much money in hand before, and my mother tucked it away in her sewing box.

Without any discussion, we all assumed we wouldn't share the news with my father.

He was not reliable with money, especially when he'd been drinking.

He could also be mean. I think Bella was the only one in the family who hadn't felt the crunch of his fist at some point. It was worse when he drank, and that year, he'd begun drinking more than he used to. Last winter, on my sixteenth birthday, when he'd shoved my mother for letting the whiskey supply run out, I hit him back. Liam intervened before things got out of control, but it was close.

At one point, my mother convinced my dad's cousin, Eamon, to go to the foundry where my father worked and ask them to pay his wages directly to her. It wasn't an uncommon story—a man drinking away his wages before his family ever saw them—but the factory refused.

My mother developed a clever coping strategy. When my father's drinking and abuse began to escalate, she would disappear into the confessional with Father Flannery for a long time, far longer than would normally be necessary. We would all begin to fidget, kneeling out in our pew, awaiting our turn with the priest, wondering what sins a woman like my mother could possibly be confessing.

"Sins of the heart," I said to Bella on one such occasion, loud enough that my father could hear. "I bet she's confessing anger and resentment."

Sure enough, she would eventually emerge, and my father would drag himself into the confessional, only to come out later, stricken and shamed. Things would be better for a week or so, until the cycle started again.

The night of our financial windfall, my mother explained the chicken dinner by saying that I'd picked up daywork, which was true in its way.

Liam wasn't home that week to enjoy our good fortune. He was deployed by the Defense Forces on coastal fortification work in preparation for either an English or a German invasion. Both seemed about as likely, and the people of Dublin were divided on which would be the lesser evil.

Chapter Four

SEPTEMBER 1939

Bella spent much of the following week with Mrs. Gleason, learning what she could of the kitchen arts while my mother and I strategized about how to ensure Bella might be invited back to serve on Sundays regularly. With last week's earnings, we bought her a proper cook's cap and a presentable pair of indoor shoes.

We still had enough left over to put in a healthy store of potatoes, cabbage, and root vegetables and to make another pot of chicken stew, which we shared generously with Mrs. Gleason. Rumors of rationing had pushed prices up on everything, and some food staples were becoming hard to find. Even middle-class women were standing in long lines outside of shops, but the newspapers said it was caused by hoarding, as no rationing had gone into effect yet.

I found odd jobs as I could. It had been over a year since I'd graduated from the O'Connell School with my secondary certificate, but I'd yet to find any work in the office-based fields I was now qualified for. No one would look beyond my poverty.

Instead, I relied on occasional work as a day laborer and would harvest shellfish from the bay when no other work was to be found. That week, I laid bricks at one of the new council housing buildings going up around the city and fantasized about how it would be to live in one.

By Saturday night, Bella and I had worked ourselves into quite a state. She was nervous and excited, and so was I. I fooled myself into believing it was because of the importance of the increased income. Seeing Otto again had nothing to do with it.

The plan for Sunday was that immediately after Mass I would head to the bay to harvest the mussels, and Bella would prepare herself at home.

But, instead, I ended up committing a sacrilege.

It started in the wee hours of Sunday morning, when I was abruptly awakened from a deep sleep. I'd been dreaming of harvesting mussels, plodding through the sucking mud of the bay, reaching high overhead to scrape and cut the mollusks off the breakwater. Unexpectedly, Otto was with me, harvesting by my side. It was a warm day and we both went without shirts, sand and grit sticking to our chests. Otto was right next to me, almost touching. I could feel the breath of his exertions and hear his soft grunts as he worked. He looked up, over my shoulder behind me, and said, "I want that one." He smiled and reached up over my head toward the rocks above me, leaning into me as he did so, his chest taut against mine.

I startled awake, gasping, feeling myself spend in my drawers, pulse after pulse. Next to me, my father let out a choked snort and rolled over, puffing cheap whiskey and tobacco into my face. Thank God, my brother wasn't home. Even sleeping crosswise at the base of the bed, as he tended to do, he would have known.

Then the horror of the timing struck me. It was Sunday morning. I'd confessed yesterday and Mass was just a few hours away. I couldn't receive Communion after having sinned without confessing first. I thought about what I knew of sins, both from the priests and from the schoolyard.

I supposed this *might* not have been a mortal sin, if I wasn't aware that it was happening, if I'd played no role other than being "steeped in lust," as Father Flannery would say. But he was clear on this. The sin of self-abuse was a mortal sin if done intentionally and for pleasure; it perverted God's plan and made a mockery of the sacred procreative act.

Perhaps I'd only pissed the bed? Both my father and my brother, deep in drink, had done that. It was disgusting and annoying, but not a sin. I rubbed my fingertips together and felt the oily slickness and realized that no, I hadn't pissed the bed. And, given the mess in my hands, I must have played *some* role.

No, it was certain. I had sinned.

I'd confessed the sin of self-abuse to Father Flannery nearly every week since I was twelve. I imagined most boys did, and he probably tired of hearing it. It was always a perfunctory affair. "Resist evil in your heart, child. Say ten *Hail Marys.*" But this was different. Otto made it different. Would I need to confess the nature of my dream?

Again, I felt an instinctual need to keep Otto hidden from the world, even from the confessional. Or, perhaps, *specifically* from the confessional.

But what to do? If I'd committed a mortal sin, I couldn't take Communion, and to ask Father for an emergency confession on a Sunday morning, when he was preparing for Mass, was a heavy burden to put on him. But sitting out Communion had its own risks, as everyone notices and rumors spread.

I decided to get up early and hurry to Saint Michael's Parish, where no one knew me. I would beg a confession from the priest there and make it back to Saint Agatha's in time for Mass.

It didn't work out that way. The priest at Saint Michael's had no time for me, and the same was true at Saint Brigid's. By the time I got home, I was late to Mass and ended up taking Communion anyway, compounding my mortal sin with *intentional* sacrilege and thereby most likely damning my soul to hell.

Later, I'd come to learn that the priests were right. Sin really does build upon sin.

Chapter Five

SEPTEMBER 1939

Having started down the path of sin and sacrilege, was it any surprise that I added pride, or maybe it was hubris, to my spiritual burden that morning?

Whatever its name, I paid a boy to do work I was capable of doing myself. I'd ridden my bike down to the harbor as I always did, bread and cheese tucked away for Eamon, my bucket lodged in the bike's basket and my knife in my belt. Eamon looked at me sheepishly, and I saw the crowd of children already working the breakwater. "I'm sorry, Jimmy. I can't accept your offer today. I couldn't hold them back, could I? Not with the food shortages."

"Of course you couldn't. You did the right thing." I pressed the bread and cheese on him anyway. "How are you making out?"

"All right," he said. "I've got steady work, unlike others." He frowned after he said that, realizing a bit late that I was one of the ones without a regular job.

"No worries," I assured him. "I've been working on one of the new council estates, and Bella's managed some housework here and there."

"Well, good for you, then."

In fact, once I thought about it, I realized I didn't *need* to be down there with the others, scraping food off the rock pilings. At least not this week. I hopped back on my bike. "I'll be seeing you, Eamon."

I began pedaling down the dock, away from the street, toward a young boy struggling with a filled bucket a quarter his size. "Lad!" I called. "Wait a moment." He seemed grateful for the excuse to put his bucket down. "Are those mussels you've just collected?"

"Aye," he responded, perhaps suspiciously. And I didn't blame him.

"I'll buy them from you." I named a price, not an extravagant one, but more than fair, and more than he would get at the market if he'd intended to sell them.

I was surprised when he said, "Sorry, but food's tight; my family needs these."

"But I have my own bucket," I replied, nodding toward it in my basket. "You can dump your mussels in there, I'll pay you, and you can go collect another bucketful for your family's dinner."

He looked at me as he puzzled his way through this offer, no doubt suspecting a trick of some sort. But I saw the moment he realized he could pocket the money and none would be the wiser.

"All right then, but give over the coins first." Smart lad.

We made the exchange, and I wedged my now full bucket into its wire cage. The boy whistled a soft tune as he headed back to the rocks, his bucket empty and his pocket full.

I was walking my bike down the dock, passing by the harbormaster's shack. I gave a wave to Eamon, who had eyed me curiously through the interaction with the boy, and turned back to the road.

And there was Otto.

★

He was dressed in a ridiculous fashion with tall sturdy boots and the sort of coverall you might see on a factory worker. He wore a wide-brimmed hat and carried thick gardening gloves.

"James," he called out to me in surprise. "You're finished already? I must have read the tide chart wrong."

"What are you doing here?" I thought my tone might have sounded accusatory. "Why are you dressed like that?"

He looked down at himself, then back at me and smiled. It was the same smile he'd given me in my dream last night, a crooked one that created a dimple in his left cheek. "I was going to help collect dinner," he said as if that was both evident and sensible. He leaned forward, inspecting me. "Why are you so clean?"

"You were going to *help*?" I had another uncomfortable recollection of my dream. "You can't help." I looked down the bay at the group of children working the rocks. "You can't go down there."

"Why?"

"Because they're harvesting food to feed their families. It's obvious you don't need to do that. It would be like…like you're making fun of them…or something." It was all still new to me at the time, Otto's blindness to class and culture.

Otto's face fell. He looked stricken. "Oh, I'd never intend... I didn't mean to offend. I didn't think."

I managed to get him turned around and had both of us heading back to the street. "I know you didn't mean anything by it. It was actually sort of a nice idea. It just would have looked bad, you know?"

"See? This is what I was trying to explain to my father. *This* is the sort of thing I need to learn. Not Latin and trigonometry. The Reich needs leaders in the new territories who understand the people and culture."

New territories? What does that mean?

Before I could ask, Otto said, "Come on, let's get these home." We walked along the bay again, following the same route we'd taken the prior week. I explained about how I'd bought the mussels from a young boy and what a windfall it would be for him; plus, it kept me from getting filthy.

"You were like some sort of sea creature when I first saw you coming out of the bay. I pointed at you and said to my father, 'Look, it's a kraken!' You had seaweed hanging off you everywhere and were covered in mud. My father laughed and said you were probably harvesting mussels. That's when I remembered about the mussels he loved so much in France. I didn't care for them. I just wanted to meet you, so I had to make something up."

That sent my head spinning for sure.

"What? You just made all that up, about wanting mussels for dinner?"

"Yes! I know, it was clever of me." He looked ridiculous walking through the city in his boots and coveralls, but he held his head high and waved his arm to indicate the two of us. "And it all worked."

"But…but, why?" I asked. I was struggling to understand what was going on.

"Well, like I said, I wanted to meet you, for one thing." He looked over at me. "You really were a sight!" When I didn't respond, he continued, "And, well, I sort of thought that maybe you wanted to meet me too? I mean, you know, the way you were staring at me, peeking up over the rocks while my mother was trying to squeeze the life out of me."

I didn't realize he had seen me, and it never occurred to me that he'd pay any attention if he had. A warm flush crept across my face, and I briefly wished I hadn't bought the mussels, so Otto and I could be scraping them off the rocks together right now. He looked at my face and smiled again.

"And I was bored. So very bored. You don't know what it's like, James. Even before so many went home, there were no other boys my age. And my teacher left in the beginning of the summer. And now my father says they're having difficulty finding another."

"You have your own teacher?" This was such an odd idea to me. My class at the O'Connell School had over thirty boys in it.

"Yes. There are no schools here that would be appropriate for me. My government pays the expense of private instruction for the children of all staff at foreign offices. Last year there were two of us, although Karl was much younger than me, so we were never friends."

We continued walking north along Dublin Bay. I was balancing my bike with its heavy bucket, and Otto was humming softly to himself. What was a "kraken," anyway? And did this mean Otto thought we could be friends? Was that even possible?

★

We arrived at Otto's at the same time the ice man was pulling his truck into the alley. A small group of children paraded behind it, eager to gather ice chippings to suck on or to throw at one another. After shaping a block of ice suitable for Otto's icebox, he used a pair of oversized metal tongs to carry it into the kitchen. I wondered if those tongs came from the foundry where my father worked.

I emptied the mussels into the sink and covered them in cold water while Otto paid the ice man.

"Otto," I began cautiously when he'd returned from seeing the ice man out, "that's at least five times what he should be charging you for ice." I didn't want to ruin my own good fortune, but I hated seeing Otto taken advantage of like that.

"It is?"

"Yes. Didn't your father negotiate this contract?"

"No, my mother handled all of this, and I don't think she was good about it. I've been telling my father we need to get organized. It's all fallen to me." He looked around the kitchen. I thought he was embarrassed. "We're low on coal too, and I don't even know who's supposed to deliver it or if I'm supposed to reach out to them somehow." He sank into the chair by the table and leaned his head back, letting out a long sigh. He looked defeated. "I need help, James."

He sure did. I imagined they were being overcharged across the board. The thought bothered me in a way it wouldn't have just a week earlier.

Otto looked over to the bathing tub in the corner. "I was going to suggest you have a bath this time to get the sand and grit off, but no need now, I suppose." If Otto's morning had gone as he'd planned, we'd both be in need of baths right now. How would that have gone, I wondered.

An idea popped into my head. It was crazy, but... "I can have a talk with the ice man, get him to charge something more reasonable, if you'd like." Otto looked up at me from his seat with a hopeful expression on his face. He was silent for a minute or two, thinking. Then, as if he'd made a decision, he rapped his knuckles on the table in front of him and stood up.

"I would be extremely grateful if you did that, James. I'm going to talk to my father first. He's at work. They're all working endless hours now that the war's on—though you'd never know it by how dull *my* life has become. I never see him except for meals anymore." He looked around the kitchen, then walked to the bathtub and placed his hand on the rim. He appeared to be about to say something but changed his mind. "Well, it seems there's nothing left to do here. Shall we go collect Annabelle?"

As if I'd let Otto see how I lived.

"No, I'll go home and get her. You can go tell your father he should be home in three hours for dinner."

As it happened, that was the day everything changed for me. For us.

Sometimes, major turning points in life are only recognizable in hindsight, after some distance and consideration. Not this one.

Otto talked to his father and explained about the ice man, and the coal delivery, and the food shortages. By the following day, Bella had regular employment and a new career as a house-maid, and I'd been hired too. As a…a house manager, I supposed. After all, one doesn't hire a companion for one's sixteen-year-old son.

It was a win for everyone. I was able to save the Werner family a great deal of money on services they'd been grossly overcharged for, and Bella and I now earned twice as much in a week than my father did working full-time at the foundry in a month.

My mother was ecstatic, but it was a terrible secret for the three of us to keep.

Chapter Six

FEBRUARY 1940

No invasion came that autumn, and by Christmas, it felt as if the tension of waiting for one had reached a boiling point. Sporadic shortages of goods left everyone in a foul mood, and merchants throughout the city made only half-hearted efforts to decorate their stores. Petrol was officially rationed, but I didn't know anyone who had a car, so it meant little to me. Food availability had evened out somewhat, but everything was much more expensive.

My father drank too much and more frequently, and Liam became more radicalized as hundreds of IRA men were rounded up and imprisoned under the Emergency authorizations.

Bella and I had secret pouches sewn into our underclothes where we stored our money. My mother feared that my father would find it anywhere she hid it in the house. Bella harvested the remains of the Werners' herb and vegetable garden, and we buried a tightly sealed tin of money there as well. Bella turned out to have a knack for cooking, and Mrs. Gleason was thrilled to teach her and to benefit from our new good fortune.

I turned seventeen in February, and when Otto learned it was my birthday, he insisted on a small celebration. "It's so gloomy here in the winter," he explained to his father, giving him an excuse for the celebration that was about his son and not about me.

Mr. Werner had Bella purchase a bakery cake. It was extravagantly rich in butter and sugar, and we were permitted to take most of it home with us. My mother brought a generous slice up to Mrs. Gleason, and the rest we took down to the laundry in the basement, thereby avoiding awkward questions from my father.

Other than that, we kept a low profile at home, and to my knowledge there were no rumors about our improved circumstances.

Otto and I spent more and more time together. I helped with his English and taught him Irish culture. He taught me about the world beyond Dublin. If Mr. Werner was concerned that his household manager was becoming more of a friend to his son than was appropriate, well, it was easiest for him not to see it.

Meanwhile, as winter melted into spring, my spiritual descent into eternal damnation continued unabated.

I hadn't again committed the sacrilege of receiving Holy Communion without confessing my sins first, but I hadn't developed the courage to go to confession either, especially as my propensity to commit the sin of self-abuse had only worsened as I spent more time with Otto. Worse, I lied to my family, saying that I was taking Communion at Saint Mark's on Sundays because it was closer to my work at the Werners.

Eventually, it became too much for me, living in a grace-less state, piling mortal sin upon mortal sin. I prepared myself as best I could and went to confession to clear my soul of both the sin and the sacrilege. It didn't go as I'd hoped.

I knelt in the darkness of the confessional booth, my face inches from the thick mesh screen, sweat dripping down my sides as I tried to clear my mind, focusing on the scent of wax and incense. The small wooden partition behind the screen slid to the slide, and I saw the vague outline of Father Flannery's profile.

"Bless me, Father, for I have sinned. It has been nearly six months since my last confession."

"Six months? That's a long time. What are your sins, child?"

"There are two mortal sins, Father." I knew not to delay at this stage. It was best to get straight to the point, no matter how embarrassing or shameful. "I've committed the sin of self-abuse, Father, then deepened my shame by taking the sacrament of Communion without having confessed." I was fooling myself, hoping to get away with this partial description, hoping he didn't do the math.

He was silent for a moment. "And why have you not sought absolution for your sins prior to now? Have you continued to take Communion?"

Well. This was the heart of it, wasn't it? I had hoped…but no, nothing can be hidden from God. "Father, I have not taken Communion. But I have committed the sin of self-abuse more than once since then." Being around Otto every day had…confused me. I was plagued by inappropriate thoughts and feelings.

"You know that a confession must be full and complete, as well as sincere, to remove the stain of the sin?"

"Yes, Father."

"How many times have you committed this sin since your last confession?"

I had hoped it wouldn't come to this. But just in case, I'd made an effort to reconstruct the history last night, scratching out notes with dates and times, estimating when I couldn't remember, then burning the evidence when I was finished. I realized I had let myself fall into the depths of depravity.

"Seventy-three, I think. I may have missed a couple."

There was a barely concealed gasp from behind the screen.

"You realize that had you died with this mortal sin on your soul you would have been damned to hell for eternity?"

"Yes, Father."

"And yet you persisted, regularly, all that time?"

"Yes, Father. I'm truly, heartfully sorry. I want to repent."

"This is very serious. Most young men find it difficult to resist this sin completely, but rarely have I seen the devil so fully in control of a lustful heart as he has taken hold of yours."

I swallowed and waited.

"You understand that committing this sin even once is in an affront to God? A perversion of his sacred plan for the union of a man and a woman?"

"Yes, Father."

Father Flannery shifted his position behind the screen. "Do you…think…of the same girl? Each time?"

Otto. God help me, I thought of Otto each and every time. His smile, his eyes, his hair, his hands.

"Yes," I lied, maybe. It was the same *person* each time, after all.

"When this urge comes upon you, have you tried shifting your focus? Think instead about marrying this girl. Envision raising children together, going to Mass as a family, taking Communion."

Was this a suggestion? A question? Obviously, I couldn't think of Otto that way. I was getting light-headed and increasingly certain I was lying. In the confessional! I snapped. I couldn't sever my relationship with God forever this way.

"It's a boy," I whispered.

In the end, Father Flannery refused to offer me absolution until I had successfully completed penance and proven that I could challenge the sinful urges taking control of my actions. True, I had expected more than having to say ten *Hail Mary*s, but I hadn't expected two solid days of fasting—water only—and a daily journaling requirement on the holy sacrament of marriage and how it fulfills God's plan.

I really did try.

On the second day of my fast, I arrived at the Werners' late in the afternoon. I was light-headed, but determined, and felt good about the progress I'd made fighting off the devil and recommitting myself to Christ. Imagining myself married and raising a brood of Catholic children didn't really do it for me, but reflecting on Jesus's suffering on the cross did. "You don't want that horrific pain and agony to be in vain, do you, child?" Father Flannery had asked. No. No, of course I didn't.

I've thought back frequently to that afternoon at the Werners'. Had I arrived early? Was I late? Had Otto forgotten I would be there that afternoon? Had Otto *planned* what happened?

I stepped through the shed and into the kitchen. Otto was in the tub, leaning over with his back to me, naked, his spine outlining an elegant curve, his shoulder muscles contracting as he vigorously scrubbed his hair.

I let out a sound. A cough, maybe? Otto turned and looked at me, wet curls slapping his face, and he smiled. "Oh, James," he said. "Good. You're here."

There was no such thing as privacy in my world. Growing up, I was accustomed to nudity of all sorts. On wash days, the basement of our building would be filled with men and boys waiting their turn at the tub. So why was seeing Otto naked so…arresting?

It had been nearly two full days since I'd eaten, and a wave of dizziness came over me. I stumbled to the chair and sat down just in time, closing my eyes and focusing on my breath. This was a test, clearly. God was testing me, and once I made it through, I could be absolved of my sins and returned to a state of grace.

"James?" Otto called, a note of alarm in his voice. A splashing sound caused me to open my eyes even as I told myself not to. Otto was climbing out of the tub and reaching for his drawers at the same time. He slipped them on and, still soaking wet, padded over to where I sat. He pulled up a chair and turned it to face me. He sat down, knees bumping mine, and reached his hands forward to clasp mine. "James. What's wrong?" he asked, peering into my face.

I was cursed. Here he was, nearly naked and touching me. His thin underclothing wet and clinging to his form.

I closed my eyes again, willing myself to feel Jesus's crown of thorns, the blood dripping into his eyes. The nails in his palms.

"I haven't eaten," I managed to say.

"What? Do you mean since breakfast?"

"No. Since the day before yesterday."

"What?" Otto exclaimed. "Nothing at all?" He was angry and not bothering to hide it.

"I'm doing penance," I admitted.

Otto was already on his way to the icebox even as I said that. "Ridiculous," he muttered, opening the door and removing a bottle of milk and a plate of leftover chicken. He brought it to me.

"Drink this," he commanded, thrusting the bottle at me.

He was my Eve.

"I can't," I said. "I need to finish my penance or Father won't absolve my sins."

Otto rolled his eyes at that. "Sins. The more I learn of you people, the more odd I think you are. Drink this," he told me again, waving the bottle in my face. I shook my head against the idea.

He leaned right over me then, getting me wet, as he was still dripping himself. "Listen. I'm bigger than you, and I'll hold you down and force you to drink this if I have to." He *was* bigger than me, even more so than when we'd first met, six months earlier. Yes, he was a few months younger than me, but he'd shot up over the winter and had to be at least six feet now. I thought about Otto holding me down and squirmed uncomfortably.

"Please," I begged. I didn't know what I was begging for.

He stood, then took the milk bottle and placed it on the table next to me. "Fine. But I'm not giving up. Tell me what these sins of yours are that require you to starve yourself."

Could I tell Otto? Not about his role in all of this, obviously, but about what sins tormented me? We'd become friends, in a way, as much as two young men from different stations and cultures could be. Perhaps he'd have a perspective or, better, a solution that I couldn't see. I didn't think he would judge me or reject me out of hand.

"All right," I told him. "But first, please put some clothes on."

He huffed but crossed the room to grab his towel, which he wrapped across his shoulders before coming back to sit in front of me again. He was still mostly naked. He saw my look but shook his head. "I don't want to go get dressed right now. You'll close down again if I leave you alone. Tell me what happened."

I needed strength for this. I sent a quick prayer to the Virgin Mary and began.

"You'll be disgusted," I whispered. "But please hear me out, and promise me you won't repeat this."

"I promise, James." He leaned forward and peered into my eyes, his concern clear. "What have you done that is so horrible?"

I took a deep breath. "Recently, I've been failing to resist temptation. Father Flannery says it's the devil seizing my heart and that it's very serious and that my soul is in jeopardy." I'd been looking down, but I risked a glance up at him to see his reaction so far. He just looked at me, expressionless.

"Go on."

"I've been committing the mortal sin of self-abuse. I know it's wrong, which makes it even worse, because I do it anyway. A lot. I don't know how to stop."

"I don't know this word, self-abuse. Are you…harming yourself, somehow?" He glanced across my face and arms, looking for signs of injury.

"What? No! Self-abuse is a sin. It's the sin of…um… pleasuring yourself?"

I realized this was going to be harder than I'd thought. I suspected his private teacher didn't teach him the words for mortal sins.

He shook his head and frowned. "I'm sorry, James. I know this is important to you, but I don't understand."

I felt myself turning a deep red and wished that I'd never started this conversation. But I knew Otto and knew he wouldn't give up.

I moved my hand over my crotch and mimed what I was talking about, a quick pass, just two brief strokes. "Self-abuse," I repeated, shame flooding through me. And then it occurred to me: What if Otto didn't know about self-abuse? What if he was a better person than I was and had never been tempted to that particular sin?

Otto's eyes lit up. "*Wichsen*?" he asked. A German word I didn't understand. "Oh, what's the English word…wanking? Yes, that's it, I think." He demonstrated a more thorough miming of the activity than I had managed, complete with a twisting of the wrist and circular thumb movement that hinted at an advanced technique. Even that triggered a sinful reaction in me.

"Yes." I looked away. My face was burning brightly.

"These priests make you starve yourself for wanking? That seems like a stiff penalty." He laughed. "Look, I made an English pun!" He seemed delighted by that, even though I'd confessed to something that would doom my soul to hell for all eternity.

"You're serious though, aren't you?" he asked, sobering quickly when he saw my distress. I nodded.

"But…but all boys wank."

"Maybe," I allowed, "but we're supposed to at least try not to. It goes against God's laws. And…well, I've been doing it a lot, even knowing it's sinful. Like, several times a week." I couldn't look at him after this. I was afraid I might cry I was so filled with shame.

"Well, I think your priests might be mistaken. Where's the harm? I do it almost every day. My last teacher said it was normal for teenage boys."

What? Otto committed the sin of self-abuse daily and didn't think it was a problem? How could this be? He wasn't Catholic, of course. Maybe it's not a sin for non-Catholics? But that can't be right, can it? Sin is sin, no matter who commits it. Although, just by not being a Catholic, Otto was going to spend eternity in hell anyway, so maybe it didn't matter?

"Is it not a sin in your religion?"

"I don't know. Maybe it was at some point. I guess in our modern religion we just don't worry so much about sins that don't hurt other people."

Suddenly, his wide smile bloomed on his face. I realized that while he was talking, I had, without thinking, reached over to the table, picked up the bottle, and taken a long drink of milk. "Good," Otto said. He picked up a piece of chicken and tore a sizable bite off for me. "Here," he said, handing it to me.

I ate it because at that point I was beyond redemption. I couldn't even fast for two days, and the things Otto was saying confused me and, if I was honest, aroused me too. He was a good person. Surely he and all the other Protestants couldn't *really* be condemned to hell, could they? What kind of a God would do that?

In hindsight, I think I was just waiting for a trigger, something to open my eyes to all the thoughts and doubts that had been stirring in my mind for years. Something to make the alternative *real*.

"Back home, a few of my friends and I would wichsen together. It was just for fun. But then one of them found a girlfriend, and right after that I moved here." He scooted his chair closer to mine. We were still facing each other, and now his knees were between mine. His tone was light, but I could tell something serious was going on in his head. "Don't Irish boys do that together sometimes?"

I remembered all the times when I and the other boys from my building would…wank…behind the pigsty in the back courtyard. Other than the privy—and no one spent more time there than absolutely necessary—it was about as much privacy as we could find, and frequently there would be a group of boys involved, some keeping watch while others quickly relieved themselves into the muddy filth. I'd been one of those boys on many occasions. But it was still a sin, to be confessed the following Saturday.

But what I'd been doing was worse than that. I was no longer just a boy scratching an itch, laughing with the others, thinking about girls. No. I was nearly a man, day after day, thinking of Otto. And here he was now, his left knee gently nudging the inside of my right knee, a question on his face.

"Yes," I conceded. "Sometimes they do." But not like me. Not with a sinful heart.

Otto smiled at me again. "Let's do it now," he said, which, if I was honest with myself, I'd suspected was coming. *Wanted* to happen. "You'll see it's not so bad. It'll be fun, and then you can relax about it." He didn't wait for me to respond. I think he knew I'd do my best to say no. Instead, he pressed his knees farther apart, tightly against mine, and slid his hand up his thigh to his crotch.

I had already delivered my soul into hell, but Otto had just slapped a padlock on the gate and swallowed the key.

Chapter Seven

MAY 1940

By May, Dublin had begun to settle, just a little. It's hard to maintain a level of imminent panic and anxiety over such a long stretch, and it had been nine months since war was declared. Still, people kept asking, when would the war *really* start? When would the invasion come? Would there be bombing? And, most importantly, would Ireland be able to retain its neutrality?

Many people had thought the war would be over by now. Instead, it was like it had been announced, then put on hold. The IRA was more of a problem than either the English or the Germans, and I was concerned my brother was getting in too deep with them.

"My father assures me it will be over soon," Otto told me one afternoon, one of the first warm, dry days of the season. We were walking along the Liffey, *taking our leisure*, Otto called it. What a world I had entered!

"The Reich has already settled into Poland, Denmark, and Norway. The low countries will be next." He glanced over and gave me *the look*, the one that said *I probably shouldn't have told you that*. "But Father says after that, France and England will likely just surrender, and then we'll be done." It seemed so simple when he put it that way. But, from what I read in the paper, I couldn't imagine the people of Belfast simply surrendering. Let alone the people in London.

"I'm going to ask for a post in Ireland." He flinched then and looked away from me. That was the look that said, *Shit, I* really *shouldn't have said that.* "Northern Ireland, I mean." Neither of us said anything for a moment. "Would you like that?" he asked. "We could both move to Belfast. There'd be plenty of work for you there after the war. I could probably help with that."

I didn't like to think about *after* the war. I'd come to an uneasy truce with myself and with my soul. My plan was to live life recklessly during the Emergency. Yes, I knew I was piling up a tally of mortal sins, but surely others were too. Once things were back to normal, after Otto went home and the country settled down, I could go back to normal too. I'd reconcile with the Church, be in communion again.

God would forgive me, but I knew I couldn't ask him to do that just yet.

And Otto. Always confident, always talking about the future.

Always bringing me in closer.

Wanking together had become wanking each other and, later still, lying together afterward, shoulders touching, which somehow seemed more intimate and frightening than the other thing. In those moments he would make ridiculous statements. "The whole future is ours, James! We can become anything we want to be." Otto made me dizzy.

But that afternoon on the banks of the Liffey was the first time he'd proposed specific plans for the future, for both of us.

"Otto, what are we doing?" I asked. "I mean, we can't make plans together. It's not like that."

He reached over and took hold of my elbow. "Stop," he said. "Come sit." He directed me to an iron bench beside a stone retaining wall. A purple flowering tree was dropping the last of its petals onto the seat. Otto brushed them off and sat, pulling me down next to him.

"I've scared you," he said. Had he? Not scared exactly. He was more disorienting than scary.

"When we can travel again, I want you to see Germany. You will come stay with my family in Dresden; then we will travel to Berlin—the new capital of the world, James! It's very cosmopolitan." He looked at me intently, as if he were communicating a secret message. "I knew an older boy back home—a man, really—who said Berlin had been quite…open, progressive even…before all this, a decade or so ago. He said when he was a teenager, he went to a club where men danced with men! Can you imagine such a thing?"

No. There was no world where that would be possible.

Before I could respond, we were interrupted by the call of a newsboy making his way down the quay, carrying his stack of newssheets in a canvas bag slung over his shoulder. "Germany invades Belgium! France to be next!" he called out, selling the papers to men crowding him for the news.

"See? Don't worry, James; it's all going to be fine."

But it wasn't all fine. Not at all.

Belgium, Luxembourg, the Netherlands—all falling within a matter of days. Otto's father spent most of his time at the legation, coming home only for the occasional meal and to sleep for a few hours. Otto and I spent nearly all of our time together too. He had thankfully backed off talking about the future—our future—so much.

"It's all going to go quickly from here on out," he said one dark afternoon in the middle of May, rain bucketing down outside. We were lying in his bed on our backs, having just concluded *wichsen time*, as Otto playfully called the mortal sin that I continued to repeat, and for which I was becoming less and less repentant.

We'd taken to having meaningful conversations like this, after wichsen time, naked and exposed. It was so easy to be honest then, or more accurately, it was difficult to be *dishonest*, to build walls between each other.

Something I'd read in the paper had been bothering me. "Belgium was a neutral country," I stated, looking up at the carved plaster molding along the ceiling where it met the walls. Otto's shoulder slid against mine as he shifted.

"Yes, but it was necessary to have a pathway for our tanks to get to France. The Belgians will be fine. Already they're finding their place in the Reich. Not too many people were hurt. It was over quickly." He didn't answer the question that I didn't ask, about Ireland. But he knew me well, and after a few more moments of silence, as our breathing returned to normal and our spend—the very heart of the sin!—chilled on our stomachs, failing in every way to fulfill God's plan, he answered anyway. "There would be no need to invade Ireland; it's not in the way of anything."

That wasn't the talk on the streets. Now that the German army was on the move, people thought that England might insist we take sides in their war, and if we refused, they might invade. Or, perhaps the Germans would invade to provide a rear front against the English.

People were hoarding food again, and prices were rising rapidly.

"And you said France would quickly surrender. But instead there's fighting there now."

"France *will* surrender. Britain too. Then the war will be over." Otto sat up then and swung his legs over the side of the bed, signaling an end to both wichsen time and to honest discussion. He leaned over and grabbed his drawers, then pulled them on as he stood. He picked up the damp cloth by the washbasin and wiped himself down, then handed it to me.

I used it and then scrambled out of bed too. I hated being naked when Otto was dressed. That made everything feel unbalanced and wrong—well, more wrong—somehow.

"I have something else to tell you," Otto said as we both finished getting dressed.

There was a mirror on the wall in Otto's bedroom, and I was momentarily caught off guard by my reflection. I was so *clean* now, all the time. I bathed regularly in Otto's kitchen, washed my hair, owned better clothes. I looked like a proper young man, with a healthy diet and a well-paying job. It was the future I'd wanted, here now, but built on what foundation? And at what cost? I looked at the bed.

As if reading my mind, or at least sensing my discomfort, Otto came up behind me and smoothed down my hair where it had been sticking up. He did this more and more lately, light touches and intimacies, not uncommon among friends, but weighted with meaning coming from Otto. We looked at our reflection together. If I were the type, I'd reach up and do something about Otto's wildly messy blond curls, but I wasn't and I didn't.

"I have a new instructor coming. He's American."

An American! There was a romanticized view of America among Irish youth at the time. So many of the Irish people had made their way to that fabled land of plenty. Liam said it was a country of the future, with strong unions and plenty of jobs. Plenty of food too.

"He's a graduate of Harvard University in Massachusetts, I think."

"When does he arrive?" I asked as I began to think through what Otto starting up his lessons again might mean for us.

"Within the week. He'll be boarding nearby, but he'll be here most of the time during the day."

Well, that would be sure to cut down on wichsen time. I was surprised by the pang of disappointment that thought prompted. We made our way down to the kitchen and to the icebox, where there were always leftovers from a meal that we could snack on. I thought Bella's plan was that I would mostly eat here, generating even more savings for the family budget.

"I think my father and your brother have the same thoughts about Americans. He thinks they're leading the way into the future. A little too democratic, he says, but they'll come around after the war when they see how successful the Reich is."

I wasn't sure about that. I knew the Irish press was heavily censored as part of the Emergency, but sometimes it felt like Otto and I were seeing two different wars playing out. I didn't say that, though. "I'll let Bella know he'll be taking his meals here and also increase our coal purchases so the office can be kept warm during the day. That's where he'll be conducting your lessons, right?"

"Yes, and…uh…we might need to move wichsen time to the shed."

Chapter Eight

JUNE 1940

By the end of May, the German army was pushing deep into France, and by the beginning of June it became clear that the fight was over. Hundreds of thousands of British troops evacuated from the coast of France back across the channel in a ragtag flotilla of every seaworthy vessel in Britain. Sixty thousand died in the battle, including a large number of Irishmen from the North. Public opinion in Dublin turned sharply against the Germans.

But not in our house. My father continued to want nothing to do with the war or politics; he was satisfied if he had his drink. Much to my mother's annoyance, Liam had become an assertive champion of the Germans. I think it was mostly a matter of "the enemy of my enemy is my friend." The IRA was sympathetic to the German cause, and my brother was being drawn tighter into the IRA's network. As for me, I was painfully aware that the circumstances of the Emergency and my association with the Werners had been a godsend for me and my family. I avoided any political opinions.

By the end of June, France had fallen. Well, most of it, anyway—the important parts—Paris and the entire Atlantic coast, from which Germany would surely launch its invasion of England. Food began to disappear from store shelves. The shortages were even worse than they had been in September at the beginning of the war.

The Werners tried to keep a low profile. Otto told me they were no longer welcome at the pub, and even general shopping had become uncomfortable. I took over most of the public-facing household duties, and Bella was busier than ever, grocery shopping for the Werners and preparing all of the household's meals. Two other staff members of the German legation had approached her about part-time help.

The only fly in the anointment was Dr. Fulman, the American who'd arrived in May to take up Otto's education.

It was late May, before France had fallen, before Dunkirk, before it became clear that the war was, finally, coming to the British Isles. Mr. Werner had been called to a meeting at the legation, so Otto and I had gone to the harbor to meet Dr. Fulman's boat. Passenger shipping had become risky by then, with German U-boats making increasingly bold attacks on merchant convoys. There was always an air of relieved excitement when an expected ship finally steamed into harbor.

Dr. Fulman carried little luggage—just two trunks and a satchel—and was surprisingly young. I guessed he was in his twenties. He wore a light-colored suit and a flat, round straw hat. Otto, tall and lean, with his wild blond curls under his German Alpine hat, stood out from the crowd of Irishmen, and Dr. Fulman spotted him right away. He waved at us, and we walked over to him just as the porter was placing the second of his two trunks on the dock.

He rummaged in his jacket pocket and pulled out a crumpled wad of bills. "Good Lord!" he exclaimed. "I still only have

American money. Will this do?" he asked, carefully extracting a bill. The porter's eyes widened, but I stepped in.

"Allow me, Doctor," I said, handing the porter an appropriate coin. He nodded his thanks as he took his tip but gave me a look suggesting I was a traitor to my race.

"Oh, thank you, young man," said Dr. Fulman, who then appeared confused as to whether he should next address me or Otto. Otto saved the day, as he usually did, by stepping forward and extending his hand.

"Good afternoon, Dr. Fulman, and welcome to Dublin. I am Otto Werner, your student. I'm grateful for your willingness to make the trip, under the circumstances."

"Oh, excellent, Mr. Werner. I'm so pleased to meet you, although if you could put a word in with your people and ask them to stop trying to blow up civilian ships, I'm sure all of us poor saps would sleep a little better. All the U-boats and the 3:00 a.m. alarms and the life jackets. It's a bit much, really." He smiled as he said this, but it was such an outrageous thing to say to Otto that even I was left speechless.

"And who do we have here?" he asked, turning to me. You could forgive the mistake. I didn't *look* like a servant, and I think Otto and I behaved in ways publicly that would imply friendship, although, to a stranger's eye, that would seem unlikely given our obviously separate stations. I often wondered what people thought when they saw us together. I glanced at Otto for help.

Otto stepped in. "Dr. Fulman, this is James Brennan. James is a local chap who assists me and my father in managing the household."

"Well, that *is* interesting. Local chap, you say? I wasn't informed such a role exists. I've been briefed on valet, butler, underbutler, and footman, but I don't recall how to address a *local chap*." He actually winked at me then. Otto was still bristling from the earlier admonition, and this just put him further into the uncomfortable space of not knowing how to control a situation.

That was *not* a space Otto enjoyed.

"But no worries," Dr. Fulman continued. "No need to stand on ceremony on my account. Please, just call me Mr. Fulman, or even Howard if you could bring yourselves to do so, and I'll call you Otto and James."

I didn't see much of Otto for the first week after his new teacher's arrival. When I was at the Werners' residence, I was busy renegotiating coal and ice deliveries and laying in supplies for Dr. Fulman, mostly educational materials like writing pads and ink pens but also items he was frustrated not to find in the house already. "It's 1940!" he exclaimed. "How can they live without a world map?"

One afternoon in early June, after Dr. Fulman had been with us for a couple of weeks, he asked me to accompany him shopping. He was looking for specific educational books on history, politics, religion, and art and needed my help to point him to the right neighborhoods in Dublin where he could find such things. In hindsight, I think this was partially a test on his part to see if I had an interest in reading and the larger world around me.

He'd heard of the O'Connell School and was pleased to learn that I'd finished my secondary education there. "That's a rigorous education. You must be proud of your accomplishment." I was, but pride was a sin, and I was still worried about how I was—eventually—going to dig myself out from the mountain of sin I'd already buried myself in, so I said nothing. We continued walking down Grafton Street toward what I knew was the city's most renowned bookseller. I'd been in once, in my O'Connell School uniform, so I hadn't been chased out. But it was still an uncomfortable memory because I hadn't been welcomed—more like suspiciously tolerated.

This was a different experience.

A clerk came up to us right away. "Good afternoon, sirs," he proclaimed brightly. "How can I assist you?"

"Good afternoon. I'm Reverend Fulman, and I need to expand an unfortunately narrow library for my young student."

Reverend?

"Oh, very good, Reverend. You've certainly come to the right place." The clerk, who obviously misunderstood *me* to be the student in question, turned to me directly and asked if I was most interested in history or philosophy. It was a trick question though, because he asked me that question in *Latin.*

I felt Dr.—no, Reverend—Fulman stiffen next to me. He was clearly as surprised as I was and hadn't intended to set me up. He was about to speak when I interrupted. "Philosophy, I think. It's necessary to understand philosophy if one is to learn from history," I replied in Latin. The O'Connell School was big on Latin. So was the Catholic Church.

"Oh, very good," beamed the clerk. He turned back to Mr. Fulman. "I see the young gentleman has a strong foundation already. Let's go explore what texts would best expand his education."

For the next hour I pretended to be Otto, not actually, of course, but I knew him well enough that I tried to look out for his best interests as we selected study materials. Dr. Fulman set me loose to browse at one point, and I was deeply engrossed in a comparative study of world religions when he found me sometime later. This was an amazing new world for me, so many ideas tumbling through my mind. I was so drawn into what I was reading that I startled when I heard his voice right next to me. "Is Otto interested in the study of religion?"

No. In fact he deftly managed to deflect all talk of religion, probably for fear that it could risk our wichsen time together.

"No," I replied, not bothering to hide my disappointment as I closed the book.

"But you are," he said. It wasn't a question. "Bring it; we'll add it to our library."

We were enjoying a pleasant late-afternoon walk back to the Werners'. The package of books and other supplies would be delivered there, so we were unburdened and unhurried. I asked the question that I had been turning around in my mind since we'd entered the bookshop. "Are you a priest?"

Mr. Fulman laughed at that and stopped walking. He turned to me. "Oh, James! Hardly. It's actually quite a funny idea if you knew the truth." This being Dublin, we had stopped right outside of a pub—the Croaking Frog. "Come on, you've earned a drink today. I'll buy you a pint."

"What do you know about Unitarians, James?"

We were sitting at a small corner table, the surface stained and sticky. A thick smoke hung in the air. It was a rare treat for me to drink beer, and I was nursing my Guinness, feeling somewhat light-headed already.

"Nothing," I admitted.

"Well, we're a religious organization, best known for our belief in the oneness of God. Hence the name."

"A religious organization? So, you *are* like a priest, then?"

"In a way, yes. I'm a trained minister. But we're different than Catholics. We Unitarian ministers view our key role as guiding people to their own understandings about what's right and what's wrong. We believe everyone is capable of this—of developing a strong, personal sense of morality. Holy texts aren't the only source of wisdom, not by a long shot."

That sounded nice, but I didn't think it would help much in the real world. Then I remembered something from a couple of years back. "Wait, wasn't your lot involved in bringing all those kids over from Germany? The Jewish kids?"

"Yes, along with others, the Quakers particularly." He seemed pleased I'd connected his church to that. "We called it the Kindertransport. Over ten thousand Jewish children are in the United Kingdom right now, thanks to that effort. Quite a few even here in Ireland. Well, up north that is, on a refugee farm near Belfast."

Liam and Bella had argued about the Jews once. She said it wasn't fair to uproot them, that they hadn't done anything wrong. Liam said we couldn't know what was really happening because the government censored the press and was always trying to make the Germans look bad.

Otto and I had talked about the Jews too. He confessed that he didn't understand what was supposed to be so bad about them, but he acknowledged his government viewed them as troublemakers. His father wouldn't talk to him about it, saying only that the Nazis were using the Jews—somehow—to consolidate their power.

"I don't think I understand enough about what's going on," I admitted.

"No," he said. "No one seems to be paying attention." He frowned into his nearly empty pint glass. Mine was still half full. "You'll need to, though. Things are going to get bad. Even here."

I didn't ask what he meant. I didn't want to think about things getting bad. I mean, I knew the war was going to get worse for England, but Otto was still certain it wouldn't drag on. And for me, everything was heading in the right direction. In fact, Bella and I had now saved up enough money that my mother said she thought she might be able to get us out of the tenement and into one of the new council flats. They had running water and flush toilets.

We sat quietly for a minute, each deep in our own thoughts. The only thing truly wrong in my life was my inability to confess my sins. I worried about that a lot. Perhaps this was an opportunity?

"I know you said you're not a priest, but are you able to hear a confession?"

He picked up his glass and drained it. "Not on one pint, I'm not! Same again?" he asked, nodding at my glass. *When did I empty that?*

Howard—because he *insisted* if we were drinking together, it had to be as equals—brought our fresh pints back to the table.

He plopped into his seat and pulled it even closer to mine. "You know," he said, "I can't absolve you of your sins in the Catholic sense. But in my tradition, it only takes your own will and conscious to be in communion with God. We don't believe in the middleman."

That made sense, didn't it? Why wouldn't God forgive my sins if I confessed them and was sincere? And here was a priest—of sorts—telling me it would be enough. I knew better, but I chose to believe him; I so wanted to relieve myself of this burden.

"Plus, it just might help to talk about your problems. I've found that many people can come to see a path forward if they can talk it through. This isn't a confessional, but I promise I'll keep whatever you tell me in confidence."

That was enough for me—a forgiving ear willing to listen without judgment.

Once I started, I couldn't stop. I ended up telling Howard everything. How I met Otto, what we'd been doing together, how I unsuccessfully tried to confess my sins. I tried to make it sound like it had been mostly my idea, what Otto and I did together. I didn't want Howard to take a dim view of his new student.

It took a while, and most of our second pints, for me to get through it. He sat quietly through most of it, asking short but relevant questions now and then. When I'd finally finished, I felt so much lighter. Still, I had to ask. "Do you think I can ever reconcile with God? Do you think I'll spend eternity in hell?"

He cocked his head. "What was that? Sorry. I was still trying to grasp how much money he paid you for a bucket of mussels. Could you repeat what came after that?"

I gasped but quickly realized he was joking.

"All right. Stay right there. Breathe." He got up and went to the bar, then returned shortly with two more pints. "I *never* drink this much," he said. "But under the circumstances…" He took a deep swallow, as did I.

"So, I'll start at the end. No, I do not think you will spend eternity in hell." I let out a breath I hadn't known I'd been holding. "I don't think there is a hell. Not the way you're thinking of it, anyway," he continued. "I'm glad we got that book for you. You'll find it illuminating. I believe, and most other Unitarians do too, that all the major religions and spiritual philosophies hold some elements of truth. They all have something to teach us."

He paused, considering his next words. We both took a sip of beer. "Did you know that Buddhists think in terms of earthly suffering and how to overcome it? They think, fundamentally, all suffering is caused by a person's resistance to change. To know that nothing can ever be as you'd like it to be. Everything always changes, and people crave things to be different than they are, thinking, 'If only I could have such and such, then I'd be happy.' But it never works that way."

I wasn't following that. I frowned and lifted my pint. It sloshed as I raised it unsteadily.

Howard vigorously rubbed his face. "No. That's stupid. I can't start there." He took another swallow. "Way too much beer to start there." He drummed his fingers in a new puddle on the tabletop. "Let's try this. Jesus never mentioned anything about confession, did he?"

I thought about that and realized for the first time how little I knew of what Jesus actually said. "I don't know," I replied honestly.

"Fair enough. But if he did, there was never any record of it. In fact, the Bible instructs Christians to 'confess your sins to one another,' like what you just did with me now. Confession as you're thinking of it, as a sacrament, wasn't even invented until hundreds of years after Jesus's death. It's entirely a creation of the Catholic Church. Jesus was a Jew, after all."

What? A Jew! Think of that. I made a mental note to ask Otto if he knew that.

"In fact, Jesus said the way to God was through him. Not through a priest or through the sacraments of a church that didn't even exist when Jesus was alive."

I was drunk and confused and relieved, and my mind felt blown open. I may have swayed a little and reached out an arm to steady myself.

Howard picked up our half-full glasses. "We need water," he said, heading to the bar, taking away the beer.

My mind was racing with the implications. I could be forgiven for my sins simply by being sincerely contrite, by acknowledging them, even privately? That would change everything. Still, I wasn't ready for what Howard said next when he returned with our water.

He placed the glasses down on the table, and they seemed to glide of their own accord through the puddles of beer. "And besides," he continued as if he hadn't been gone, "I don't think what you did comes anywhere near being a sin. You did nothing wrong. There's nothing to forgive."

"But...but...self-abuse." I'd said that too loudly and glanced guiltily around. No one seemed to have heard. I lowered my voice to a whisper and leaned in. "And with another boy too. Surely that's a sin."

"Well, it certainly isn't accepted in our culture, but it hasn't always been that way, and even today there are societies where it's more commonly accepted." He thought for a moment. "There's two different things going on here. What you call self-abuse is simply masturbating—the Americans call it jerking off. It's a totally normal and even healthy thing for a young man, as long as it doesn't become an obsession."

God, could that be true? How wonderful that would be.

"The other thing is more problematic. Boys exploring their sexuality together isn't too unusual, but at your age, it starts getting more toward what most people would condemn as an unnatural relationship. Homosexuality."

I'd heard the word, and I knew what it was. I was upset that he would apply that word to me and Otto. It meant buggery and perversion. Men dressing as women doing unspeakable things to each another.

But, but…I did *feel* something for Otto; it wasn't just wichsen, or wanking or jerking off, or whatever it was called. I had already come to see it as something larger than what the boys do behind the pigsty. But it wasn't…*that.*

"Enough for now though," Howard said. "You needed to unburden yourself, and you did. You're a good man, James. Have no worries about your soul." He drained his glass of water. "And we've had far too much Guinness to have a philosophical discussion about sex."

I finished my water too.

But Howard wasn't quite finished with me.

"You've done well for yourself, James. You've managed to turn many disadvantages to your benefit and the benefit of your family. You should be proud. But…" He looked around the pub. It had mostly emptied while we'd been there. "Things are going to get bad, James. Very bad. I know Otto thinks the war will be over quickly, and I don't know if his father believes that, too, or if it's simply what he's telling Otto. But it won't be over quickly. It's going to get ugly. I don't know if Ireland will be dragged further into it or not.

"But there are dark, dark things happening in Europe, James. Those lucky Jewish children we rescued were just the tip of the iceberg. Keep your eyes and ears open. Remain on guard. There *is* real sin in the world, James, and you won't be able to avoid it coming closer to home."

Chapter Nine

JULY 1940

As we entered into July, Otto and I fell into a new pattern. We saw each other less; he was busy with his studies, and I was helping my mother navigate the Dublin Corporation's byzantine regulations for a housing application.

We still found wichsen time here and there, always in the shed, but it wasn't quite the same. For one thing, we couldn't lie down in the shed. The most we could manage was to sit side by side on the dirt floor, backs against the wooden wall. And there was no washbasin there, so on the occasions when we'd forget to bring a damp cloth, cleanup was a challenge.

Still, it was private, and in some ways the new constraints mirrored the distance that had developed between us once Otto's lessons had resumed.

There were secrets between us now.

On my part at least, but I suspected Otto had his own too.

I didn't tell Otto about my pub visit with Howard. It felt like a small betrayal; I thought Otto might resent the time his teacher had spent with me. To make matters worse, Dr. Fulman was providing me instruction too. It was an informal arrangement. He would leave a book for me in the kitchen, usually on politics or religion, with a note marking the page of a specific lesson or essay. Every few days, when Otto was studying in the office, Dr. Fulman would come find me, and we'd have a brief discussion of what I'd read.

Bella missed nothing. Well, hopefully, she missed what Otto and I did in the shed, but other than that, she was always right on top of things. "That Dr. Fulman has certainly taken an interest in you," she said to me one day as she was scrubbing bed linens in the Werners' washing tub. I was at the kitchen table, reading about Henry the Eighth and the Church of England, so I could hardly deny it.

"I'm fortunate," I acknowledged. "It's like having a private instructor."

"It *is* having a private instructor," she corrected, "and without spending a shilling." She shook her head. "When I think back on this year…" She continued her work, then seemed to change the subject. "Otto is a pleasant young fellow." I didn't respond. It wasn't actually a question, and I wanted to see if she'd say more before I jumped into such dangerous waters. I noticed she was washing what I'd come to think of as Otto's wichsen towel. Well, mine and Otto's. I felt my face flush.

"We're not taking advantage, are we?" she asked.

"No," I said. And I meant it. "I know we're paid more than we should be, but honestly, I've saved them more on the delivery contracts, and how would they eat without you? You know it's uncomfortable for them to be out at the pub."

"That's good, then," Bella said. "I'd hate to give all this up. Our prospects, I mean. Things are looking up for us, Jimmy, aren't they?"

"They are, yes. Although…there is the war."

"I know, but not here. And Liam says even if the Germans *do* come here, it won't be a bad thing. He says it'll be good to knock the English down, once and for all."

I thought about what Dr. Fulman had said, and how he expected things to get bad, and how we didn't have a full picture of what was going on in Europe.

"And the Werners are nice people, don't you think?" Bella continued.

I agreed they were. I thought about our two families and how different they were.

"How do you think Liam's doing?" I asked.

"I worry about him," she said. "The IRA has been doing all those bombings, and I'm worried he's going to get involved in that."

"Me too," I agreed. "And Dad's not helping things either. I'm surprised he can still hold a job."

"You know, Jimmy, we have skills now. I could pick up more work. Other people who work with Mr. Werner have already asked. Maybe we could afford to get a place? A couple of rooms somewhere?" Bella was folding the wet linens and piling them in the wicker basket, preparing to take them out to the courtyard to be pegged on the line. "Do you think Otto will stay on here, in Ireland, after the war?"

"I guess that depends on how the war goes."

By the end of July, it was clear that the war wasn't going well at all, at least not for the British and, consequently, not for the

Irish either. The Germans had blockaded key commercial harbors in England and had begun an aggressive bombing campaign of shipping convoys, severely restricting already tight supplies of coal and wheat into Ireland. My family was fine; Bella and I had money, and my sister was proving to be a thrifty shopper. But people around us were beginning to go hungry.

Anger at the Germans was rising once again.

One evening I stayed behind at the Werners' after Bella and Dr. Fulman had left for the day. Mr. Werner had to return to the office after his evening meal, so Otto and I were able to spend time together alone, outside of the shed.

We were in his bedroom, and Otto was standing naked by the washbasin, wiping the remains of our wichsen time from his belly. When he came back to the bed, instead of handing me the towel as he would normally do, he lay back down, propped on his side, and began wiping the mess from my belly. This was new and intensely intimate. When he was finished, he ran a finger along my chest, which was also something new, and even more intimate.

"Look at how hairy you're becoming," he said, swirling his finger through the damp strands of black hair on my chest.

His touch was electrifying and unnerving.

He must have felt my tension. "Relax," he whispered. "It's just us. We're good." But he withdrew his hand, pinching me quickly on the nipple, and plopped back down at my side.

We stayed like that for a while. Just when I thought that perhaps Otto had dozed off, he tilted his head toward mine and asked, "Is it bad out there?" It was such a broad question, but I thought I knew what he meant.

"It's getting to be," I replied. "Your blockade has limited food and coal supplies. People are starting to go hungry. They're afraid."

"Please don't call it *my* blockade. It's not like I'm personally out in Portsmouth Harbor with a gunboat."

"I know. Sorry. But, Otto, what if your father is wrong? What if the British don't simply surrender or negotiate a peace? What if the fighting gets really bad, like it was with France?"

"Well, then Britain will fall just as quickly as France did. There's no one as powerful as the Reich."

"You know, we Irish feel a kinship with our brothers up north. Just because they're part of Great Britain doesn't mean they aren't Irish. People here are worried for them too."

Otto turned on his side to face me now. "Well, I think those Irish should fight the British too. Maybe this war will be the opportunity to finally achieve a united Ireland, under Germany's protection, so the British never come back."

Germany's protection? I didn't like the sound of that. We were a fiercely independent people. Would the Germans allow an independent neutral Ireland to exist after they annexed the rest of the British Isles? I had my doubts, but I didn't want to ask Otto.

"I think your IRA has the right idea," he said. "Support Germany in the war, then reap the benefits when it's all over."

"Please don't call it *my* IRA." I supported a united Ireland, but I didn't approve of the IRA's declared war against Britain or its violent strategies.

"All right. Your brother's IRA, then."

Even as he said it, I could tell Otto realized his mistake. "It's late," he said immediately. "We should get up now." He slipped off the bed and began pulling on his drawers. "I'm wondering if tomorrow we might—"

I interrupted him before he could continue, as he must have known I would. "What do you know about my brother and the IRA?"

"Nothing," he protested as he continued dressing, and I quickly followed suit. Otto asked innocently, "Didn't you tell me about his interest in it?"

"No," I said. "His *interest* in it is dangerous. I would *never* have told you something like that."

"Oh." He tried to wave it off. "Perhaps Annabelle, then…"

No, not Bella. She would never share something like that with Otto.

"No, Otto." I approached him and grabbed his bicep, gripping it tightly. "Tell me what's happening here."

He looked down pointedly at my hand on his arm, then raised his face to look me in the eye. I didn't let go, and he didn't break his silent stare. "You're going to leave bruises," he said in a low, deliberate tone. Not objecting, exactly, more…surprised.

I had grabbed him without thinking. I wanted to force him to pay attention, to answer my question about Liam. But now I found that I couldn't let go. Something was changing, the energy shifting between us. I squeezed his arm even harder, and a new smile appeared on his face, not his sunbeam, dimple-producing smile, but something calculating…dangerous.

"I think I *like* this new, bolder James. Where have you been hiding?"

Then, rather than pulling away, he leaned in and kissed me.

★

When I arrived home that night, my head spinning with what had happened with Otto, of what it meant, or didn't mean—he'd kissed me!—I was waylaid by Bella, who'd been waiting for me on the stoop. "Jimmy, my God! Where have you been?"

"At the Werners'. What is it? What's wrong?"

"Don't go up there. Father's there, and Eamon. He's drunk. I left when the yelling started."

"But what's happening? Why is he home at this hour?"

"I don't know, Jimmy, but I'd stay away if I were you. Wait here with me until they leave." She shifted over to make room on the step.

"No. I have to go up there. I'll find out what's happening." And with that I bounded up the three flights of steps, barely managing to avoid a dog and her pups huddled in one dark corner of a landing. When I reached our hallway, I noticed the stench, as I always did now that I'd become accustomed to a way of living that wasn't mired in filth. The next thing I noticed was the shouting. My father's voice, slurred but loud, even through the closed door at the end of the hall.

I braced myself and entered my home.

It had been torn apart. Furniture was knocked over, drawers emptied, my mother's sewing work strewn across the floor.

"There's the bastard!" my father bellowed when I stepped into the room. He lunged—to strike me, I thought—but nearly fell before Eamon managed to catch hold of him.

"Keeping money from me! Me! And working for those goddamned Germans." The stench of whiskey hung around him in a fetid cloud.

I glanced at my mother, and she shook her head, a quick side-to-side movement, but mostly stared at the floor.

"And I had to learn of your disgrace from my own cousin." He spat on the floor toward my feet. At least that explained why Eamon was here.

"What are you talking about?" I asked. "I earn honest money and provide food for our family, or haven't you noticed you've been eating better recently?" Eamon flinched when I said that and tightened his grip on my father, who struggled, sloppily, to break free.

"And forcing your mother into your scheme, making her hide money from me." It was then I noticed her sewing box, broken apart on the floor, all of its little boxes and bags open, the contents dumped. I sent a silent prayer of thanks to Saint Brigid for giving us the wisdom to hide our wealth. Most of it I'd hidden in a jar tucked behind a loose wall shingle in the Werners' shed. Whatever my father had found here was a small fraction of what we'd managed to pull together.

I turned to Eamon. "What's going on? What have you told him?"

"Sorry, Jimmy. I'm not trying to turn on you, but a father has a right to know what's happening with his son. I told him how you took up with that German molly boy and how you've been spending all your time with him."

Molly boy? I told myself he couldn't possibly know. He was just being insulting, cutting at me.

Otto kissed me tonight.

Eamon looked between my father and my mother. I suspected he was hoping for support, but my father looked like he was struggling not to vomit, and my mother continued studying the floor.

"And how do you know where I spend my time?" I asked.

For a brief moment, Eamon looked uncomfortable. But then he forged ahead and said, "I told that kid you bought the mussels from to follow you. Offered him first rights to the rocks the next day."

"Buying mussels from other boys!" my father spat. "He thinks he's above us. And keeping money from his own father. And now getting me fired!"

What? He was fired?

My mother finally spoke up. "You were fired because you're a drunk, not because Jimmy works for the Germans."

He made another lunge for me, but Eamon kept a tight hold on him.

"And it's not like I work for the German government; I just manage the household for a family that can't handle it on their own. Sure, I might be taking advantage a little, but it's honorable work I'm doing."

Eamon turned to my mother. "Tell him about the priest," he told her.

My mother sighed and looked up at me. "Oh, Jimmy." She had been crying, and her eyes still shone with tears. "Father Flannery came to see me. About you."

Oh my God. He wouldn't share my confession with her, would he? He couldn't! I felt my face flaming.

"Look at the wash of shame on that sinner!" My father thrust an accusing finger in my direction.

"He told me you hadn't been to confession," my mother continued, "and I explained you were going to Saint Mark's because it was closer to your new job." My mother let out a sob, and when she could continue, she said, "But Eamon had that boy follow you, and you're not going there either. Oh, Jimmy! Your soul!"

Otto kissed me tonight. "I talked to a priest and confessed my sins." It was a small lie, maybe. Dr. Fulman wasn't technically a priest, but he was a minister, just not Catholic. I knew that wouldn't be enough though.

"You're lying!" accused my father.

"Stop!" my mother cried out through her tears. She came to me and grabbed my hands. "Jimmy, you need to be in God's grace. Confess your sins and take Communion. I'm *begging* you. Father Flannery said he'd absolve your sins if you did your penance. He's worried about you. *We're* worried about you."

"And give me the goddamned money!" my father added. He was fading fast. It was only Eamon's grip that was keeping him from slumping to the floor.

My mother squeezed my hands. "Can you go somewhere safe for a few days?" she asked. I nodded. "And for Jesus's sake, Jimmy, confess your sins to Father Flannery. Please, son."

Otto kissed me tonight. And I kissed him back.

Chapter Ten

JULY 1940

I wanted to go to Otto that night, but how we'd left things was too confusing. I wasn't anywhere close to understanding what it meant or what I wanted. Bella was distraught when I filled her in on what had happened upstairs, or at least most of what had happened. I left out the part where Eamon had called Otto a molly boy and left out my concern that Father Flannery might have revealed my confession, or hinted at it, anyway.

"I'm going to find someplace to stay for a couple of days—away from this madness. If you give me your money, I'll keep it safe for you." She reached into a coin purse tied beneath her apron and handed me most of what was in it. "He stole the money she'd hidden in her sewing box. Oh, and he was fired."

Bella started crying then too. She hugged me, a tight embrace as she sobbed into my shoulder. "Don't abandon me, Jimmy. I can't make it through all this without you."

"I won't. I swear."

"Hush. Don't swear."

I had to smile at that. "All right. I *promise*, then. I'll protect you." I grabbed her shoulders and leaned her back from me so

I could look her in the eye. "I don't think he knows about you working for the Werners. Don't mention anything about it."

★

It was still surprising to me that I had become presentable enough I could appear on the doorstep of a boarding house and be welcomed inside rather than run off the stoop. Howard came down to meet with me, and we went for walk where I filled him in on what had happened. It was a damp, warm evening, and coal smoke hung thick in the air. He was easy to talk to, even without the Guinness. It helped that we were walking side by side through the city streets and not facing each other.

He told me about how things were going in Europe and about his church's efforts to help refugees escape. He said the plight of Europe's Jews was worse than any of us were told and that many were being taken to camps set up in the countryside. Others were being abducted too, he said: political opposition, Polish refugees, the mentally ill. "Homosexuals," he added, pausing in our walk to look at me when he said that.

I told him my parents were concerned about me, morally. I didn't tell him I had my own concerns, or about the kiss. "The love of God is in all of us, James," was all he offered. Still, it was a confession of sorts, and I felt better afterward.

Later that night, he snuck me into his room. It was easy to do because we didn't need to go inside the main house. His was the only room on top of the garage and had its own entrance around back, behind the building. We went through an open archway, with bicycles stored just inside, and up a long narrow stairway directly to the room's door.

It was a small, chopped-up space squeezed under a sharply slanting, unfinished ceiling. The garage below was open air, and the entire situation seemed beneath his station. There was a water closet, of sorts, tucked into a corner, barely concealed behind a curtain on a rod.

Although I was still in awe of the entire idea of an indoor flushing toilet, I'd spent enough time at the Werners' to recognize this as a less-than-ideal setup. I wondered if he felt he couldn't afford better or if there was something else at work.

He noticed me looking at the space skeptically and told me it suited his needs. He liked the privacy, he said, and when he spoke with friends back in America—he indicated the bulky shortwave radio set up in the corner—he didn't need to worry about disturbing other boarders. He also said the landlady was relieved to rent to a minster, who wouldn't be inclined to have "prohibited female guests." He winked at me.

He piled up a few blankets for me on the floor.

Tomorrow I would talk to Otto. I'd left in a hurry after our kiss. Fled, more accurately. We needed to figure out what we were doing.

"Did you see this?" Otto exclaimed excitedly, waving a newspaper in front of me as soon as I came into the house. I supposed that meant we weren't going to talk about what had happened between us yesterday.

"What is it?" I asked, taking off my new hat and placing it carefully on the top peg of the stand in the corner.

"It's from your IRA. It's their *War News* publication. Listen!"

I sighed. We were back to it being *my* IRA. But then the memory from last night—before the kiss—came back to me.

"Your brother's IRA," Otto had said. I still needed to ask him what he knew.

Otto opened the paper wide and shook it to straighten the pages. Even as he read from it out loud, he was walking toward me so I could see for myself. "If German forces should land in Ireland, they will land as friends and liberators of the Irish people. Germany desires neither territory nor economic penetration in Ireland but only that it should play its part in the reconstruction of a free and progressive Europe."

He moved beside me and held the paper so we could both see it. He glanced up at me. "This is so exciting, James!" He looked down and continued scanning the paper. "They go on to say that the Third Reich is an energizing force of European politics and the guardian of national freedom. Isn't that wonderful? An energizing force!" He folded the paper, more like crumpled it, in his haste to hand it over to me. "With the Irish people behind us, the war with Great Britain should be over in no time."

I took the paper and began to fold it carefully. "Otto—"

"Read it!"

"I will. It's just…the IRA isn't the 'Irish people.' They're a militant group. Not everyone thinks this way." I recalled my father's and Eamon's distrust of the Germans and their anger at my employment here.

"Maybe," he said. "But even so, it's good to know that if German soldiers had to…be here…for a while, it wouldn't be too upsetting. For the people, I mean. It would be fine."

"No, Otto. No matter how many ways you find to avoid using the word *invade*, it would *not* be fine. Ireland is a neutral country. There should be no soldiers here but her own."

Otto deflated and I felt badly for having caused it. He'd been so excited.

"Do you think German soldiers are going to come to Ireland?" I asked him. I realized I'd whispered the question, afraid, maybe, of making it real.

"Well…" He didn't finish, which told me what I needed to know.

I walked over toward the sink, keeping my back to him.

"But…Otto…"

"I don't know, honestly. I asked my father that same question. He didn't think it would come to that." Otto rushed to interrupt me. "But he did say that after England falls, Ireland should be reunified into one district."

"One *district?*" I asked. I was getting angry and wasn't whispering anymore. "Ireland isn't a *district*. It's a country. An *independent* country."

"Yes. Yes, of course, James! That was my mistake… My English is so bad still… I shouldn't have used that word. *England* will be a district; Ireland will be a country. But a unified country! That's what people here want, right?"

"Well, yes," I said, turning at the sink now to face him. "But not at the point of a gun by a foreign power. We want to control our own destiny."

"I'm sorry, James." Otto put his hand on my shoulder. Was he sorry about our argument or sorry about something he knew was coming?

He turned me to face him, and we stood that way for a while. He didn't take his hand off my shoulder. I was angry at him for not understanding and angry at the Germans for turning my world upside down. And yet…why did a part of me hope that he'd lean forward and kiss me again?

Otto did lean forward, but rather than kiss me, he placed a hand under my chin and tilted my head up so we were looking into each other's eyes, and he whispered, "I don't regret what we did last night."

I wanted to say I didn't regret it either, or maybe say I *did* regret it, because I wasn't yet clear in my own head which was the truth, maybe both. Instead, I said, "I was kicked out of my father's home last night."

He pushed away from me with a shocked look and a soft gasp. "But, he couldn't know…about us?"

Us. What the hell are we, anyway? But no, it wasn't that.

"He found out I was working for your family. I think he was mostly angry I kept the money from him. And our priest told them he was worried about me." I didn't say that Cousin Eamon had called Otto a molly boy or that my mother was worried for my soul.

"Where did you stay? Why didn't you come back here?"

"Howard put me up for the night."

"Howard? Who's How—? Do you mean Dr. Fulman? Has he invited you to call him Howard?" Otto seemed distressed by that idea.

"Yes. He was very kind." He frowned when I said that, then pursed his lips and scowled, creasing his forehead.

"I don't think I like that," he said.

I wasn't sure why he wouldn't, but then I'd kept my relationship with Howard a secret from Otto, sensing somehow this would be his response. And I was right.

"Did he behave appropriately?"

"What? Of course he did."

"Well, don't stay with him again. Stay here."

That was absurd. "Otto, I couldn't possibly stay here. This isn't a boarding house; I *work* for you."

"You *work* for my father. You're my friend, James. At least, I think of us as friends. Don't you?"

I hadn't thought of us that way, but once Otto presented the idea, I realized it was true. It had been true for some time now. And thinking about us as friends was easier than thinking about the other thing between us.

"Yes," I said, and I hoped I didn't sound as surprised as I felt.

"Good," he said, flashing his dimple smile—the one I liked, not the sly, calculating one. That one scared me a little. "I'll think of something." He put both hands on my shoulders and said, "Now, wichsen time?"

★

Later that morning, sitting side by side on the dirt floor of the shed, still basking in the relaxed, unguarded moments after wichsen time, I finally remembered to ask, "What did you mean last night about it being 'my brother's IRA'?"

Next to me, I felt Otto roll his shoulders and heard his neck pop. He turned his head to look at me and asked, "Am I going to have to sit here and just wank you nonstop in order to avoid the difficult questions?"

I smiled at the idea. It had its appeal. "You could try," I suggested.

He laughed. "I like you this way. Loose, joking."

"You're not going to distract me this time, Otto." We were sitting with our shoulders touching, faces just inches apart, and he looked down pointedly at my lips. No, not this time. I scowled at him, and he got the message, sighing and leaning his head against the wall.

"Okay, the IRA," he began. "You know they declared war against Britain last year, yes?"

"Yes," I said. There had been a lot of bombings since then. I thought most people in Ireland were coming to resent the IRA. It was already complicated enough to be caught between the English and the Germans.

"Well, the IRA has reached out to us to offer their support, given that we're both at war with Great Britain."

"What kind of support?" I asked.

"Anything. They said they could provide intelligence, and if we gave them weapons, they could also conduct attacks throughout the United Kingdom."

So presumably Belfast too. Once again, Irish fighting Irish.

"And my brother?"

Otto squirmed, then stood, fastening up his trousers and brushing the dirt off his backside. He held a hand down to me, and I grabbed it. As he pulled me up, he said, "The IRA had provided us—the legation staff, that is—with a list of names of members who will work with us. Your brother's name was on the list."

Oh, Liam. I'd suspected he was in that deep, but I hated having it confirmed this way.

"He's kept that from the family," I told Otto. "I want you to know that we wouldn't support him in that."

Otto looked like he was mildly offended. "We're not bad people, James. As your brother's paper noted, we're fighting for a free and progressive Europe."

I thought of everything Howard had told me. "But, Otto," I said. I wasn't sure how to continue. I didn't want to betray Howard, but I wanted to learn what Otto knew. "There are rumors. About the Jews—"

"Stop," Otto said. He held up a hand to emphasize his command. "I know. My father has told me what's going on. And it must seem strange to outsiders. But the Jews have been holding us back since the last war, and even before that. They controlled all the banks and have been choking our economy. The Nazi Party has been retaking control of our country and its finances. A few communities are being relocated—for now—where they'll be taught how to be better citizens. And where they can work productively in the meantime to support the Reich."

He presented this as if it made perfect sense. Maybe it did to him. And maybe that was all it was. Not that it wasn't bad enough, but maybe Otto's father was right; maybe it was just temporary. And, after all, hadn't England set up its own internment camps for Jewish refugees if they had come from Germany? I was sure I'd read that in the paper. I'd have to ask Howard about it.

I wanted to ask Otto about the homosexuals but didn't dare to raise that topic for fear of where the conversation could go.

Chapter Eleven

AUGUST 1940

I didn't go back home right away, but I saw Bella each day at the Werners, and she kept me up-to-date. My father hadn't found a job yet, and he was drinking whenever he could get whiskey or beer. She said our mother looked exhausted.

I slept where I could: in friends' hallways, once in the laundry of our tenement building, once in the open, on the sand above the tide line of the bay. On that night, I saw planes in the distance, presumably German bombers heading toward Liverpool or Manchester. Increasingly, the Germans were expanding their bombing campaign to include industrial manufacturing, and civilian deaths were starting to mount.

Otto and I didn't kiss again, at least not right away. We were likely both unnerved about what that kiss could mean. Neither of us was ready to go there, to acknowledge out loud what we both privately thought. Sexual play between youths was different than two men kissing.

I wanted to kiss him again.

I know he wanted that too.

In late August I had two days off. Bella and I took the train to Cork to visit cousins the first day, and on the second, I took my mother to the council housing office. She was next on the waiting list for one of the new flats, and she had to complete the paperwork. The new housing was luxurious—four full rooms, including a kitchen with a bathing tub, and a private flushing toilet in the hallway. "You'll have your own room, Jimmy! Imagine that," she'd said, and it was then that I realized she didn't intend to have my father with us.

"I will not have drink in my new home, Jimmy. Not a drop."

When I returned to the Werners', entering through the back of the shed as I always did, I thought something looked odd. I had an uncomfortable feeling and immediately went to check that the jar filled with my money was still safely hidden behind the wall board in back of the top shelf along the side wall.

But the shelves were gone!

There had been four of them, sturdy wooden shelves two feet deep, one above the other, attached to the wall with metal brackets. The shelves had been filled with old gardening equipment, boots, and boxes. No one had cause to search them or retrieve anything stored there.

The shingle on the wall behind which I kept my hidden jar was hanging loose, exposing the empty space.

I frantically scanned the room, hoping the jar might be sitting out. All of the items that had been stored on the shelves were stacked against the opposite wall. But the jar was nowhere in sight. That was nearly all our savings. Bella and I had a fraction of it buried in the Werners' herb garden and sewn into pockets in our underclothing, but without the money in the jar, we'd have to start all over.

I felt myself beginning to panic. I became dizzy, and my hands started to shake. Where was the jar? It had to be here somewhere.

The door opened, and Otto stepped into the shed from the kitchen.

"James," he called out. "I'm so sorry. I meant to be here when you arrived. Your money is safe. I have it." Relief flooded through me. Otto came and hugged me. "You're so upset," he said. "It's my fault for not warning you, for not being here. Come, sit." He guided me to a crate on the floor and helped me lower myself onto it.

"I meant to surprise you," he said, rubbing small circles high up on my back, between my shoulders, as I leaned my head down and concentrated on my breathing. Everything wasn't lost after all.

"You managed that just fine," I replied. "What has happened?"

"I'll show you when you can stand again."

"I can stand." I proved it. I was upset, though, and angry at the shock. I turned to Otto. "What happened?"

"Here," he said. "Move forward a bit." He held my shoulders and nudged me away from the crate, then let go of me and reached down to slide the crate forward. "Look." He took hold of a wooden peg on the wall behind the crate and pulled. A part of the wall moved forward a few inches, and then everything coalesced at once in my mind, and I realized what I was seeing.

It was a new wall, made up of a row of panels that were the former shelves, now standing upright and set next to each other along the entire eight-foot width of the shed. If Otto hadn't just pulled one of the panels away, the wall would have appeared as one solid length.

He'd created a fake wall.

Once he'd slid the panel aside, I saw that behind it was a small space, about three feet deep and running the entire width of the shed. A kitchen chair and small chest of drawers sat at one end, behind the now open panel, and when I stuck my head in, I saw that a narrow cot filled the rest of the space.

"Welcome to your new secret bedroom," Otto whispered in my ear.

I examined his handiwork. It was masterful. He'd attached a small board along the ceiling and had nailed three of the four shelves to it, leaving only the one end piece as a way in or out. If you didn't know to lift it away by the wooden peg, you'd have no idea it wasn't simply a solid wall.

"Come see," he said. He stepped through the two-foot-wide gap and opened the top drawer in the chest, pulling out a torchlight. He motioned me in. It was a tight squeeze, barely room for the two of us to stand together. There were two more pegs on the interior of the panel, one at the top and one at the bottom. Otto used the pegs to maneuver the door back into place.

"There, safe and sound," he said. He placed the torch on top of the chest.

I couldn't believe he'd done all that. It was quite clever, and I was surprised to learn Otto was that handy. "I did it all myself too." There was a definite note of pride in his voice, deservedly so. "No one else knows it's here. Your jar is in the drawer. You can hide it again wherever you'd like."

He'd done all that for me. To keep me safe and to keep me near him.

I felt an upswelling of…something…for Otto then. A tenderness that was almost painful.

There was less than two square feet of space in front of the chest between the chair and the base of the cot. Otto's hand was on my arm to steady us, and the soft yellow light of the torch beam created deep, shifting shadows. My breathing was returning to normal, and we were close enough that I thought Otto could feel the rising and falling of my chest.

"I'm so sorry I frightened you," he whispered. "I only want to protect you."

"I know," I said. And it was true. We had something between us. I looked down at the cot. What we had went far beyond wanking together. I didn't know what it was, and I knew I didn't want to put a label on it. I was too afraid to do that. But I knew I wanted to nurture it, protect it. Encourage it.

"Otto, I'm scared." We were both whispering.

He put his other hand on my shoulder. "It's fine. You'll be safe here."

"No," I said. "I'm scared about what's between us."

Then I leaned forward and kissed him.

If he'd been at all reluctant, Otto didn't show it. Instead, he deepened the kiss aggressively. I was shocked by how arousing that was, and I stopped thinking and started feeling. Otto moved his hands to my hips and pulled me closer. Then he backed into the corner and dropped into the chair. He reached up a hand, which I moved to take, thinking to help him back up, but instead he took the torch from atop the chest and turned it off.

In the blackness that descended, he reached for my hips and pulled me closer. He deftly undid the fastening on my trousers and managed, in one motion, to lower them and my drawers to my knees.

I felt his hot breath on my belly and then lower.

A series of thoughts flashed through my mind.

The first was *Oh, is he going to…?*

The second was *Oh my God, this is amazing!*

The third was *Oh, ah…ah…ah…*

I'd lost all capacity for thinking.

The cot wasn't really wide enough for the two of us, but the space was so narrow that the walls kept us from tumbling off the sides. We'd been there for three hours, neither of us wanting to break the magic of our new intimacy. We'd both had another go at this new thing between us Otto had introduced, and I added it to my expanding list of sins I wasn't sorry for. Not at all.

We kissed again too. A lot. The walls had come down between us, and we couldn't seem to stop touching and stroking each other, learning each other's bodies.

"But what does this *mean*?" I mumbled at some point, immediately grateful when Otto responded, "Shh. It doesn't matter."

★

It wouldn't be until the next day that I learned what was happening at that very moment, a hundred miles to the south.

As Otto and I held each other on that small cot, Kitty Kent was sitting down to lunch at the Shelbourne Co-op. The co-op was attached to the Campile Creamery, which was highly regarded for the quality of the butter it produced.

Earlier in the summer, German troops had discovered empty boxes of Campile Creamery butter at Dunkirk, raising, in their eyes, the very real possibility that perhaps Ireland wasn't quite as neutral as it claimed to be.

As Otto and I were leaving our new hiding spot, heading into the kitchen to raid the icebox for ham and milk, two German planes were flying low over the railroad tracks heading into Campile. The workers at the co-op, who had mostly finished their lunches, stood outside, marveling at the spectacle. The planes passed the village, then circled and flew back. The first bombs were dropped by the rail station, damaging the tracks and destroying an empty house. Puzzlement turned to horror, and the workers fled into the surrounding fields.

Inside the canteen, Kitty, her sister Mary, and their colleague Kathleen were enjoying a late lunch and were unaware of the commotion outside.

They may have heard the telltale whistling sound of a heavy bomb speeding toward them—a sound that Londoners would soon come to dread—or they may not have. Perhaps they were laughing with each other or had the radio on. In the end, it didn't matter.

Their bodies were recovered from the rubble later that afternoon.

★

Otto and I learned of the incident late in the afternoon, when Mr. Werner came home unexpectedly from his office. Had he come home an hour earlier, he would have found me in the kitchen's bathing tub, which would have been difficult to explain.

As it was, he had the same startled look on his face whenever he saw me in his home, as if he'd forgotten about me and had to let all the pieces of the story fall back into place. *This is the boy I pay to collect mussels, manage the household contracts, keep my son company.* I sensed it was all a little too complicated for him, and I suspected he knew something wasn't quite right. Somehow. But that was as far as it went. In the end, he always had the same reaction—a head nod and a clipped "Brennan."

On that afternoon though, I was alone in the kitchen when he entered. "Where is my son?"

"I'm not sure, sir. I suspect he's studying in his room." In fact, I knew Otto had just left the kitchen only minutes earlier, naked and flush from his bath, but I decided I probably shouldn't know that. "I was just finishing up here with a new coal delivery contract."

"Right, thank you. I'm afraid I need to dismiss you for the day. There's been an incident, with casualties. Otto and I will be going to the legation office. Oh, and please find Annabelle and tell her not to come today." As he was heading out through the door and into the dining room, in search of Otto, he turned and said, "I'm sure Otto will arrange for appropriate payment."

"Very good, sir," I said and went into the shed to wait for Otto, who I was sure would fill me in before he left with his father.

Otto only managed a minute or two with me before leaving. He was distressed as he described how German bombers had killed three Irish girls. The Germans were worried about how the public would react, and all legation staff and their families were asked to spend the night in the office for their own protection.

No one thought to tell Howard, who showed up for Otto's afternoon lessons shortly after the Werners left.

"Good afternoon, James," Howard said as I let him in through the front door and then into the kitchen. "Where is everyone?"

"I'm sorry, Dr. Fulman, there's been a last-minute emergency, and Otto and Mr. Werner had to leave for the office. They won't be back today."

"Oh my," he said. "Nothing too serious, I hope? And we're back to Dr. Fulman again?"

"It feels odd to call you Howard, here in our employer's home."

"James, you've slept on my floor. We've been drinking together. We've talked about sex together!" I blushed at that, which I think was Howard's intention. "You *must* call me Howard. Well, when we're alone, anyway. Wouldn't want to shock the Germans."

And Otto *had* seemed shocked by the familiarity and even more upset that I'd spent the night with Howard.

"All right, Howard, I'll try to conform to your sense of American egalitarianism." It was a word that Howard had taught me, and he beamed in pleasure when I used it correctly.

"We'll make a Yankee out of you yet." He took off his hat and sat in a chair at the table. "Sit," he said, indicating the chair opposite him across the table. "What's the emergency?"

"It's not good. German bombers killed three girls down in County Wexford. They said they bombed a creamery."

Howard frowned. "That's *not* good; you're right." He thought for a moment. "This could change everything," he said.

"Otto's father said it could have been an accident."

"He told you about it?"

"No, he told Otto before he took him off to the office."

"And yet Otto found time to tell you before he left?"

I blushed again. Dammit, I wished that didn't happen to me.

He cocked an eyebrow. "I see," he said, and I felt exposed, as if he *did* see. All of it.

He tilted his head. "You look…different." *Yes, I've learned exciting new ways to commit mortal sins.* No. He couldn't possibly know what Otto and I had been doing all morning, so I didn't respond to that.

"Do you think this will mean war between Ireland and Germany?" I asked. "I'd hate to lose my job." And I'd hate to have a war come between me and Otto, now that there was something big between us.

"I don't know. We'll have to wait and learn more. I suspect Ireland would like to avoid war."

I agreed, and Howard decided we should work on my own studies while we were both here. We had been talking about women's suffrage and, in Ireland particularly, the difference between women's civil rights and how religious institutions consider and treat differences between the sexes.

"Ireland has allowed women to vote since its independence twelve years ago. But the Catholic Church still considers women unfit for clerical service. Which is fine, right? Different standards for civic life versus religious beliefs. After all, you can choose your religion, but you can't easily choose your country, right?" Howard said.

What a thought! Could I simply choose my religion?

"Did you choose your religion?" I asked.

"Yes, I did," Howard answered. "Even in the United States it's not that easy though. I was born a Methodist but became a Unitarian in college."

"Why?"

"That's a big question," Howard stated. "And there were lots of reasons. But I guess, in the end, I thought personal conscience should dictate morality." He looked at the table, as if he should have a drink in front of him.

"We do seem to have the kinds of conversations that require alcohol, don't we?" I asked.

He smiled. "Was it that obvious?"

"Yes! I happen to know there's an unclaimed bottle of whiskey in the shed." Unclaimed because Otto had brought it. I supposed he intended it for us, soon. Maybe to see what limits we might be able to cross. The idea excited and scared me at the same time.

"Bring it on, young man!"

And so we started drinking. As it tended to in such moments, the conversation eventually turned from religion to sex.

"So, your religion believes any form of sex is okay?"

"Well, no. I wouldn't say that Unitarians believe that generally. In fact, most would balk at that, I'm sure. I'm saying that Unitarianism puts the obligation of figuring out right and wrong on the individual, not on a priest or a book. And some Unitarians, well, just a few right now, believe that any form of sex, if it's respectful and consensual, is just fine.

"The point is, you need to be true to yourself and not worry about what other people would tell you is right and wrong," he concluded.

I tried to imagine a world in which what Otto and I had done this morning was not a sin. I could *almost* believe it. It made so much sense when Howard explained it.

Then I wondered how Howard had gotten to be so smart. "Have you ever had sex like that? A relationship that wasn't okay by other people's standards but that you thought was fine?" I asked, which just showed how much I'd had to drink. It was Howard's turn to turn a deep red. I'd never seen it on him before.

"Well, that's…that's…"

"Hello?" Bella was in the shed. "I'm here," she called out, then came through into the kitchen.

I'd forgotten to get to Bella first and tell her not to come.

"Oh, Dr. Fulman. Good afternoon, sir." She performed one of her ridiculously awkward curtsies, and God help us, Howard and I both burst out laughing.

She eyed the bottle of whiskey on the table. "Ah, so that's how it is then, is it?"

She put down her shopping and unwrapped her shawl. "Am I correct that you both wouldn't be doing this if the Werners were home?"

"That's correct, miss. Sorry," Howard said. "See, James? It was smart to give them the vote"—which set us both off again.

"And are they coming back this evening?"

Howard and I both shook our heads. Bella went to a cabinet and pulled out a glass. She placed it on the table in front of me and said, "Well then, pour me in while I get supper together."

We filled Bella in on what little we knew of the bombing while she put the meat she'd brought in the icebox to prepare when the Werners returned tomorrow. We enjoyed a light supper of bread, cheese, and apples. And whiskey. I'd never seen my sister drink before, and she revealed a sharp wit and slightly bawdy nature, which embarrassed me but delighted Howard.

"So, brother"—she'd leaned forward with her elbows on the table—"tell me about our young German fellow. He's a strapping lad. Is he seeing anyone? Interested in anyone particularly?"

Predictably, I flushed a bright red, and Howard nearly choked on his whiskey.

Bella looked back and forth between us. "Uh-huh" was all she said.

Both Howard and I deflected that line of inquiry, and we spent a couple of hours talking about many things. We talked about the war, and what was happening in Europe with the Nazis, but also America, and religion, and communism.

When it was time, Howard said, "I'll see your sister home. Word is probably starting to spread about the bombing."

Bella thanked him and rose, just a little unsteadily, to her feet. "Will you be all right, Jimmy? Where are you staying?" I noticed Howard seemed interested in the answer, too, and I wondered if he would have invited me back to his room again if we'd been alone.

"Oh, I'm fine," I told them. "Don't worry about me."

The following day all of Dublin was up in arms about what had happened at the creamery. I went home to be with my mother and Bella, in part because I didn't want Bella going to the Werners' that day—I didn't think it was safe. Already a crowd had gathered in front of the German legation to protest the killing of the girls. The Germans insisted it had been a mistake, but the rumor of the empty butter cartons at Dunkirk had spread along with the news, and most seemed to think the bombing was revenge for providing assistance to England.

As the morning progressed, more than a few young women in our building began claiming kinship, albeit distant, with one or another of the dead girls. Stories soon began circulating about how sweet they were, how innocent. How each had touched the lives of friends and relatives, near and far. I imagined the same scene played out in every tenement in Dublin and even in the parlors of the better garden terrace flats.

That was one of the best things about being Irish, high or low—we didn't let the facts get in the way of our truths.

Chapter Twelve

AUGUST 1940

When I think back on the Campile bombing, I think of it as a turning point. Not a turning point in the war, because it wasn't. In fact, the incident quickly faded from memory as the world shifted its attention to the horror unfolding in London.

No, it was a turning point for me and Otto. We were in too deep to walk away from each other, which we could have done had the Campile bombing happened even a week earlier. Should have done, maybe, even as our relationship moved from boyhood ambiguity to something more fundamental, some adult shared secret. To living outside the norms, and to being able to destroy each other.

"It was a mistake," Otto insisted two nights later, when we finally saw each other again. We were in the shed, but not in my hideaway, as I'd come to think of the space behind the wall. The shed felt like neutral territory, as much mine as his, and it was a good place for this discussion.

"It was broad daylight in the middle of the afternoon," I protested. "How could it possibly have been a mistake?"

"Pilots get lost sometimes. And everything looks different up there." He was trying for a light, forgiving tone. I still didn't know if he believed his own claim, and it didn't really matter. Within weeks everything was going to change, and he wouldn't be able to pretend anymore. But neither of us knew that at the time. "If they thought they were flying north instead of south, Ireland's coast would have seemed to be that of England."

"And *then* it would have been all right to kill three girls working at a creamery? Because they were English girls?" I was exasperated and angry and getting even angrier that Otto was trying to calm me down.

"James, people die in war. It's going to happen." He rubbed his hand through his hair, and God help me, even then I was struck by his beauty, by the thrill that he was mine for the taking. "It's not like we're deliberately targeting civilians," he continued, unaware of the effect he was having on me. Or, perhaps, he was deliberately manipulating me. "I bet they were aiming for the railroad." He paused then, as if he knew he should stop there. But he couldn't help himself. "And if the creamery hadn't been supplying the enemy—"

"No. Stop," I interrupted. "Absolutely not. The English are *not* our enemy."

"No. But they're ours. And you need to decide where you stand." He said this with a sense of finality, as if it were up to me to determine the future.

"Fuck off, Otto. I stand in Ireland." We'd reached a stalemate, and I turned to gather my things. I would not be staying here tonight, and there would *definitely* not be any wichsen time. I picked up my bag—I'd taken to carrying a few necessaries with me all the time, as I never knew for sure where I'd be bedding down—and I remembered the package in it.

Shit.

Liam had been to see our mother and Bella the same day I was there, after the bombing. We didn't speak much anymore. I suspected Liam thought Otto was a corrupting influence on me, and if anyone could read between Father Flannery's lines, it would be him, eager as always to see the bad in me. But as he was leaving, he'd slipped a thick envelope under my waistcoat.

"Give this to your German fellow," he'd said; then he was out the door before I could question him.

I took it out of my bag and held it out to Otto. "Here. I really hate giving this to you, especially now." I wasn't sure if by *now* I meant after the Campile bombing or after he'd been such an arse. Probably both. "It's from your IRA." I spat out the words and turned to the back door.

"James, wait. I'm sorry."

But I was having none of it.

I headed to Howard's. It was still early in the evening, so I hoped it wouldn't seem like I was begging for a place to stay. I just wanted to talk.

I went behind the garage and climbed the narrow stairway to Howard's door.

Halfway up I heard voices. Howard's quite clearly, and another, seeming strangely distant. I shouldn't have, but I paused on the top step to listen. I wasn't trying to eavesdrop, exactly. I told myself I was trying to determine whether or not he had company so I'd know whether to knock or simply leave unnoticed.

The voice that wasn't Howard's sounded garbled somehow. Then it clicked into place, and I realized it was the shortwave radio and he was talking to someone who wasn't in the room with him. Standing right at the door, I could hear both sides of the conversation. I should have left then.

But I didn't.

It was a woman's voice with a heavy accent. Spanish, maybe.

"Well, you'll need to *find* a way. She'll be there soon, and you'll have her, and you'll need to move her," she said.

"But I have nothing set up here. Not yet. I'm *trying*," Howard responded. I'd obviously joined in the middle of an argument.

"Try harder," she said softly, as though acknowledging the weight of the task she was asking.

There was silence at that.

"I don't know who else to ask," she said. "The others are scrambling to reestablish themselves—"

"I know," Howard interrupted.

There was more silence and then a loud radio interference sound, which Howard must have managed to dampen somehow. "I'll think of something," Howard said. But there was no response. And after Howard tried again—"Elsa? Elsa?"—he gave up.

I crept down the stairs and slept that night on the sands of Dublin Bay.

Chapter Thirteen

SEPTEMBER 1940

Otto and I tried to avoid each other the next few days, which was hard to do in the Werner household.

It had been a week since the Campile tragedy, and things were returning to normal. Mr. Werner was home for dinner most nights, and Howard was back during the afternoons for Otto's lessons. I never mentioned to Howard what I'd over-heard outside his door, though I was burning with curiosity, and once or twice he caught me staring at him with a puzzled look on my face.

I had taken to using the kitchen as my office, and I had just returned there after my third fruitless trip that day to dif-ferent coal suppliers, trying to secure a more reliable source. The Werners' coal company had twice failed to deliver in the last month, and they were claiming such limited supplies that they couldn't commit to a next delivery date. But it was Sep-tember, and I felt an urgent need to prepare for the cold months ahead.

But the entire city was low on coal, and although I had the Werners' money to throw around, I was frustrated in my efforts to find a new supplier. I had my papers spread out before me on the kitchen table and concluded I would need to talk to Otto about the situation. It would be dire soon if we couldn't find a solution.

And, well, I had missed Otto. I enjoyed spending time with him, had become uncomfortably fond of him. And I missed the wichsen time too.

Bella came into the kitchen just as I resolved to find Otto, talk to him about the coal situation, and maybe spend some bonus time reconciling.

"His lordship requests an audience with you in his study," she said, rolling her eyes but also smiling playfully. It seemed neither of us could resist Otto's charms for long.

I leapt to my feet, perhaps with unseemly haste, and was halfway to the door before I thought to go back to the table for my notes. "He needs to see this," I explained to Bella as if rushing off to meet Otto had been my idea.

I passed Howard on the stairway. "He's all yours," he said to me as we squeezed by each other on the steps. "I'm only taking a quick break though, so don't get too comfortable."

I entered the study and found Otto sitting in one of the two wing chairs in the corner. I was glad he wasn't behind the desk, and I happily accepted his waved invitation to take the seat next to him.

I sat and crossed my legs at the knee, waiting for Otto to say something. He looked at me, and I sensed he was waiting too.

"I'm sorry," we both said at the same time.

He smiled sadly but then looked away. "Oh, James. You have nothing to be sorry for."

"That's true," I replied, which triggered a more robust smile from Otto.

"Except maybe for being a hotheaded Irishman—"

I began to object, and he held up a hand to stop me. "I *am* sorry, James. What I said was awful. There was no excuse for my government killing those girls, and even if it was a mistake, I shouldn't have tried to shrug it off or make you feel even more uncomfortable—about choosing sides."

He took a deep breath, then continued. "Yes, civilians are going to die in war. It's inevitable, but we should avoid it when we can. And Ireland isn't at war, so those girls should never have been in the line of fire in the first place. And while it's true that the IRA has killed more Irish civilians—"

I began to interrupt him, but he stopped me again.

"But, the point is that's *your* business, not Germany's. So, I'm sorry for having hurt us."

I nodded.

"And I want you to know that we're not evil. We wouldn't intentionally kill civilians. That's barbaric."

"But, Otto, the Germans are bombing British ports every day now, sinking ships and even bombing factories. Civilians *are* dying."

"Well, yes. But it's all part of the war effort. They're not being targeted because they're civilians, they're just...what's the word?...collateral? Yes, collateral damage." I frowned at that, and Otto rushed on. "And as soon as Britain concedes, this will all be over, and things can get back to normal."

"All right," I said. I wanted to say more but couldn't think of the words.

"But wait," Otto continued. "The most important thing is that it *killed* me to know you were angry. I hated us being apart. You've become important to me, James. Extremely important."

I reached across the narrow table between the chairs and took his hand. "You're important to me too, Otto. I was miserable these last few days. Let's not do that again."

His smile lit up the room, sunbeams and dimples rained down on me, and I was disgusted by how easy it was for him to control me like that.

"Well," he said, reaching into his waistcoat and pulling out a small package. "I was hoping you would say that." He put the little box on the table between us and sat back. "This is for you. Open it."

I picked it up. It was small enough to balance on my palm, and I turned it over, admiring the delicate tissue paper wrapping, a soft moss green with the tiniest little shamrocks. A velvet ribbon in a deeper shade of green tied it together. I'd never held anything so beautiful before.

"What…what is this?"

"I told you. It's for you. It's a gift. Open it, please."

I carefully undid the ribbon, thinking Bella or my mother might like it for their sewing, then carefully tried to pry open the flaps on the sides without damaging the paper.

"Oh, for God's sake, James, just tear the paper and get on with it. I'm a bundle of nerves—in case you haven't noticed."

The paper tore—it was going to anyway—and I was left with a delicate metal box with a hinged lid and the smallest clasp I'd ever seen.

"It's beautiful," I said, because it was. I held it up to get a closer look, turning it this way and that, admiring the craftsmanship.

"If you make me come over there and open it because you can't work a simple clasp, this won't be nearly as special as I was hoping."

I opened the lid, careful not to damage the hinge.

Unbelievably, there were more folds of tissue paper inside, soft greens and buttercup yellows. I nudged the wrapping aside with my finger and could see Otto's impatience building out of the corner of my eye.

Finally, I saw a metal link chain, and as I pulled it out of its nest of paper—a longer chain than I would have thought possible for such a small package—I found a pendant dangling from the end. A claddagh, cast in a dark metal. Exquisitely detailed hands holding up a crowned heart, enclosed by a round, roped frame.

"It's made out of iron," Otto added, sounding nervous now.

I turned to look at him. I didn't know what to say. So much was happening.

"The shop girl said my sweetheart might think it's too masculine. I disagreed."

I dangled the claddagh at eye level; it was intricately detailed both front and back. It was extraordinary.

Sweetheart, I thought. "Is that what I am?" I asked.

"If you'd have me, yes. If we can build a world where it's possible. Yes."

I felt a hot, unmasculine tear run down my cheek.

"Otto," I managed before choking up and going mute again. "I don't think…" I couldn't finish the thought. I couldn't find the words to tell him how much he meant to me. But he misinterpreted my silence.

He panicked. I could see it in his eyes the moment it happened. He waved his hands about and stood abruptly.

"Oh, I'm so sorry. I've made a terrible mistake. Please…forget this entirely." He dragged his hand through his hair, took a step toward me, stopped, then paced toward the door before freezing in place again just a few steps away. "I've completely ruined everything. I just thought…well…it doesn't matter. Obviously, I was mistaken. We can go back to how it was…or…or nothing at all if you'd rather…I…" He trailed off and turned from me again.

I stood and went to him, gripped his shoulders, and turned him to face me.

I was crying now, full-on, and so was he, but for different reasons.

"Goddamn you, Otto! I was going to say that I don't think I've ever wanted anything as much as I want you."

We kissed then, forcefully. Our tears turned to muffled laughs, and we both began hiccupping. We pushed ourselves apart.

"Can I put this on you?" he asked.

"Yes. It's beautiful. Thank you."

He turned me around and draped the pendant around my neck. He fastened the clasp behind me and smoothed the chain, running his fingers across my shoulders and chest, although the chain was finely made and didn't require the attention. The claddagh itself sat low enough on my chest that it wasn't visible beneath my shirt.

"I would rather it had been a ring," he whispered into my ear.

"Maybe someday," I said. "Maybe you and I can make that world, where we could be sweethearts."

Chapter Fourteen

SEPTEMBER 1940

The following week, my mother received notice that she'd been approved to move into the Galway Arches, the newest council housing complex. It was farther out from the city center and south of the Liffey, near the Guinness factory. The four-room flat would be available in a month, and we excitedly started planning the move.

No one told Father.

Liam was twenty and deployed with the Irish Defense Force, so he wouldn't be coming with us. I would have one of the two bedrooms, and Bella would continue to share a bedroom with our mother. We were sitting in our North Strand flat, planning the move. Our rooms—the whole building, really—looked worse and worse every time I visited. I didn't know where our father was, and I didn't ask.

"You know," Bella said in a far too casual tone, "James and I could afford our own place now and still make sure you're cared for."

"Nonsense!" my mother replied immediately. "No daughter of mine is leaving my house until she's been safely married."

Then, to my immense horror, she added, "Now that we'll have a respectable home, you should invite that young German fellow over to meet me." Bella shot me a quick look that I couldn't interpret *at all*.

"Well," I began, "he *is* our employer. I'm not sure it would be—"

"Nonsense!" she said again. "The father is your employer, and the young man has been extremely helpful to our family. He'd be an excellent prospect. And Bella is a beauty who has already proven her house skills. And she'll be nineteen soon. Beyond time to get serious, I should think."

"Please don't talk about me like I'm not here," Bella complained. Then she shot me another *totally* indecipherable look. "But he sure is handsome, and kind too. Though maybe a bit arrogant."

"Nonsense!" my mother said for a third time. "That's just the German in him. They're a very domineering people."

If my mother had any idea just how domineering Otto had been the night that he'd given me the claddagh, afterward, in the privacy of my hideaway, she'd drop right through floor.

"But the war," I finally managed. "Surely we need to see how that goes before we start considering marriages." No one had a response to that, but based on the pounding Germany had given Britain the prior week, all but destroying her navy, we were fairly certain how the war would go, and how quickly too.

Even though it was early September, Saturday felt more like November, with a heavy, windswept rain battering the city. It was early evening, and Bella had just finished preparing supper for the Werners, a slow-cooked beef stew that suited the weather. I was overseeing the work of a tradesman who was installing a new stove in the kitchen, or I should say, *attempting* to install an *old* stove in the kitchen. It was a small turf-burning contraption, the kind that hadn't been used in decades, and the worker was having a hard time fitting it to the new flue, which had to be specially built to fit the old stove.

But the coal gas that supplied the newer stove was in critically short supply, and the city had implemented severe restrictions on the hours when gas could be used. Coal itself, for the heating system, was even harder to find, but those of us who grew up poor knew a thing or two about Ireland's riches, both from the sea and from the bog, and I believed I was ahead of the curve in acquiring an old turf stove—just in case.

Otto had scoffed, especially as the job dragged on and we saw how ugly the ancient contraption looked sitting in the modern kitchen. "The war will be over before you even fit the flue," he'd said, "let alone find turf to burn."

"Hush, you," Bella had responded, which was amazing, all things considered. She'd become relaxed and familiar with Otto lately—too familiar—but Otto didn't seem to mind. In fact, he seemed to enjoy it.

"Think of all the extra work for you, dearie," Otto shot back and winked.

The worker dropped a wrench, and I caught him staring, slack-jawed, at the three of us. What a sight we must have been—a lowborn Irish house manager, just seventeen, a mouthy maid not much older, and a wealthy German youth keeping the others company.

The bell rang at the front door, and Otto stood to answer.

"I'll see to it," Mr. Werner called from deeper in the house.

A few minutes later, he entered the kitchen, looking pale and shaken.

He did a double take when he saw the antique turf stove, and for a moment it appeared that he would ask about it. But, instead, he shook his head as if to clear it, nodded at me—"Brennan"—then turned to Otto. "This just came." He handed Otto an envelope and turned to my sister. "Good evening, miss. That smells wonderful. I'm afraid it will just be Otto for supper tonight, though." *And me*, I thought, *and Bella. We all eat here now, but you'd have no idea.*

"But I'm afraid I'm going to have to ask you to leave off for now. You should hurry home. And go directly. It's not a night for delay."

"And you there, man," he called to the workman. "Are you almost finished?"

"Another hour or so, I'd say, sir. I need to widen the flue sleeve."

Mr. Werner turned to Otto, but he was busy with the note, and when he saw his son's expression, he turned to me instead. "Is this…whatever it is"—he waved his hand to indicate the stove and the workman—"absolutely necessary right now?"

I turned to the man on the floor. "Can you come back tomorrow, then? There's a Jameson's in it for you if you can." I said it quickly and with enough of an accent that both Werners couldn't have understood a word.

"Aye, 'tis an odd job you've got here for sure, lad."

He began packing up, and Mr. Werner pointedly looked at Bella, who hadn't yet moved to leave, until she began cleaning the kitchen mess. "Leave it," he said. "You should go now, miss."

I could tell Bella wanted to stay and learn what was going on, but she had no choice in the face of such a direct dismissal. "Yes, sir," she replied and reached for her shawl. She brushed against me as she wrapped it around her. "Let me know what's going on," she whispered. I nodded.

After both Bella and the workman had left, Mr. Werner turned to me. "Brennan, I—"

Otto interrupted him in German. They had a tense exchange, not arguing exactly, but heated. They both seemed distressed, Otto even frightened. He'd left the note on the table, open and balanced on its creased hinge so I could have read it if it had been written in English. They both raised their voices, but it still didn't seem as if they were angry at each other.

"Wait, please," Otto said to me, and they both left the kitchen. I could hear them continuing their conversation as they went upstairs.

I stood, crossed the kitchen, and went into the shed. As I suspected, Bella was waiting there for me.

"Well?" she asked.

"I don't know," I admitted. "But it's something big, I think. Does Mrs. Gleason still have her radio?" I asked. Bella nodded. "Check in with her this evening, see if there's any news. But until we know more you should follow Mr. Werner's advice and head straight home."

"What about you, Jimmy?"

"Don't worry about me. I'll be fine. Wait here. I'll grab a jar of stew for you to take."

It only took me a moment, and I was back, pressing the stew and a loaf of rare white bread into her hands. "Be careful," I said. "I'll see you tomorrow."

I went back into the kitchen and heard Otto and his father still arguing upstairs. And it *was* arguing now, voices raised, accusing tones, an occasional shout from Otto.

They spent at least ten minutes in that mode, moving from room to room, voices rising and falling. It was mostly Mr. Werner doing the talking, and toward the end, he seemed calmer. I thought he might be providing instructions.

As I waited, I examined the progress made on the stove installation. I was down on my knees, bent over awkwardly, peering up into the dark, sooty flue. I was probably just being paranoid. Burning turf! Like it was the Middle Ages or something.

I wondered if, no matter how comfortable I ever became, I would always fear being one meal away from poverty.

I heard the kitchen door open and was surprised to see Mr. Werner rather than Otto. I scrambled up from the floor, brushing off my trousers and pulling down my waistcoat to smooth it. "Sir," I said.

He looked at the stove. "Otto explained to me about that contraption. If you'd asked me a week ago, I would have said you were a lunatic. Now, well...I'm afraid to say it might have been smart planning on your part."

Well, not paranoid, then. Good.

"Brennan, I know this is a terrible imposition, but I need to spend the night at the office. There are things happening...with the war...that require me to be there. Otto is upset. Understandably so, but still. I'd rather he not spend the night here alone, and he's…resisting…coming along with me. Would it be horrible of me to ask you to spend the night here with him?"

Without all the sex, I assumed he meant.

I fingered the claddagh beneath my shirt. "Of course, sir. It would be my pleasure."

★

A little while later, I heard Mr. Werner leave. Otto had not returned to the kitchen, so I picked up the note and went looking for him. I found him in the study, standing by the oversized map of Europe that Howard had put on the wall.

He didn't turn to look at me.

Instead, still looking at the map, he said, "He didn't know either. My father. It's important to me that you know that."

"All right." It was all I could think to say. I'd never seen him like this, and I wasn't sure how to proceed. He hovered his finger over the surface of the map, moving it in tight, small circles.

"I didn't want to leave this in the kitchen, so I brought it up here." I dropped the note, which I'd tucked back into its envelope, onto the desk. Otto turned and looked at it, but he didn't say anything.

"Would you read it to me so I know what's going on?"

"No. I can't read it to you. Its classified, and I could be executed."

He let that sink in for a minute. His country was at war, and his father was high enough up that he had access to dangerous information.

He looked up from the envelope and offered me a faint smile.

"But I'll tell you what it says."

★

Otto walked to the desk and removed the note from the envelope. He scanned it again and put it back down.

"The Germans...*we*...are about to start bombing London." He looked at the clock on the mantel above the cold fireplace. "*Have* started bombing London."

I thought about that. The bombing campaign had been going on for over a month already. It's why everyone assumed Germany would win the war quickly. Otto's father said that Britain's naval forces had been largely neutralized. Once its air force was destroyed, there was little Britain could do to prevent the invasion from across the channel.

"I don't understand," I admitted. "I thought the bombing campaign was almost finished. Haven't your—what are they called? Luftwaffe?—already established dominance?"

"Yes. Britain should have negotiated peace by now, but it hasn't. And now we have to finish it."

"Finish it?"

"Right. My government believes we need to—what is the English word for it? Demoralize, I think—the population so there's no common support for the war to continue." He looked at me then, waiting to see how I'd react.

I thought I understood, but part of me—a big part of me—didn't want to. "I'm not sure I know what demoralize means?"

"To break the will of the people, to push them down so far they want to give up. That they'd do anything to stop the suffering." Otto looked at me to see if I understood.

"Does this mean you're going to be bombing more than just military targets?" Not that that wasn't bad enough. Lots of civilians had died already in those attacks. Collateral damage, as Otto referred to them.

"More than that, James." He came to me then and clasped one of my hands in his. "I didn't *lie* to you. I didn't know." He took a deep breath. "There's going to be an invasion, like in France. But first, our Luftwaffe is going to bomb London, for as long as it takes to weaken the country as a whole. To break its will.

"We're going to *target* civilians, James."

Chapter Fifteen

SEPTEMBER 1940

We turned on the radio in the study. BBC was broadcasting a music program, something modern and snappy, like you would hear standing outside of a music hall.

We sat in the corner chairs and listened for a few minutes. Otto was fidgeting and wringing his hands, and every now and then I'd try to say something to calm him. I knew him well enough that I found myself supplying his own lines: "It should go quickly from here at least" and "Maybe it won't be so bad."

The music stopped midstream, and an announcer's voice, stern and authoritative, interrupted. "This is a BBC news bulletin. London is under a sustained bombardment by German airplanes. We have reports that fires are spreading rapidly in the city, especially in southeast sections. The attack has been underway for nearly an hour and shows no signs of abating. Eyewitnesses report at least two dozen German bombers are involved."

"No," Otto murmured. "It's more than that."

The announcer continued. "All residents are urged to seek shelter immediately until the all clear is given. We will return with updates as we receive them."

The music began again.

I looked across the table at Otto; he wouldn't meet my eyes.

"Do you hate me?" he asked.

I stood from my chair and then knelt at Otto's feet. I took his hand in mine. "Otto, listen to me. This is not your fault, none of this. You are a *good* man. I know you don't approve of this. You don't need to convince me you don't support it."

He let out a sigh and sank to the floor next to me, wrapping me in a tight embrace. "I was afraid I'd lose you, James. I really was."

"Never," I whispered into his ear. "We're in this together. We'll help each other through it, no matter what."

I wanted that to be true.

The music on the radio kept playing and playing, and we remained on the floor, silent but touching, waiting for something to happen.

Finally, it got to be too much for Otto.

"I need to show you something you're not supposed to see," he said. "I don't want there to be secrets between us. Not anymore."

He stood and pulled me up. "Come," he said, leading me into the hallway and to a closed bedroom door. He opened it and led me inside. "This is my father's room. Only he and I are allowed here. Bella knows never to go in. We clean it ourselves. Well, I do."

There was a wide bed with a heavy wooden frame, but it was otherwise sparsely furnished, with just two end tables and a matching wardrobe. There were windows on two walls and, next to the bed's headboard, another door, which was closed. Otto went to it and pulled it open. "This is a walk-in closet, but my father uses it as his home office, where the secret work gets done," he explained.

It was big for a closet but small for an office. There was an overhead light with a glass shade in the ceiling and a metal lamp with a curved gooseneck sat on a desk wedged against the wall. Most of the desktop was occupied by a shortwave radio, with several large round dials, switches, and buttons.

A BBC-type microphone sat on a stand next to the radio, and padded headphones rested next to it.

"We can communicate with the whole world here. I mostly use it to speak with my mother and sister, though. We have one at the legation, but we're afraid it's monitored. And my father thinks your government won't let us keep it much longer anyway."

I was impressed by the setup but worried that Otto was showing it to me. This could get us both into a lot of trouble. Me, probably, more than him.

"Otto," I began, "I don't think I should be seeing this, right?"

"No more secrets, James."

I thought of the smaller version of this radio I'd seen in Howard's room and the conversation I'd heard while I stood outside his door. I wasn't ready to tell Otto that. "Right," I said, "no more secrets."

Otto sat on the small round stool in front of the desk and turned on the radio; the dials glowed a soft yellow, while a squelching sound filled the small room.

"The thing is, James, now that I know the truth about what's happening, I need your help. To fix it." He began turning first one of the big dials, then, after checking an open notebook nearby, a second.

Fix it?

"You can't fix it, Otto; it's war."

"Well, I can't stop the war. But we can make a difference. Especially here in Ireland, I think."

I looked at him quizzically and wondered if I would regret promising to keep his secrets.

He continued to slowly turn the dial, pausing occasionally to focus on what he was hearing. He talked to me at the same time as he worked the radio. "My father told me the code name for this invasion of Britain getting underway tonight is Operation Sea Lion. Isn't that a stupid name?"

I didn't have an opinion, so I didn't say anything. I was still trying to figure out why he thought we'd be able to make a difference in Ireland and, more importantly, why we'd need to.

He spun on his stool to face me. "But he also told me there's an Operation Green."

★

"Green?" I asked, a sinking feeling building in my gut.

"Yes, green. As in the color of Ireland," he replied.

"Are you telling me the Germans plan to invade Ireland?" I may have sounded panicked. I knew I felt that way.

"That's what my father just told me, yes. I was angry. I think he's known for a while."

I began pacing the room, looking about frantically, as if the Germans might be here already. Well, of course they were—Otto was sitting right there. He'd turned back to the radio. He wasn't using the headphones, but the voices were all speaking German, so I couldn't understand. He would jot down notes, then tune to a different frequency, listen for a few moments, and then take notes again.

Finally, he put his pen down and turned back toward me again.

"This is going to be bad, James. We've sent three hundred and fifty bombers over London this afternoon, and five hundred more fighters to protect them. The casualties will be high."

"Will that happen here?" I asked.

"I hope not," replied Otto.

We spent the next several hours going back and forth between the BBC, which was still mostly music with occasional bulletins, and the German communications on the radio. I made us stop to eat some of the stew, and we shared a bottle of beer.

Eventually, at two in the morning, with the bombing raid still underway, we decided we'd had enough. "We won't learn anything new until tomorrow. Or, later today, I guess," said Otto. "Come on, let's go to bed." We went to his room, and even though I knew we'd be alone for the night, I wasn't sure what was expected at that point. Would Otto want to have sex? I didn't, and as much as I didn't want to refuse him, I was ready to tell him no if I had to.

I was about to suggest that I would just head down to my hideaway in the shed when Otto interrupted my thoughts.

"Will you sleep with me tonight, James? Just sleep? I want to have you with me." Yes, that felt right.

We cleaned up in the bathroom, stripped off our trousers and shirts, and climbed into Otto's bed. He draped an arm across my chest and pulled me tightly into his side. Despite everything that had happened that day, we both fell asleep immediately.

Chapter Sixteen

SEPTEMBER 1940

The next morning, we learned that several hundred civilians in London had died that night.

And, although Otto told me the plan was to keep up with the bombing until Britain either surrendered or became so demoralized that an invasion would be a quick success, neither of us could have envisioned just how bad it would get. Night after night of bombing, week after week, month after month—tens of thousands dead, much of the city destroyed.

But even back then, in September of 1940, when the war had only started to hit home, Otto was inconsolable. "All of those innocent people," he would say, as if he were personally responsible for each of their deaths.

His father came home briefly that morning, just to clean up and change. Otto and I were in the kitchen, eating cold ham with our tea. The Werners exchanged a few words in German, and the father nodded at me. "Brennan."

The two men left me alone, and I tried to ignore the increasingly loud conversation that followed them through the house. I was fairly sure I heard my name a few times, which was alarming. I sent a quick prayer to the Virgin Mary that it wouldn't be obvious I'd been in Mr. Werner's office. Then I realized it was tempting fate to seek her help when I'd been ignoring God's commands for so long.

After Mr. Werner left, Otto and I read through the papers again to see if we'd missed anything the first time. We hadn't.

"I don't know what to do, James. I don't know how to stop my country's army from coming here."

I didn't know what to do either. The stakes were much higher for me and my family than they were for Otto and his. "How long do we have?" I asked.

"It's not clear. My father says no one in Germany wants an actual invasion of Ireland. He says it will just be an occupation while we subdue Britain. There's concern that British rebels could escape here and run a resistance operation. So we need to be in control here, too, until it's all over."

"But how long will that take?" I asked again. I needed to make my own plans to protect my family.

"We just don't know. Operation Sea Lion—the actual invasion of Britain itself—won't begin until the British air force has been eliminated. And Operation Green won't start until the British invasion is underway. My father says that we thought the RAF had already been more or less eliminated, but air resistance to our fighters and bombers is proving to be more— what's the English word? *Robust*, that's it—than anyone was expecting."

I thought about that. Perhaps the English were functioning as a shield for Ireland. That made for a pleasant change.

"Are you saying there might *not* be an invasion of Ireland, if England beats back the Germans?"

Otto sighed, then walked to the ugly turf stove in the corner. He nudged it with his foot. "But that's the thing, James. The British *can't* beat back the Germans. We're unstoppable. The only question is how many innocent people have to die before the English realize that."

★

I wanted to do something for Otto; he was taking all of this so hard.

I was beginning to feel hopeful again. Although Otto couldn't conceive of it, I thought the British and Irish people *did* have the resolve to resist a German invasion. Maybe Ireland would be safe after all. Still, that was a mixed message as far as Otto was concerned, and I didn't want to press the point.

Instead, I walked over to him and gripped his elbow. "Come with me to the shed," I told him.

"Oh. Um…James, I'm not sure that's a good idea right now. And didn't you say the stove fellow would be back soon—"

"Not for *that*," I interrupted. "There's something I want to show you."

He let me lead him into the shed. "Wait here," I instructed as I pulled aside the fake wall and slipped into my hideaway. I returned quickly with a bag in my hand.

Otto lifted an eyebrow.

"Do you know what tomorrow is?" I asked him.

"I *do*," he said, the sly smile he used on me making a welcome appearance. "I'm surprised *you* know what tomorrow is."

"What's that supposed to mean?" I demanded, pretending to be affronted but actually feeling pleased that he'd been thinking about tomorrow too.

"Well, just that you're not a particularly romantic chap, right? More of a practical fellow, I think," he said.

"Yeah. Piss off, Otto. Here." I thrust the crumpled bag into his hands. "Happy anniversary."

He gripped the bag. His eyes were shiny. "This is…lovely. I can't believe you'd remember such a thing."

"I can't believe it's been a whole year!" I said.

"You've changed a lot from the sea monster I first glimpsed arising out of the bay, caked in muck."

"And you've changed from the shining golden boy I first glimpsed, with your silly hat. You must have shot up six inches since then."

Sadly, I was still holding at only five foot six.

"And you've gotten…hairier, I think," Otto decided.

I knew he was just being funny, but I *had* gotten hairier this year. I liked the way the black hairs on my belly and chest contrasted with Otto's smooth pale skin, especially when we were lying side by side, glistening with sweat after wichsen.

"And you still wear that silly hat," I added.

"It's not a *silly* hat. It's a fine Tyrolian." He tried for indignation, but he couldn't help his smile returning. "I *still* can't believe you remembered."

"Open it," I said.

He did and pulled out— "An Irish flat cap!" he exclaimed, a brilliant smile lighting his face. "Oh, James."

"Now you'll have a proper paddy cap to wear, so you won't stick out like a sore thumb. Nothing to do about all those blond curls, though."

He slicked his hair back behind his ears, as much as he could at least, and fitted the cap on his head, tugging the flat brim down over his forehead. As I'd hoped, the soft mossy tweed, flecked with rust, complemented his golden hair and sky-blue eyes perfectly. The whole effect was…unnerving. He was extraordinary, and I was once again struck by the circumstances that had brought us together. It hadn't been my intent, but I felt myself responding, a heat growing in me.

He must have seen it in my eyes.

"Maybe a quick visit to your hideaway wouldn't be such a bad idea after all," he whispered.

We'd finished, but only just, when the knock came on the shed's door.

I opened it, expecting to find the laborer from the day before, here to complete the work on the stove, but instead found a small boy. He looked to be about seven or eight.

"My da sent me. He said I'm to speak to the Irish bloke and not the Nazi."

Out of the corner of my eye, I could see Otto stiffen at the term. "That would be me, then," I responded, without inviting him in.

"My da says Jameson's or no, he won't be back to work for any stinkin' Nazi bastard, and good luck findin' an honest Irishman who will." Then he just stood in the doorway. Waiting to see if I'd respond?

"Good Lord, you'll not be wanting a tip for that, will you?"

"He said there might be one in it for me." He stood his ground. Poor sod. Probably hungry too. I considered giving him a heel of bread.

Otto stepped into view and the boy's eyes went wide. "Well, he was wrong," Otto proclaimed, shutting the door in his face. There was a hard *thunk* as the boy kicked the door before running off.

Chapter Seventeen

DECEMBER 1940

That autumn was horrible.

The nighttime attacks on London intensified. "The Blitz," the press called it, and the bombing raids soon expanded to other cities too. Plymouth, Manchester, Birmingham, Coventry.

And the Irish kept asking, "Are we next?"

Certainly, our brothers up north thought they would be, and for good reason. Belfast was a manufacturing powerhouse and shipbuilding center. The Germans would have to target it eventually. Dublin swelled with Catholics from the North, eager to remove themselves from such a ripe target.

There was *some* good news though, when my mother and sister and I finally left the tenements of the North Strand behind us. Our new four-room flat was luxurious, and I even boasted to Otto that the bathing tub in our kitchen was larger than the one in his.

Even though I had my own room, I still found myself staying in my narrow hideaway at the Werners' more often than not. Did Mr. Werner sometimes wake up in the middle of the night to the sounds of his son creeping down the stairs? Did he pass his empty bedroom and wonder? Maybe. Probably. But if he did, he never made a point of seeing it, not clearly.

Christmas that year was a subdued affair. My mother found holly sprigs to place in the kitchen. At the Werners', Otto insisted on a tree of sorts, a deformed little spiky thing, which he propped in a bucket in the shed because his father didn't want "such an absurd fire risk" in the house.

One December evening, he wrapped his head in a scarf, put on his paddy cap, and joined me and Bella on a shopping trip through the street vendors to find paper decorations for the tree. All three of us enjoyed a modest amount of whiskey as we decorated the tree, and Otto taught us German carols. He placed a small framed picture of his mother and sister on the shelf next to the gardening tools, behind the tree, and Bella and I both carefully didn't notice his damp eyes when he sang "O Tannenbaum" to them.

It was comfortable—the three of us together—and for the first time, I had the sense Bella might have had an idea about me and Otto. Not the complete picture, I sincerely hoped, but a sense that there was something…more.

Bella insisted that the family visit Father on Christmas Eve, but it was an uncomfortable, brief trip. The building's other tenants were polite but distant. Only Mrs. Gleason seemed honestly pleased to see us and cried when we presented her with an orange spice cake. Father had remained sober for the occasion, but it was obviously difficult for him, and the new socks and scarf we offered were greeted with "Did you bring me any money, then?"

My mother hadn't told him where our new place was, and none of us wanted to ask how he'd managed to keep this one on his own, with no money and no job. Those old tenement houses were being demolished as quickly as possible, replaced by modern council housing as soon as it could be built. I'm not sure anyone was actively collecting rents in the North Strand tenements by then anyway.

On Christmas morning, Mother, Bella, and I exchanged simple, practical gifts and enjoyed ham and eggs for breakfast. Bella had even managed to get oranges, and I'd located a source of good chocolate sweets. Even without the shortages and price increases, we couldn't have imagined such an extravagance a year ago, and we were all grateful.

Mother didn't mention anything about church or Mass, which I counted as a blessing because it was the topic I most worried about.

She did, however, *insist* that Otto come for tea on New Year's Day.

Later on Christmas Day, snuggled tightly against Otto on the cot in my hideaway, I explained about the invitation.

"Oh dear," he said.

"I know," I replied. "I couldn't put her off again."

Otto rolled partially on top of me. "Did she say, 'James, bring your sweetheart to dinner. I want to meet him'?"

I pinched him in the side. "That's not funny."

"Sure it is. You just don't have a sense of humor." I pushed him off me. "But why *does* she want me to come for tea? Don't get me wrong. I'd love to meet the woman who raised you. I bet we'd have a lot to talk about."

I groaned. "Otto, for an occasionally bright young man—"

I was interrupted by *his* pinch this time.

"Ouch." I raised myself up on an elbow and twisted to look directly at him. My claddagh pendant slid over the side of my chest. "She wants you to meet *Bella*. Well, she knows you've *met* Bella, but she wants to introduce you formally, in a social setting."

Otto looked puzzled, but I saw the moment the penny dropped.

His eyes widened, and he sucked in a breath. He mumbled something in German that sounded like a curse.

"But, James…" he began, then stopped.

"I know," I said.

"She knows I'm not…not…"

"For God's sake, Otto, don't say it out loud!"

"Catholic," Otto concluded.

I dropped down flat on my back. "Yes, Otto, she knows you're not *Catholic*. Jesus, you can be an arse sometimes."

He sighed, then rolled to his side and looked at me. My pendant was still draped over my side, and he lifted it, then placed it squarely in the middle of my chest. He let his hand linger there, trailing his fingers down the thick line of black hair to my stomach.

"Annabelle will make a lovely match, though. She's a lively, modern girl," he mused.

"Otto, we're lying here naked, and your hand is inching toward my privates. Please don't talk about my sister."

"Who?" he asked, all innocence and sparkling eyes, then crept his hand lower to close the gap.

An hour later we heard Otto's father banging about in the kitchen. We both froze until we knew he'd gone through the dining room, probably up to his office.

"I should go," I said. "It's Christmas Day. I have no legitimate reason to be here. We could get caught."

Otto climbed awkwardly over me and crawled to the end of the cot. There was no graceful way to get out of the tight space, but I enjoyed the show just the same.

"This feels legitimate to me," he replied as he began dressing.

"You know what I mean." I didn't like being the one to always question what we were doing.

"I know," he conceded. He held a hand out to me to help me clamber off the cot. As I was pulling on my drawers, he said, "You know, we never talked about whether either of us might get married someday. Have a family."

No, we hadn't. And that was my fault; any time Otto tried to talk about the future—our future—I would shut him down.

"Oh, I don't know. I suppose we might," I replied, as if we were speaking of something inconsequential. I could tell Otto wasn't happy with that, but he took the hint. We probably both realized this wasn't the time for that discussion.

Looking back on that time now, I'm glad we didn't force the issue. No good would have come from confronting the hopelessness of our situation. Not then, anyway.

Chapter Eighteen

JANUARY 1941

All week I worried about New Year's Day. And why would Otto have said that Bella was a good match? I mean, she was, certainly, but I guess I'd hoped he would have said, "Oh, James, don't be silly. I have no interest in Annabelle." Yes, that would have been better.

At one point midweek I caught them conferring together, standing next to each other at the sink, heads inclined toward one another, whispering. I wasn't proud of the wave of jealousy that rolled through me.

Howard knew something was wrong too, but I didn't want to talk to him about it. He may have sensed my discomfort since he avoided me most of that week.

I spent New Year's Eve with my family, and I had never seen my mother happier. Neighbors from throughout the complex came visiting, and we made for a proper family, polite, clean, well situated. No one asked about Father, and we didn't offer.

The next morning was a frenzy of preparation. We cleaned baseboards and water pipes, and I'm sure I rearranged our sparse furnishings at least three times before Mother was as satisfied as she could be. She looked with disappointment at the tea service. I didn't blame her. The set had the mismatched, chipped look you might find in the poorest of tenement houses—because, well, that's exactly what it was.

I was glad, then, that she'd never been exposed to even middle-class finery, so she wouldn't understand just how impoverished we appeared. I felt a sudden surge of tenderness and affection for her and vowed to set her up for proper entertaining before the year was out.

I was banished from the house while Bella bathed in the kitchen and dressed. I took a long walk along the Liffey and passed the bench where Otto had first tried to talk to me about our future after the war, about how he could get a post in Ireland. And I'd shut him down right away, as I did each time he tried to talk about us, together.

No wonder I was nervous about this afternoon. How many times could I keep turning Otto away and expect him to keep coming back? Maybe Otto and Bella *would* be good together. We could still be friends, couldn't we?

I returned to the house and joined my mother in the parlor.

"I have a parlor now, Jimmy! Isn't it a wonder?"

There was a tea table in the middle of the room, with a small couch on one side and two straight-backed chairs opposite. It was a cozy space and smelled of the pine oil we'd used that morning to shine the wooden molding. An electric light bulb covered by a soft yellow globe hung from the middle of the ceiling. The tea set was laid out, and Bella had managed to find white sugar this week, which sat proudly in its bowl on the table.

"Now, Bella and Mr. Werner will sit on the couch," my mother said, and for a moment I thought, *Otto's dad is coming*? I was that nervous. "You and I will take the chairs," she continued. "Bella will serve tea."

Otto would be here soon.

"Well, how do I look?" asked Bella as she came into the room.

Radiant, I thought.

My sister was beautiful, and I didn't know why I'd never really seen it until then. She wore a muted-pink dress in the new, modern style, with a shorter hemline that came just below her knee and oversized round white buttons from the waist to the neckline.

She stepped into the room and gave a slow turn. My mother and I both expressed our admiration, and I stood as a gentleman would for a lady. She smiled at me, but I realized then she was nervous. This meeting meant a great deal to her. So she was serious; she welcomed the opportunity to have Otto court her.

My stomach sank at the thought.

I wanted my sister to be happy. She deserved to be. So did Otto.

She took my hand. "Jimmy, can I speak with you in the kitchen?"

I let her lead me there, and when she spoke next, it was in a voice choked with emotion. "I won't do anything without your approval, Jimmy. You know that, don't you? You're my little brother, but you're like a father to me. If you say no, Jimmy, then it's no."

I couldn't imagine seeing her with Otto, watching them get married, holding their babies. But I couldn't imagine a world where I could be with Otto either.

"Bella—" I began. But the doorbell interrupted me.

Bella hurried back to the parlor as our mother headed to the door.

"Wait," said Bella. "I forgot to mention I invited an associate of his too. I should have said something earlier."

"What?" my mother asked, shocked. "Why on earth would you do that? This tea is to provide an opportunity for you to impress Mr. Werner." She was angry but whispering, as she already had one hand on the doorknob. "Of all the ridiculous things. We'll talk about this later," she hissed, then schooled her face and opened the door.

Huh.

Bella stood behind our mother, quivering with nervousness, while I made the introductions.

"Gentlemen! Come in. Welcome to our home." Otto stepped through first. "Mother, may I present Mr. Otto Werner, the young man you've heard so much about, and the son of my employer."

"Welcome, Mr. Werner," my mother managed, still unsettled by the abrupt change in circumstances.

"It's so good of you to invite us, Mrs. Brennan. I'm afraid it's been difficult for my father and I to maintain much of a social life."

My mother looked confused. Understandably so, as the man behind Otto wasn't nearly old enough to be his father.

"And, Mother, may I present the Reverend Fulman, Mr. Werner's private teacher. Reverend Fulman is an American."

"Reverend? American?" my mother asked, brushing her hair back with her hand. "Oh, well, yes, please come in."

"Thank you, ma'am," Howard said.

"Dr. Fulman, may I take your hat?" I asked.

"Doctor?" my mother mumbled.

"Yes, ma'am. I'm both a reverend and a doctor, but I can't help with any aches and pains; I'm not that kind of doctor. My degree is from the Harvard Divinity School in Massachusetts." He handed me his hat—the American one, made of straw with a wide brim—and Otto handed me the paddy cap I'd given him.

"I…" Mother began, then stopped. I'd never seen her this flustered.

"And, Miss Brennan!" Howard exclaimed. "How wonderful to see you in your own home. You look lovely." He turned to my mother. "I see now where Miss Brennan gets her beauty; why, you could be sisters!"

I saw Otto roll his eyes, but no one else was facing him. My mother blushed, which I was fairly certain I'd never seen before, and I turned to Bella, who was blushing more than anyone and—oh!—the way she looked at Howard. And the way he looked back! My God. How had I not seen this? Otto caught my eye again and smirked this time.

The door to our flat opened directly into the parlor, so once hats and coats were taken care of, there was the question of seating.

"Bella, would you prepare the tea, please, and, Mr. Werner, please have a seat on…" My mother waved her hand toward the sofa and chairs, then trailed off, confused as to how she should proceed. She glanced between our two guests and the couch.

Bella stepped into the breech. "Jimmy, could you go into the kitchen and get a chair for Mr. Werner? Reverend Fulman will sit on the couch, and once we're situated, I'll bring in the tea."

It was short work to retrieve a chair, and Bella was seating herself on the couch when I returned. Howard hovered next to her but kept glancing at my mother, who hadn't moved since everyone arrived. I could almost see the wheels turning in her head.

I realized Howard was waiting for my mother to sit first. As I was putting the kitchen chair down, I said, "Mother, please have a seat." She seemed to realize she was holding things up and sank into the chair opposite the couch, across from where Howard promptly lowered himself next to Bella.

Otto was about to take the kitchen chair I'd just brought in, but I redirected him to the more comfortable parlor chair. Bella had made her point about the seating arrangements, but there was no need to force Otto to sit on the rickety kitchen furniture.

My mother was a clever woman, and she recovered quickly. "So, Reverend Fulman, how old are you?" She was also very direct.

"Twenty-five, ma'am," he replied. "And, if you would, please call me Howard. We Americans don't stand much on formalities." If Otto kept rolling his eyes like that, they'd get lodged in the back of his skull. "James and An—I have been on a first-name basis for some time now." He'd been about to say, "James and Annabelle and I," and I could see my mother caught it too.

She narrowed her eyes. "Is that so?" She turned to me, and I'd swear I saw accusation on her face. "Tell me, *Reverend* Fulman, have you spent much time alone with my daughter in that house?"

Howard blanched, and Bella squirmed next to him. She reached out to grab his hand but thankfully stopped herself in time.

Another, horrifying, piece of the puzzle fell into place for me. All those hours Otto and I thought we'd been so clever, spiriting ourselves away in my hideaway, with no one the wiser, I'd been leaving my sister alone with Howard, unsupervised. No wonder we'd never had any close calls, and neither Howard nor Bella had ever asked where we'd been.

I was a fool, and a bad brother.

Then, Otto did what he *always* does and stepped in to save the day. This time with an outright lie, but at that point, why not?

"Oh goodness, no, Mrs. Brennan!" he exclaimed. "James is like a mother hen that way, so protective of Miss Brennan all the time. Why, once I went into the kitchen to grab a snack from the icebox while your daughter was cooking, and James told me quite sternly afterward that I was not to be alone with her for any reason. He insists on always being in the same room. I'm surprised he manages to get any work done for us at all."

There was so much wrong with that, starting with mother hen but certainly not ending there. My mother was slowly nodding. I'm sure she had no idea what my job was at the Werners' or how it filled so many hours. In fairness, it didn't. Most of my time was spent with Otto, securing my place in hell.

Otto wasn't quite finished.

"I'm sure James is just as insistent with Howard. Isn't he, Howard?" I knew Howard had never invited Otto to use his first name. He'd told me once he feared it would undermine the student-teacher relationship. Well, here we were.

"Oh, he is, yes," Howard replied, not missing a beat. "James would never just go off somewhere and disappear while his sister was left unchaperoned."

Now it was my time to squirm.

"Well, that's good," my mother allowed. She nodded to me, acknowledging that I'd done the right thing, even though it was all a lie, and I'd done nothing of the sort.

She turned back to Howard, Otto all but forgotten. "So, Reverend, not a Catholic, then?"

"No, ma'am. I am a Christian minister, though. I think God and Jesus should guide all of our lives." Nicely done, I thought. It sidestepped lots of issues—how many beings *are* God and Jesus, anyway? Is *guide* the same thing as *command?*— allowing my mother to choose to believe what she will. My mother wouldn't be interested in parsing any of that, though. There were Catholics, and then there were non-Catholics.

"I'm a Lutheran," Otto chimed in helpfully, clarifying for my mother that she'd lost that battle before Howard had even joined the war. And why was I only learning then that Otto was a Lutheran? If any of us survived this tea, I vowed to ask Howard what that meant.

She nodded and turned to Howard. "And are you permitted to marry?"

"Oh yes, ma'am. Marriage of clergy is encouraged." Then he pulled out his ace. "As are children."

My mother brightened. "So you'd like to have children someday?" She glanced at Bella.

"Oh yes. Dozens."

Bella froze, but then Howard laughed. "Well, at least two or three, anyway."

That broke the ice, and the conversation flowed smoothly after that. Bella brought the tea and served it with delicate lemon cakes she'd baked in the apartment's gas oven. Our own gas oven! It was still a marvel for all of us.

After some time passed, my mother said, "I'll clean up. Jimmy, why don't you entertain Mr. Werner, perhaps with a tour of the complex? We'll leave Annabelle and Howard alone for a few minutes." So it was Howard now, after all!

I led Otto out the door and into the hallway.

"You knew about this, didn't you?" I accused.

"I only found out this week." As we walked down the hallway to the steps, Otto let his hand brush mine. "They make a nice couple though, don't you think?"

I supposed they did. Howard's unconstrained American style suited my sister. "Am I terrible brother?" I asked.

"The world is changing, James. We all need to figure out a new way of being in it."

That was cryptic, but it mirrored my own feelings. I felt light and free. A weighty burden had been lifted from my heart when I realized Bella wasn't interested in Otto. I didn't want to pick that burden up again.

"Would you have allowed me to court your sister?"

"It would have torn me apart." It was the truth, too, no matter how much I'd told myself I just wanted her to be happy and that I'd be able to be friends with Otto afterward.

"That's not an answer," Otto observed. And that was the truth too.

Chapter Nineteen

JANUARY 1941

If the first day of 1941 started out on a hopeful note, the next few days—the rest of the year, really—was one disaster after another.

On January 2, Mary Ellen and Bridget Shannon, and their niece Kathleen, were killed when the Germans dropped a bomb on their house in Carlow. Other bombs dropped harmlessly in several other counties in eastern Ireland that day. There was an outcry, but not nearly as intense as the public reaction to the Campile Creamery bombing five months prior. No one wanted to antagonize the Germans and bring London's fate to Ireland.

The following day I was eating breakfast with my mother, Bella having already gone off to the Werners', when we heard planes overhead. We looked at each other, eyes widening as we put down our forks. There was a muffled boom and the room shook, our teacups jostling on their saucers.

I rushed to the window but couldn't see evidence of an explosion.

"I'll head out and find Bella. Make sure she's all right," I said.

"Be careful, Jimmy, and if you get to the Werners', tell them to stop bombing Ireland. We're not in this war."

"I'll see what they can do."

Once I was outside, I saw rising smoke just a couple of blocks away, so I headed in that direction. A crowd had already gathered at Donore Terrace on South Circular Road, a complex not unlike the Galway Arches where we lived. A large section of the building had collapsed, and already a dozen or so men were helping disoriented victims make their way onto the street.

Many more people were simply standing about, and I concluded there was nothing I could contribute, so I continued on in search of Bella. By the time I got to the Werners' and saw that my sister was safe, Otto had already learned of the bombing and that dozens had been injured.

Bella was shaken when she learned of the incident, and as she was frying up the eggs and ham, Otto told her he would serve the food at breakfast. I didn't know if he wanted to spare Bella or his father, whom Otto later told me was embarrassed enough by the recent bombings that he preferred not to have to engage with his Irish employees.

Howard rushed in, disheveled and wild-eyed. When he saw Bella, he pulled her into a tight embrace. "I was so worried," he murmured, "when I saw that they'd dropped bombs so close to you." He looked over Bella's shoulder and scowled at Otto.

I still wasn't comfortable with the entire Howard/Bella thing and how neglectful I'd been as it developed. At the end of the New Year's Day tea, Howard had respectfully asked both me and my mother for permission to court Bella, which we'd readily granted. Still, seeing them holding each other was a bit much, although I supposed the circumstances warranted it.

"Otto," Mr. Werner called from somewhere in the house, upstairs, I thought. "Come here, please."

"I'll tell him breakfast is almost ready," Otto said to Bella and then left us alone.

Howard and Bella stepped apart. "That was a neat trick you pulled at tea," I said to my sister. "And you"—I turned to Howard—"all the times we talked about…everything…and never once did you think to tell me you were interested in my sister?"

Howard at least looked uncomfortable at that, but Bella huffed. "You know how Mother is, and it worked out in the end, anyway."

"Did it?" I asked. "Are we at the end already?"

"Ha," she said. "It's not as if you haven't been keeping a few secrets of your own now, is it, Jimmy?"

"Annabelle—" Howard started, but he was interrupted when Otto came back in.

"My father says he feels horrible about what has happened these last two days and thinks you should both take the day off, be with your family."

"That's funny, because my mother said I should ask him to please stop killing Irish people." Sure, that was a little unfair, but I wasn't in a mood to accommodate Mr. Werner's sense of guilt.

Otto turned red and stared at the floor, causing me to immediately regret my words. "Otto, I'm sorry. None of this is your fault. We all know that."

"I wish there was something I could do," he mumbled.

"That time might come," Howard said cryptically. Before I could ask about that comment, he turned to Bella and said, "Come on. Mr. Werner would be more comfortable without us here."

Some residual instinct of brotherly concern rose in me, quite late to the game. "You *will* take her directly home?" I asked.

Howard opened his mouth to reply, but Bella beat him to it.

"Jimmy—" She came to me and placed her hand lightly on my forearm. "—I'm nearly nineteen." I thought she was going to say that she was old enough to make her own decisions, but I knew our mother wouldn't share that opinion and was ready to tell her so. But, instead, she had something else to say entirely. "And it's so unfair that I'm expected to be controlled and under supervision at all times when you get to go off—who knows where—doing whatever it is you two do, with no one the wiser!" She looked pointedly between me and Otto.

Good God.

She'd removed her hand from my arm during that speech but then pointed an accusing finger at me. "Why should you be able to do as you please while I'm expected to remain a prisoner in my own home? Maybe some of the pressure to conform should be on you for a change."

She couldn't know the full extent of my relationship with Otto, could she? Behind her, Howard gave a slight shake of his head. I took that to mean he hadn't betrayed my confidence.

I was fairly certain she didn't know everything; otherwise, what she just said could have felt like a threat to expose me, and I was certain Bella wouldn't do that. Howard seemed extremely uncomfortable, and he gripped her arm. "Annabelle—" he began. But then I saw his eyes, and Bella's too, go to Otto behind me.

I turned to look at him, and I was surprised by what I saw. There was a fierceness in him. It was unnerving to see. Though I was certain, or nearly so, that Bella hadn't just threatened me, Otto felt differently.

"Miss Brennan," he addressed my sister, holding himself stiffly, almost formally. "Are you *threatening* James?"

"Why…no, no…of course not…" Bella had turned white.

Howard held her steady and said, "Now, Otto, I don't think—"

But Otto interrupted him. "I will not allow James to be threatened, by anyone, for any reason. Please, Dr. Fulman, my father is right. You should go now."

Once Bella and Howard had left, I turned to Otto. "That was a bit rough, don't you think? She's just a girl."

"It was *not* rough," he insisted. "She knew exactly what she was doing. She threatened you, James. She threatened to expose us. I won't have it, even if she is your sister."

He walked to the sink and stood there with his back to me. "I've put you at such risk. I can tell Howard knows about us, and now, I think, your sister too. And my country is dropping bombs on your city! I just wish I could protect you."

I wanted to go to him, but it was quiet in the house, and I didn't know if Mr. Werner might suddenly appear.

"When can we be alone?" I asked quietly in case Mr. Werner was just on the other side of the door. I was suddenly feeling paranoid.

Otto understood. He splashed water on his face, then turned to look at me. "He'll be here another few hours at least," he whispered. "Can you come back this evening?"

I nodded. I raised my voice to a normal volume and tried to sound calm. "I'll be going now, Otto, if there's nothing else you need?"

"No, nothing. Thank you, James. We'll see you on Monday."

I thought I heard a soft movement in the dining room.

Chapter Twenty

JANUARY 1941

When I arrived home, I found Bella and Howard having tea with my mother in the parlor.

Howard stood and shook my hand as if we hadn't seen each other less than an hour ago. "I'm sorry to have intruded without an invitation, but Annabelle seemed distraught, and I wanted to see her safely home." My mother seemed pleased that he did, and Bella looked better than she had right after Otto accused her of threatening me.

"We were just telling Mrs. Brennan about the bombing at Donore Terrace. Terrible thing. Thankfully, no one died."

"When will this all end?" my mother asked, theatrically, I thought, considering the thousands of women in London who'd been sleeping in crowded tube stations each night for months. Still, this morning's bomb could have just as easily fallen on us.

"Hopefully soon, Mrs. Brennan." Howard stood. "Thank you for the tea, ma'am. I'll take my leave now." He turned to me. "James, will you walk out with me?" Howard and I hadn't had a chance to talk since the surprise New Year's Day revelation, so despite my discomfort, I agreed.

We walked away from the crowds at Donore Terrace. Instead, we headed up to the Liffey and strolled along the quay, again passing the bench where I had learned of Germany's invasion of France less than a year earlier. We were mostly silent as we both thought through how best to proceed.

"Quite a mess this morning," Howard offered.

"Are you talking about the bombing, or Bella, or Otto?"

"All of them?" he asked.

I sighed. "You're right; it's a mess all around."

"It's nearly noon," Howard said. He indicated a cheerily lit pub at the corner. "And it's frigid out here. Can I stand you a pint?"

"A tea would be nice," I countered.

Once we were settled at a small table by the window, with two cups of tea and a plate of biscuits before us, Howard started again.

"First, before anything else, James, I want you to know I would *never* have revealed to your sister what you told me about you and Otto."

I believed that, *had* believed it, even before. Bella was smart, and she was just intuitively hitting the mark, even if she wasn't positive what that mark was.

"I know," I said. "I trust you, Howard."

He let out a breath. "That's good! If we're to be brothers, we need to trust each other."

"Are we?" I asked, not hiding my surprise. "Has it come to that, then? So soon."

He looked away from me, down at the table. "Er...perhaps it's not as soon as it appears to you. Despite Otto's covering for you on New Year's Day, it *is* true that your sister and I have had plenty of time...alone...to gradually reveal our feelings for each other."

It was my turn to look away. I truly had failed to look out for her.

"James, look at me." I did. "Annabelle knows her own mind. She's strong-willed and seems to be confident she can look after herself. But I want you to know I would *never* do anything to put her in jeopardy, of *any* sort."

We were dancing around it, but so much had already passed between me and Howard I decided to simply ask.

"So I won't need to be sending her off to a nunnery for nine months?"

Howard blushed. "Not unless the science has changed significantly since I learned the basics, no."

"Well, that's good. I'd hate to see her ruined."

Howard bristled at that. "The world is changing, James. Annabelle would not be 'ruined' no matter what choices she makes." I considered that. It's what Otto had said, talking about Howard and Bella. Maybe they were right.

I thought about me and Otto, about the impossibility of our being sweethearts. Maybe the world needed to change even more than it had.

"You, on the other hand," Howard continued, "seem quite ruined." He leaned back in his chair, studying me.

"Is that what I am? A ruined man?" I was surprised to find the idea somehow appealing. Freeing, even.

Howard chuckled. "I suppose not. I shouldn't joke that way. But you are in quite deep, aren't you? Much deeper than I'd expected."

I looked into my teacup and nodded my agreement.

"I thought so. Otto's reaction this morning was surprisingly...aggressive. I think he might be in even deeper than you are."

"It does seem to be a mutual obsession," I agreed.

"Where do you fellows disappear to, anyway? You go off for hours in the afternoon, then show up again as if you were never gone. I kept thinking you might be in the shed, but when I look, you're not there."

I know, I thought. *We've heard you checking.* I didn't want to tell Howard about my hideaway. It was like a game for me and Otto. No matter what we're doing, we freeze, and don't move an inch until he's gone. I considered how I should respond.

"No, wait," Howard interrupted before I could formulate my reply. "I don't want to know. I'd rather not lie to your sister. I think she thinks you two are out getting in trouble somehow—with cards or something—not the actual trouble you're getting into." He grinned.

"The good news," I said, "is that I won't be sending myself off to a nunnery either."

"Still, there are risks to what you're doing. Legally, physically...emotionally."

I wondered what he thought we were doing and what physical risks he envisioned, but I wasn't going to ask *that*.

"I'd hoped this would be just a phase for you, James."

I was taken aback. Hadn't he been the one to talk about defining your own morality? Then again, wasn't I the one who kept refusing to look squarely at what Otto and I had? To acknowledge it for what it was, whatever that was?

I swirled my nearly empty cup, studying the tea leaves there.

"You're only seventeen?"

"I'll be eighteen next month."

Howard sighed. "And Otto?"

"He'll be eighteen in May." Otto was a few months younger than I was, which bothered him a little because he always thought of himself as in charge.

Howard looked off to the side. "Old enough to know your minds, then."

Hardly.

"I suppose," I replied. "If only I *did* know my mind."

"James, look at me, please." Why did I keep avoiding his gaze? "When I said I'd hoped it was a phase for you, it's not because there's anything wrong, morally, with your relationship. I've watched you two together for over a year now. You're *everything* to each other! I just didn't understand how *romantically* involved you'd gotten."

Is that what it was? Romance? I guessed so, ever since wichsen time turned into lying together, caressing, kissing. Ever since we began fixing each other's collars, surreptitiously brushing hands, even in public.

"I was only hoping it would just be an adolescent thing because if it's not—if this is who you men are—it will make everything harder for both of you."

"I understand," I said. "And I don't *know* who we are. Or what any of this means. I only I know I can't keep pretending we're just fooling around, you know?"

"Well, after what I saw this morning, I'm certain Otto is not just fooling around. He's devoted to you." He drained his cup and set it back on its saucer. "But I have to say I didn't appreciate him talking to Annabelle that way. He frightened her."

Yes, he'd frightened me, too, a little. "I'll talk to him," I said.

"Good! Now, there's something else I need to discuss with you, but not in here."

★

What? We could talk about my relationship with another man—discreetly, of course—in a pub but needed privacy for this other thing?

We began walking through the streets again. A cold drizzle was falling, and we quickened our pace to keep warm.

"I need your help," he said. "Liam's help, actually."

That was odd. He knew my brother and I weren't on the best of terms.

"I'm about to tell you something that could get me killed, so if you don't want to hear it, say so now." I suspected I knew what this was about. I kept quiet.

He waited for a moment, then nodded his head. "Good. I'm involved in efforts to smuggle refugees out of Nazi-controlled areas in Europe."

Right. "The radio," I said.

"Yes, that's how we arrange transport and safe houses."

"Jews?"

He waited a moment before responding. "Mostly, yes."

"So it's that bad, then? Over there?"

"Yes. They're moving Jews across Europe into these so-called work camps. We have intelligence that they're also killing the Jewish civilians who can't work anymore—the old, the infirm."

That was horrifying, and I wondered what Otto knew. How sheltered from the truth was he?

"What do you need from Liam?" I decided I should help Howard in any way I could, but I failed to imagine what role Liam could play.

"There's a girl we need to get to Belfast. A German refugee. Her sister made it over on the Kindertransport a few years ago, but the girl we're trying to save wasn't able to leave at the time. Now our people have managed to get her to Portugal, and we want to reunite her with her sister up north. This is new for us. We usually move refugees to the Americas. We've never tried bringing anyone into Ireland before."

I considered that and was ashamed. I'd read that my government wasn't very accommodating when it came to accepting refugees from Europe. There was too much fear of losing our neutrality.

"She'll be arriving on the Lisbon run," Howard continued, "but she has no ID. We know the IRA forges documents sometimes. Will he do it, do you think—create an identity card for her?"

There was no way Liam would work against the Germans, not when he was working *with* them to try to get arms and support for the IRA. Nearly every week, Liam would approach me about being his messenger, getting information to the Germans through me, then to Otto, and eventually to the legation office. After the first envelope, right after the creamery bombing, I'd refused.

"No, he won't." But…

An idea was forming in my mind.

What if I lied to him? What if I convinced him he was actually *helping* the Germans?

"I know you well enough now, James. You're thinking heavy thoughts. What's going on?"

"How old is she?" I asked.

"About fifteen. I think."

I thought it through as we walked. This could really work, and not just for this one girl, but lots of things. Otto and I could even use this to thwart Germany's plans in Ireland.

"I'd need Otto. Can I share this with him?"

Howard was silent. I understood. He didn't know Otto's heart like I did, and even if he thought he *could* trust Otto, it was a huge risk, bringing the conspiracy right into the center of the German government's diplomatic mission in Ireland.

"Why do you need to involve Otto?"

More secrets. I hated this, but Otto had told me about Operation Green in strict confidence. I wasn't free to reveal Germany's plans for Ireland to Howard. But that meant I couldn't reveal that Otto was actually looking for a way to help Ireland avoid that fate.

"Liam will need to think he's supporting the IRA's secret work with Germany, and Otto will need to be involved to make that part real."

Far overhead, a plane buzzed. We couldn't see it through the thick cloud cover, but we listened until it passed out of range.

"I trust you, brother," Howard said, and that brought a pleasant warmth to my heart. "Be careful though, and it's better for Otto that he knows as little as possible." He reached into his thick wool jacket and pulled out an envelope. As he handed it to me, he said, "I'd brought this this morning, hoping to catch you at the Werners'; then events got away from us. There's a passport-style photo in here."

I slid the packet into my own jacket.

I went home, my head spinning with plans. I was working through what I'd tell Otto, and what I'd tell Liam, when I walked into the parlor and found my brother sitting there, having a beer while my mother had tea, and Bella sat in the chair, sewing, like a proper young lady.

I would need to talk to her too.

Liam had come when he'd heard about the nearby bombing.

It would have been better for my purposes to talk to Otto first, to get his agreement with my plan, work with him to refine it. But Howard was in a hurry, and I decided to take advantage of this opportunity to get Liam on board.

When he was ready to leave, I walked him out.

"Where are you staying these days?" I asked him.

"With friends," he replied. I knew he meant his IRA boys, who had safe houses scattered across the city. He didn't say anything else. He knew I didn't approve of the IRA.

"Eamon says you're getting to be too close with that German boy." Yes, that sounded like Eamon.

"He's not a boy; he's a soldier." It was another lie. But hopefully Liam wouldn't question why I'd be friends with a German soldier. He cocked his eyebrow at me but looked impressed. Good.

"Is that a fact?"

"Yes. I'm learning a lot from him." That, at least, was the truth.

"Well, that's good, then," Liam said. "Did he get the package I left with you a few months ago?"

"Yes." This was the tricky part, the part I would have liked to go over with Otto first. "He said it was helpful. But I don't know more than that. He doesn't tell me much." Again, a lie. Otto told me everything.

Liam smiled to himself and stood a little taller, pleased, I thought, to have been useful for the IRA's common cause with Germany against Britain.

"He did tell me, though, that they'd lost a couple guys who were reassigned elsewhere. They need to reestablish connections with the IRA." I waited to see if he'd say anything. I hoped I hadn't overplayed my hand. "I know you and I have never really talked about…your friends. And you know I don't approve of the civilian deaths…"

"I could help him out," Liam said.

I breathed a sigh of relief. "The thing is, though, they need something from the IRA right away. I told him I didn't even know if the IRA did this type of stuff."

"What stuff? What do they need?"

"Forged identification papers. They have an agent, a young German woman they need to sneak into Britain. She has the plans for some sort of bombing campaign." I figured that would get his interest; he was always going on about how the IRA was justified in bombing British targets. Although I was concerned that he might not believe a fifteen-year-old would be working as an agent. "She looks younger than she is, so they need documents showing her to be fifteen."

"What kind of documents?"

"I don't know. The Germans were hoping you fellows would know all that," I said. "She'll be on the Lisbon ship and will need to pass through customs here at the dock. She also needs to get into Belfast on the train."

"I have friends who do IDs. I'll find out what they'd need," said Liam. "Are the Germans ready to supply us with guns?"

"I don't know. He just said 'cooperation with the IRA.' I have no idea what they're thinking. The whole thing makes me uncomfortable." Which was also true. Very true.

Liam thought for a minute, but I knew at that point he wasn't going to pass up this opportunity. In his mind, if he played it right, he could rise in the ranks of the IRA, be somebody important after the war.

"Can you get me a passport picture of her?"

"I've got it right here." I pulled the envelope out of my jacket and opened it. I wanted to make sure there was nothing inside that Liam shouldn't have. There wasn't, just a small photo of a frightened-looking girl.

"You're carrying it around with you?"

"I was going to seek you out this afternoon."

Normally, he would have called me out on such an obvious lie, but he was clearly hooked. He studied the picture. "I'll find out if it can be done. Meet me back here tomorrow?"

"Thanks," I said.

"Does your German soldier want to meet me?" His question had a note of pride as if it would be an honor to meet a soldier.

"Not yet. He said it's best these things be done through intermediaries so no one knows everything."

He nodded slowly, and if he was disappointed in that, he didn't let it show.

Chapter Twenty-One

JANUARY 1941

Bella. I needed to talk to her before visiting Otto that night.

We were in the kitchen, our own kitchen, which felt odd, as we usually only chatted in the Werners' kitchen while she was working. When I came in after leaving Liam, I'd casually mentioned to my mother that I'd seen a few of the neighborhood ladies gossiping about the bombing down in the courtyard, so Bella and I had privacy.

She was washing dishes at the sink. "I hope you won't be wanting an apology from me, Jimmy."

"I might be. What were you thinking this morning, going off like that? I was just trying to be a good brother."

"A good brother!" She threw the towel she'd been using into the sink. "A good brother would support his sister, I think. And trust her. And help her be happy. Not try to keep her locked away under constant supervision." She balled her hands on her hips. "And to not trust me with Howard is just insulting."

She was right about that. I knew Howard, and I knew my sister. There was no risk there. I had reacted out of guilt, I realized. I was ashamed that I'd missed what had been happening between them right under my nose, and I suddenly wanted to make up for that. But suggesting I didn't trust her and Howard together wasn't the way to go about it.

"Howard's been a perfect gentleman," she continued. "Too perfect, sometimes. And even if he wasn't, even if I didn't *want* him to be, it's no business of yours what we get up to."

"Bella, I'm sorry. I overreacted this morning, that's true. I *do* trust you. And Howard too. But you *are* my business. I don't want to see you hurt. And…you won't want to hear this…but your reputation is important too."

"You see?" she cried. "You of all people, Jimmy."

"Bella, I don't understand…"

"Of course you don't."

"So *tell* me," I pleaded.

She moved to the chair by the table and collapsed into it. Then she leaned back and blew out a breath. "It's just so *unfair*. It drives me mad!"

"What's unfair?"

"Everything. You. Us." She rubbed the back of her neck. "Oh, Jimmy, I *did* mean it, you know, when I said you were important to me. You *are*. And I meant it when I said if you said no, I'd agree to abide by that. But…I was talking about the big things, you know? Like, if you thought he was wrong for me, I'd trust you and listen to you."

I nodded but didn't say anything. She was leading up to what was actually bothering her, and I wanted her to find her own way there.

"But the little things! Sweet Jesus, Jimmy, I'm so *controlled*."

Was she? I didn't see it. She had a job where she worked on her own; she went shopping without supervision. I imagined she had friends. What more did a girl need?

Thankfully, I knew enough not to say any of that.

"Bella, I still don't understand."

She let out a frustrated groan. "Let's try this," she said. "Tell me, during the last month, where did you sleep each night?"

"Well…different places on different nights, I guess." I wasn't sure of the answer myself. It would take some effort for me to come up with an accounting. I'd slept here occasionally, and in my hideaway more often than not, on the sands of the bay a few times. In Otto's bed. That didn't seem like an adequate response. "You know, my job…"

"Oh, hush," she snapped. "I have a job, too, same place as you. And I'm there each morning to cook breakfast long before you show up."

"But it's different for me. For one thing, you're a girl—"

"Right," she interrupted me. "And is that the first item on a long list, Jimmy, or is that the whole of it?"

I tried to quickly think of a few other reasons but drew a blank.

"Uh-huh," Bella said.

"But it *is* different for girls, Bella. It would be a scandal if you disappeared for a night."

"I *know* that," she shouted. "That's what's so unfair!"

Oh.

"Do you…do you *want* to…spend the night…elsewhere?" I whispered that last bit. I was thinking of Howard and trying hard to remember that I trusted both of them.

She looked at me for a long moment, then sighed. "No," she admitted. "I'm not ready for anything like that." She made it sound like a failure on her part.

I was relieved. I was trying to keep an open mind, but I would have been strongly opposed to any such thing.

"But it would be nice if that were *my* decision and not everyone else's." She wiped a tear away. "Sit down. You're making me nervous hovering there."

I sat across from her.

"And when I look at you," she continued, "only seventeen and allowed all the independence you could ask for, I get…envious, I guess. Jealous, maybe."

"Practically eighteen now," I offered weakly.

"Don't." She held up her hand to me, palm forward. "You and Otto have both been on your own for over a year now."

I blushed, which brought us back to what had happened this morning. I understood her position better now, but I still wasn't sure if she realized why she'd frightened Otto so badly, and if she didn't, I wasn't sure how to tell her.

"I'm sorry Otto snapped at you this morning." I'd concluded it was safe to just raise the topic without assigning blame. "He's been under a lot of stress."

"No, I should apologize to him. And I will when I see him next. I should have been more…sensitive…to his, and your… situation."

She looked me straight in the eye and held my gaze.

"It's…complicated," I managed.

She reached across the table and held my hands. "Jimmy, just because I have to live under a microscope doesn't mean you do too. Honestly, I just want you to be happy. And I know—more than you probably think I do—about you and Otto. And if I didn't know before this morning, I certainly do now after he bit my head off to protect you! That was impressive."

I was so red in the face I felt the heat radiating off me in waves.

"Jimmy, it's all right; really it is. I don't know *everything*. And I don't want to," she hurried to add at the look of panic on my face. "I'd always just accepted what the Church taught, so I knew it was wrong, and I don't pretend to know better than that now."

Me too, I thought. *But I do know better now.*

"And Howard has talked to me about it," she continued, "with much dancing around the topic, for sure. I think he wanted to make sure I wouldn't reject my little brother if I ever found out. I think the Americans are smarter about these types of things than we are, Jimmy."

I thought of Howard's church, and its ideas about personal responsibility, and its efforts to save refugees. Bella was right about the Americans.

"But honestly? I still assumed it was wrong. None of my business, maybe, but the Church is clear about it." I sighed. She was right about that too.

"But then I came to *like* Otto, so my thinking…changed. And I didn't know until this morning that he *loved* you."

I was sure I was going to fall off my chair. With great effort I remained firmly in my seat. But I couldn't seem to speak coherently.

"Uh…uh…"

"Do you feel the same way…about Otto, I mean?"

Maybe? It was all too much, too fast. *Love?*

"I don't… I mean… It's not… You shouldn't…"

"Oh, for goodness' sake, Jimmy. Forget I asked. I *will* apologize to Otto. You two have absolutely nothing to fear from me."

I concentrated on my breathing.

"I still don't know what's right or wrong, but I do know the world's changing, Jimmy. You should take advantage of that. I'm going to."

Well, if they all kept saying it, maybe it was true.

I judged my feet to be steady enough, so I released my sister's hands and stood.

"Oh," she said. "Don't tell Howard I know about…the two of you. I'm sure he thinks I'm too innocent to even conceive of these things." She smiled and nodded to the door. It was clear she'd decided to let me escape without further interrogation.

I wobbled as I began making my way to the parlor and the exit in a daze.

"One more thing," she called. "I *think* I'm the only one who knows about your secret hiding place, but Otto is loud enough to hear from the kitchen…when he's…well, you know."

I nearly fell out the front door and blindly made my way down the stairs and into the bracing winter air.

★

It was later than I'd intended by the time I made it back to the Werners' that evening.

Otto was waiting for me, seated at the kitchen table, a bottle of whiskey and two empty glasses in front of him.

"I was afraid you wouldn't come."

I remembered the first day we'd met, when he had said that very thing to me here in his kitchen. When were we going to start trusting each other?

"I was afraid you were angry for how I treated your sister, and for the bombing."

"No, the bombing isn't your fault. You know that; *we* know that. And I talked to Bella; it's all right."

"There's more though," said Otto. "I've learned more. And I need to tell you about it."

I thought about what Howard had said and what I'd arranged with Liam. "There's a lot we need to talk about," I agreed.

He nodded. "But first." He poured a generous measure in each glass. He stood, picked one up, and handed it to me. "No matter what happens now, James, you've been the best thing that ever happened to me." He raised his glass, and I did the same; then we drained our glasses and placed them, empty, on the table.

He was nervous; that much was obvious. I was, too, because I'd committed us, or me, at least, to a perilous path with

Howard and the IRA. I realized this toast felt like it could be a goodbye, and that's when it struck me that it really *could* be. Otto might be furious that I'd arranged all these deceptions.

Part of me wanted to take him into the shed to allow us one more time together before I told him what he needed to hear. But I didn't want to trick him into having sex if I knew he might never want to see me again after I told him the truth.

He put his hand on my shoulders, leaned in, and kissed me. He took his time about it too. I began to reassess about the shed. After he pulled away, he said, "You taste good."

"I taste like whiskey," I replied with a smile.

"You taste like home," he said.

Love, Bella had said.

"Come upstairs with me." He tugged on my arm, trying to lead me out of the room.

I wanted to, but... "I think we need to talk first."

"We do," he agreed. "But let's not talk here."

We went upstairs. I thought we'd go into the study, but he led me into his bedroom. There, we kicked off our shoes and got on top of the bed, lying next to each other, touching shoulder to shoulder, but looking at the ceiling. He was right, somehow. This was a good place for a difficult discussion, intimate, but not threatening.

I chose to break the silence first. "Bella knows about us."

"Hold that for now. There's something more important I need to tell you." He took a deep breath. "And it might not matter what your sister knows...afterward."

I moved my hand between us until I found his. "Tell me."

"First, you need to know that I didn't know about this. I know I say that to you more and more about the bombing of London, the invasion, the plans for Ireland, and then the bombs here. I understand at some point it doesn't matter anymore just how ignorant I am. I'm afraid we've reached that point."

"What is it?"

"It's about the Jews. You were right. I was lied to. And when you asked me about the situation, I told you that you didn't understand, but you did. I was the one who didn't see what was really happening."

I thought about what Howard had said, but I needed to hear it from Otto, and he needed to say it out loud, and in the daylight.

"What's really happening?" I realized I might be squeezing his hand too hard and loosened my grip.

"We're removing them. All of them," he whispered.

"What do you mean removing?" I asked.

"We're moving all the Jews in Europe to these work camps, not just the German Jews. Tens of thousands of them, James. Entire neighborhoods and villages. From Poland, from the low countries, even from France."

I turned my head to see him. He wasn't crying, but his eyes shone with emotion. He didn't look away from the ceiling. I knew there was more, based on what Howard had said. I sensed Otto was leading it up to it.

"And...I think they're killing the ones who won't work, even if it's because they're too old, or...or...crippled, or something." His voice shook as he said that, overwhelmed by shame.

The thought literally sent a shiver through my body, and Otto sensed the movement. He turned his head toward me. "Maybe even children too," he whispered. I understood the urge to whisper, to not give the idea more weight than necessary.

We stayed there for at least fifteen minutes, just being together in a world gone mad.

Finally, Otto said, "I don't know what to do."

I sat up but stayed on the bed, sitting cross-legged. Otto did the same so that we were facing each other, knees touching as the mattress shifted with our movements. His cheeks were damp.

It was hard for me to understand what he must have been feeling, to be betrayed like that by your own country, perhaps by your own family.

"Otto." I tapped his knee to get him to look up. "There *is* something we can do. At least here in Ireland, like you said before."

He tilted his head at me.

"I know someone." This part was tricky. Howard trusted me to involve Otto, but he hadn't suggested I could reveal his own identity. "Someone who knows what's going on in Europe…with the Jews. He's part of network that's trying to rescue as many as they can."

Otto looked at me. "And you felt you couldn't tell me this because I'd dismissed your concerns earlier. I've failed you, James, haven't I?"

"No! You haven't failed me. I only just found out about this fellow's work myself. But we can *do* something to help."

"What can we possibly do? We're so far away."

I told him about my plans, leaving out anything having to do with Howard.

He became more animated as I went on and grew excited about the ability to funnel false information to the IRA, misinformation that might actually help protect Ireland from German attacks. He actually laughed when I described telling Liam he'd be secretly helping the Germans defeat England, when really he'd be helping me and Otto undermine Germany to protect Ireland.

"Oh, James, that's brilliant. So many complicated lies! You're extraordinary." He squeezed my knee. I was thrilled that I could make him happy like this and that he was enthusiastically supporting my scheme. *Our* scheme.

"Let me get this straight. The Irish government doesn't know it's authorizing this Jewish girl's entry because the IRA is forging those documents, and the IRA thinks it's working with the German legation to bring in an agent? When really it's just you and me playing both sides?" He was grinning, eyes dancing with pleasure.

"Right, you and me, saving the world."

"And this girl, what is happening with her?" Otto asked.

"I'm not sure, but she's going up north, I think, eventually."

"But, if she can get here to Dublin, why can't she just stay?"

"Because Ireland isn't willing to risk offending Germany. No refugees without proper identification will be allowed in. And I guess now it's impossible for Jews in Europe to emigrate."

Otto was thinking it through, nodding to himself. "But, James, this is amazing. I feel like you've given me an opportunity to be useful, finally!"

He was so excited, bouncing up and down, it felt like the bed was floating on a rough sea.

"And your brother and the IRA—what luck! We can feed them false information about British positions and German plans." I could see his mind was racing. "Oh!" he exclaimed. "I can use the legation stationery in the office, make it look like stolen official documents. There's so much we can do!"

He squeezed my knee again, this time leaving his hand there.

His gaze locked on mine. "I thought it was all over for us," he said. "But it's only just beginning."

He leaned in and kissed me again, and this time we both knew we wouldn't stop there. It's difficult to kiss and undress on top of an unsteady mattress, but we managed.

"What about your father?" I murmured into his mouth while he worked my braces free.

"He won't be back for hours," Otto said.

About half an hour later, just as Otto was reaching his climax, he began shouting—loud, foreign words, repeated again and again until he released a final exclamation, a guttural growl that still managed to be German somehow.

Bella had been right about how loud he was.

About so many things.

Love, she'd said.

Chapter Twenty-Two

FEBRUARY 1941

One bitterly cold afternoon at the end of January, Bella and I were working in the Werners' kitchen when we heard children raising a ruckus in the alley. We rushed through the shed and opened the door. A dozen or so children were running down the alley. "The Glimmer Man's coming. The Glimmer Man's coming!" they sang out, some turning down other alleyways to carry their message through the neighborhood.

"I hate this," said Bella as we made our way back into the kitchen to await the inspector.

"We'll be fine," I told her. "We've only used the turf stove for the last two days." I had managed to fit the flue on the stove myself, and just in time too. Coal rationing had limited supplies severely, and what coal was available was of extremely poor quality. For those lucky enough to have piped coal gas, like the Werners, there were only brief periods of the day when they were permitted to use it. Hence the Glimmer Man—an official inspector who went door to door checking that gas wasn't being used when it shouldn't—"not even a glimmer," as the posters put it. A warm gas oven could have your supply cut off for days.

A few minutes later, Bella was ushering the inspector into the kitchen.

"It's warm in here," he observed with some suspicion as he read the notes on his clipboard.

"Yes, sir," I replied. "I installed an old turf stove. Heats the place right up."

He looked up at me. "That was smart of you." He walked over to get a better look at it. "Looks like the one we had in our cottage when I was a boy." He walked to the gas oven and placed his hand on it. "Good," he said. "How are turf supplies?" he asked me.

"Getting better," I replied. And they were. The government was pushing to transition to turf across the country, and the effort was beginning to pay off.

"Think you could set me up with one at my flat?"

Bella smiled. I knew what she was thinking. Another job. We were doing quite well, she and I. Bella had two other families she'd met through the Werners that she occasionally worked for, and I was developing a reputation as someone who could secure fair contracts for home deliveries of all sorts. Maybe I could branch out into turf stove installation?

"I imagine I could," I answered.

"Good, then, and where can I find you?"

"I'm here more often than not," I said.

He looked at his clipboard and frowned. "This is the Werner household, yes?"

Bella and I nodded.

"I'm not one to tell others their business, but I'd be careful about getting in too close with Germans if were you." He tugged on his hat. "Have a good day."

"A little late for that piece of advice," Bella murmured. After she'd shown him out.

Bella went back to her vegetable chopping, and I went back to the bills. Everything was getting to be so much more expensive, and I was a stickler for ensuring the Werners didn't pay more than necessary.

"Speaking of turf," Bella said, even though we hadn't been.

I put the paperwork aside and looked up at her. I could tell from her tone this wasn't idle chitchat.

"I have news about Father." She continued prepping the food, not meeting my eyes as she said this.

"You haven't been back there, have you? There's nothing for us there anymore." If I could erase the tenement from our histories, I would. We needed to be focused on our futures.

"No. But Father Flannery came around to see Mother. It seems Father has gotten a job."

Well, that was good news for him, I thought. But I was sure it wouldn't last. I'd seen men that deep in the drink before, and they never managed to climb out of it, not for long, anyway.

When I didn't respond, Bella continued. "I think Father Flannery is hoping that there might be a reconciliation."

"Huh," I said. I hadn't considered that as a possibility. But I knew my mother had been increasingly uncomfortable with how she described her circumstances. It's not acceptable for a Catholic woman to simply leave her husband. "What's he doing, then? For work, I mean?"

"You won't believe it, Jimmy. He's cutting turf!"

"What? You're right; I don't believe it." I couldn't picture our father out in the weather, working the land.

"It's true though," Bella said. "There's dozens of men now, working for the parish. They take the truck each morning and drive into the countryside to cut turf, then bring it back and distribute it to parish families. They say it's happening all over the country." She'd finished chopping the carrots and swept them into a bowl.

I was familiar with what was happening, in a general way. Even outside the church, the government itself employed thousands of men in the business. I just couldn't picture my father being part of that effort.

"It's funny," Bella continued, "how we poor people are able to adjust right away, when the rich people don't know how they're going to heat their homes or cook their meals."

"Don't say that, Bella," I snapped, perhaps too harshly. "We're not poor. We're a respectable family now." It's what I'd been working toward for years. We needed to start believing in ourselves, and I couldn't have Bella dragging us back into the past.

"There's nothing wrong with—" she began, but she was interrupted by Otto and Howard coming into the kitchen from the shed. They brought a swirl of cold, damp air in with them as they removed their coats and hats. Otto rubbed his hands over the stove.

"It's gone fierce cold out!" exclaimed Howard, winking at Bella as he said it.

She blushed and looked at me. "I love it when he pretends he's gone native," she said in a stage whisper. "He just never gets the language *quite* right, though."

Otto looked between us, missing the subtext, mumbled something in German, and shrugged.

It had taken a few weeks, but things had finally settled nicely between all of us.

"You fellows have been out and about quite a bit recently," I observed, trying not to make it sound like an accusation. But in truth, I was feeling left out.

"Oh, just secret teacher-student things," Howard responded. As if *that* would make me feel better. Otto looked at me with a small smile and a gleam in his eye. I was getting worried.

I finally received the forged IRA documents from Liam and was able to hand them off to Howard. "Just in time too," he'd said. "She can't stay in Lisbon much longer."

I would be turning eighteen the next day, and the four of us went out for a pub dinner and visited a music hall afterward to celebrate. "Are you excited?" I asked Bella. "Your first time at a music hall?" She quickly looked at Howard without answering me, and he cleared his throat and looked away. Oh. Not her first time, then.

After the performance, Howard escorted Bella home, and Otto and I continued on a walk. It was a cold night, but dry, and we were well bundled and content to be out in the winter air. A stinging pall of peat smoke hung over the city, making my eyes water. We ended up walking toward the bay.

"I can't believe you're eighteen tomorrow," Otto said.

"I know. It sounds so mature."

"I should be the older one," Otto told me.

"Why is that?"

"Because I'm always the one taking charge. You'd still be standing on the dock with that bucket of mussels in your hand trying to figure out whether you wanted to sell them to us if I hadn't forced you into it."

Was that how he saw us? How he saw *me*? I had to admit there was an element of truth to it. "Well, one of us has to be cautious." I bumped his shoulder with mine as we continued walking. We came to the bay and strolled out onto the sand, away from the city lights. The smell of salt and peat and the stars overhead all made me think this was what it had been like for hundreds, maybe thousands, of years. The world might be changing, but some things stayed the same.

"I come here sometimes, when I need to think. When I need to be alone," Otto said. We stopped when we reached the water's edge. The bay was calm. Gentle waves melted into the sand just beyond our feet. "I stand here and think about how far away my home is. Sometimes, at night, I'll see planes and wonder if I know any of the pilots." I reached over and took his hand. "I know you don't like talking about the future"— Otto curled his fingers around mine—"or about us, but I do. I think about us all the time, that is. Think about our future."

I fought the impulse to pull away, to change the subject. "I think about you all the time too, Otto," I said instead. I wrapped my arm across his shoulder and pulled him in tight as we both looked out to sea, into the unknowable future.

★

The next day, to celebrate my birthday, we had a small family lunch, and my mother gave me a beautiful silk tie and matching waistcoat. "Because you're a man now and need to look the part." Liam pulled me aside afterward and handed me a package. "This is for your German fellow," he said. I knew it would be more IRA intelligence about British troops and plans, which, thankfully, would never make its way into German hands. Well, not beyond Otto's, anyway. "And this is for you," he said, handing me a second package. "Happy birthday."

"You'll have to hide it," he added as I removed it from its bag. It was a book of some sort. Was it…pornography? No, I concluded as I flipped through it. It was more of a how-to manual—with detailed illustrations—on the mechanics of "marital relations." Surely the Church didn't approve of most of these positions? I quickly looked away at one point. I did *not* want to know that much about the female anatomy. But I imagined the fun Otto and I would have reading through it.

Was I willfully blind or just naïve? Both probably. But it wasn't until that moment, on my eighteenth birthday, with explicit drawings of naked ladies in hand, that I had the shocking realization that I was without a doubt a homosexual. I was startled by the revelation.

"You're welcome," Liam said, smirking. "I knew you'd never get the information from Da. So. Feel free to ask me any questions. It's not too late, is it? Do you have someone special yet?"

I *did* have someone special. And I never wanted to see another picture of a naked lady again.

Chapter Twenty-Three

FEBRUARY 1941

That night, Howard stayed to have dinner with me and Otto at the Werners'. It was becoming more common for him to do so. Mr. Werner wouldn't arrive home until late into the evening, and more often than not, he would rush back to the legation after he ate. Howard and Otto and I would sit and talk about the world until Otto's hints that he wanted Howard to leave were too obvious even for the American to miss. On that night though, both Otto and Howard seemed distracted throughout the meal.

I was looking forward to seeing Howard go home, as it had been a few days since Otto and I had managed to carve out any wichsen time, and I wanted to remedy that situation. It *was* my birthday, after all.

Plus, I had an idea that I *might* decide to talk to Otto afterward about my realization that I was a homosexual and ask him if he thought he might be a homosexual too. But I wasn't yet committed to having that discussion. I didn't know what my being a homosexual could *mean*, for us. Or if it would even matter at all. Maybe it would just make things worse to put it out there like that. It was probably best, I decided, not to talk about these things at all.

I convinced myself that the way to proceed would be to bring Liam's book over and see how Otto responded to the far-too-detailed pictures. That should tell the story.

As soon as he was finished with his meal, Howard stood, wiping his mouth with his napkin. I was relieved he was heading off so quickly. "Gents, I've got to run out for a moment, but I'll be back in a flash." And with that he grabbed his coat and was out the door.

Wait, what?

"Why is he coming back?" I asked Otto.

"Well, we're still celebrating your birthday, aren't we?"

"Are we? All of us? I was hoping we could celebrate in private." I reached across the table and ran my fingers over Otto's hand, just in case he didn't get the message.

"And we will!" Otto said, giving me the sunbeam smile I never tired of. "But let's clean up here first so Bella doesn't have to do it in the morning."

When Howard returned about a half hour later, Otto said, "Finally! Let's go for a walk!" He was bouncing on his feet in excitement.

"I was as fast as I could be," Howard mumbled, breathing heavily as if he'd exerted himself.

What was going on?

It was cold and drizzling. "Not the best night for it though," I observed, thinking my friends had lost their minds.

But Otto and Howard were already bundling up, and Otto was grabbing my heavy winter coat and scarf. "Come on!" he urged me.

"Why are we doing this?" I complained as we made our way through Dublin's wet, smoke-filled streets.

"It's a surprise," Otto proclaimed. I'd never seen him so excited.

"And let's keep it that way until the end, Otto," Howard admonished, which scared me a little, given how much time they'd been spending together alone recently. After fifteen minutes or so of walking, we entered a recently built commercial district of the city near the financial companies and a few of the newer diplomatic offices built since Ireland's independence. There was the occasional pub, but otherwise it was mostly dark, the offices closed and locked tight that time of the evening.

The drizzle turned to rain and I'd had enough. "Gentlemen, seriously, this has gone too far. What's this about? Let's go back where it's warm."

"Well, let's just pop in here, then, shall we?" Howard suggested. "It looks like a good port in a storm." We'd stopped in front of the only office on the block with lights on inside. The glow from the lamps spilled through a large plate-glass window next to the door, illuminating the puddles on the pavement. I looked up at the door, a freshly painted green with white trim, which set it off nicely in the redbrick facade. I glanced again at the window.

Printed across the glass in modern, bold lettering was:

James Brennan — Property Management
Supply Contracts
Domestic Services
Foreign Clients Welcomed

I just stood in the rain, staring at the sign.

Otto and Howard were grinning and slapping each other on the back. "Well, come on," Howard said, retrieving a key from his pocket and opening the door, then ushering us inside. We hung our wet coats on the clothes pegs lining the entry hall and stepped into the office itself.

There was a large wooden desk, simply designed but of high quality. A series of wooden cabinets lined one long wall, and a couch with end tables filled the other. Two wooden chairs with burgundy leather seats sat in front of the desk.

There was an actual telephone right on the desk! It was a big, clunky black contraption with a thick cord disappearing into a discreet hole drilled into the desktop for that very purpose. Along the front wall of the office two upholstered wing chairs flanked the picture window with a small table between them. There was even a small potted plant on the table.

Covering the wall behind the desk was an enormous framed map of the city of Dublin, with every street, parish, and landmark identified in detail.

"Good Lord," I managed.

"Run upstairs and get us the champagne, won't you, James?" Howard asked.

"Upstairs? Champagne?" My mind was reeling.

Otto put his hand on my shoulder and turned me in the direction of an open doorway in the corner opposite the front door. "Through there," he said. "Past the WC."

Upstairs was what the new developers were calling "above-shop living quarters." It was a square room with a bed and a closet, a desk with a lamp, and, behind a door on the back wall, a bathroom. With an honest-to-God shower. I'd never taken a shower before, and I studied the small, open space next to the toilet below the showerhead and wondered if Otto and I could fit there together.

In the bathroom sink was a cold bottle of champagne. Three glasses sat on the tiny counter next to it. I brought them downstairs and found Otto and Howard sitting in the wing chairs by the window. They stood when I came in.

"How is all of this happening?" I asked. I was bewildered and couldn't quite believe what I was seeing despite what was written on the window.

Howard took the champagne to the desk and opened it. There was a resounding *pop* as the cork flew into the back hallway. He poured three glasses, and I was surprised to see how much was just bubbles. He waited a few seconds and topped them off. He handed one to me, Otto picked up another, and Howard raised the third. "To James Brennan, Property Management. May it prosper." He lifted his glass higher, and Otto and I did the same. Then we all took a sip. It fizzed in my nose and tasted bitter. I didn't like it.

"First," Howard said, at last answering my question, "we had to put the lease in my name. But now that you're eighteen, we can change that. The landlord already knows you're the real owner of the business and is expecting us tomorrow to change the paperwork." *The real owner of the business.* My head was spinning.

Otto cleared his throat. He looked a bit nervous suddenly. "Howard and I are partners, though. We put our own money in too," he said. "And Bella gave us yours and some of her own. We knew you wouldn't mind."

I'd saved up a fair amount. I had nothing to spend money on. To invest it in my own business was something I'd never even dreamed about. I shook my head in wonder.

"It's beautiful," I managed to say through my suddenly thick throat. "And generous, and…and I don't know what to say."

"It was my idea," Otto said proudly. "Do you have any idea how much money you've saved us, James?" No, I didn't. "Every month my father gives me money to run the household. Even after paying you and Bella, I've been able to set aside quite a bit. And already you've started earning more working with others from the legation. And so has Bella. You have a growing reputation. You're going to do quite well."

"And I know a few Americans who need help securing coal deliveries," Howard added. "And maybe you could even start selling some of those turf stoves. I think Otto and I are going to see a handsome return on our investments."

I looked around the space. I couldn't believe this was mine. My mind was racing with possibilities. I could do this. I really could! I knew how to run a household now and could extend that to running a business. Otto and I locked gazes, silently communicating all the things we never said to each other.

"There's a pub just two blocks over," Howard said. "Shall we have a nightcap?"

"No," Otto and I said at the same time.

"Oh, I see." Howard scuffed his shoe on the floor. "Well, as James has pointed out to me, I have a certain obligation to ensure behavioral standards are upheld—"

Otto turned to Howard and interrupted him. "What's the American word? Scram? Yes, I think that's it. Scram, Howard."

Howard scrammed.

Otto and I put our glasses on the desk, and without a word, he took my hand and led me up the stairs.

A real bed, my own business, a naked and sated Otto stretched languorously in my arms. It was everything I could possibly need.

Otto's breathing settled into a steady, deep rhythm. I wasn't certain if he was sleeping. I ran my hand softly down his flank, then pulled the cover up tightly over us both. A satisfied sigh escaped his lips. I wanted to tell him I was a homosexual, that what we had was more than just two young men finding pleasure in each other, for me at least. That I would always be this way and was never going to marry. I needed him to see me for what I was, to give him a chance to back away before getting more deeply involved in case it didn't mean to him what I now realized it meant to me.

Instead of saying any of that, I simply whispered, "I love you, Otto Werner."

He didn't open his eyes, but a gentle smile lit his face. "Of course you do, James. How could you not?" He settled deeper into the covers. "I love you too."

Chapter Twenty-Four

MARCH 1941

March of 1941 was the best month of my life.

I *almost* felt badly about my good fortune as the rest of the world slid deeper into chaos and disaster. Every single night, Londoners continued to die in horrific air raids. In Europe, the refugee crisis intensified every day, and the plight of the Jews grew more and more dire. Howard became despondent, claiming no one back in the States would listen to what was happening, or worse, they chose not to hear. But it was all so difficult; so much of what we knew, or thought we knew, was based on rumors and unconfirmed reports.

Meanwhile, my property management business was taking off.

Toward the end of the month, I convened an all-staff meeting, which meant Bella and I sat in the comfortable wing chairs and talked business. We were finishing our second cups of tea, having gone over the accounts and concluded we were in fine shape financially.

"It's time, Jimmy. I'm turning away business," my sister said, continuing her argument that we should bring on another employee. "It's the cleaning and laundry, mostly. These German men don't know where to turn. And they're willing to pay so much."

She was right. She usually was. Even I'd been having to turn away offers to take on household management duties, both from the legation staff and also from a few of Howard's American colleagues, as well as some English families too. "You've convinced me," I told her. "Let's start with Clara, as you've suggested."

Bella clapped her hands. "Perfect," she exclaimed. "I know she'll jump at the chance, as will any number of girls back in the North Strand."

With business concluded, we delicately turned to personal matters.

"Otto seems happy," she observed.

A blush crept over my face. "Yes, he does."

She sighed. "Which means you're happy too."

"I suppose so," I admitted. And it was true. I'd become alarmed by how much my happiness was now connected to Otto's. I was far too frequently concerned with what I could do to solicit one of Otto's smiles.

"You're as tight as a cockle, you are." She said this with no small amount of exasperation. "You know you can talk to me about anything."

I reached over and took her hand. "I *do* know that. It's just...well, men are bad about that whole talking thing, that's all."

"And I know *that* in spades. Howard will be the end of me yet, Jimmy. He's in something deep, and it's weighing on him. I wish he'd talk to me too."

I wondered about that. Bella was a modern woman with her own ideas, especially ideas about fairness and principles. How would she feel if she knew about Howard's work? I thought she would have been keen to help, actually, and that made me feel hopeful about their future together.

"All three of you," she continued. "Secrets everywhere. Liam too. What is it about men anyway?"

"We're beasts; that's for sure."

She laughed then and reached over to slap my arm. "You're not, really. You're all just stunted." We both looked about the shop, neither of us accustomed to the idea of our success yet. It seemed so unlikely, so spectacular.

"It doesn't seem right sometimes, Jimmy. That we have it so good when so many are suffering." She turned back to me. "I love Howard, you know, Jimmy. When he gets around to asking me, I'm going to say yes." I nodded. I'd assumed as much. Before I could say anything, she continued. "One of the things I love most about him is his compassion. His sense of being compelled to do the right thing by others."

Maybe she knew more than Howard had led me to believe? Was she dancing around the issue, trying to feel me out first?

"But he doesn't let me in. Not really. I think he thinks he's protecting me, but he's just putting up walls between us. And…well, I know more than he thinks I do."

That pulled a laugh out of me, and Bella made an affronted face in response.

"I'm not laughing at you," I insisted. "I'm laughing at the men in your life—always underestimating you. *Of course* you know more than we think you do. You always have."

She nodded. "Well I'm glad you see it now, at least. And I want to help Howard, but he needs to let me in. He's been so stressed lately. And I know it's about the work he's doing in secret. I think it has something to do with the war." She gave me a moment to respond, but I kept quiet. "Would you tell me what you know, Jimmy? The two of you are close."

That was an easy one for me. "No, Bella. Those aren't my secrets to tell."

She let out a frustrated groan.

"But," I continued, "I think Howard should tell you everything. And I'll tell him so myself. Just please understand there's real risk involved here. Yes, he's trying to protect you, but it's not because you're a woman. It's because he's involved in dangerous work."

"I suspected as much," she said. "You are too, aren't you?"

"Bella, I love you. But you need to hear this from Howard, not from me. And I think you will, honestly. I can't imagine a worthier companion than you, and I'm sure Howard agrees. Just be honest with him."

"Are you out of your *mind*?" I was nearly screaming at Howard, standing close to him, leaning in. I could feel myself losing control. I actually wanted to throw a punch. "I will *not* let you drag my sister into this!"

Otto stood by my side, uncertain as to how he should handle my outburst, poised to pull me back if necessary. The three of us were in the Werners' kitchen, which was a good thing because if we'd been in my office, I probably would have tossed Howard out on his ear.

"Oh, so you *are* Irish after all," Howard spat back, which only inflamed me further. "You want to hit me? Go ahead if it'll make you feel better. Just remember, you're the one who convinced Annabelle to talk to me about this." Otto gripped my bicep.

"Talk to you, yes! I didn't say you should *conscript* her. It's dangerous!"

"Yes, James. It's dangerous. These are dangerous times. Everyone is either at risk or choosing to make sacrifices for the greater good. It's what's called for. Even from Annabelle." I pulled against Otto's hand, but he had a firm grasp. "So go ahead and punch me if it'll make you feel like a better brother, but it's not going to stop the Germans from committing genocide."

I felt Otto stiffen next to me. "Well," he began, "I—"

"Oh, for God's sake, Otto," Howard interrupted. "We know *you're* not responsible. You're not a Nazi. We get it. Jesus."

This was getting ridiculous. We were all trying to do the right thing, after all. And the spectacle of Howard cursing out Otto took some of the wind out of my sails. I relaxed, and I felt Otto drop his hand.

"I just..." I began, the anger rapidly draining from me. "I just don't want to see anyone in my family get hurt."

"I know, James," Howard agreed. "This girl, though—Leah—she'll be killed if we don't get her to safety." Otto looked down, avoiding our eyes. Howard and I exchanged a glance.

Otto had been the brains behind passing falsified information between the IRA and the Germans, and he and I spent many hours taking my brother's "intelligence" and modifying it in ways that protected the Irish and British civilians, as well as making sure potentially useful information didn't make its way into the hands of the IRA. Still, Otto felt that he should be doing more.

Howard and I had decided early on to tell Otto about Howard's real work with the Unitarian Service Committee. We both trusted Otto, and he'd proven to be a real ally for Howard, translating smuggled documents and occasionally obtaining classified information from his father's office. But I knew Otto felt some shame for his betrayal of his country, or, more specifically, his father. And, occasionally, Otto clung to hopes that an actual genocide wasn't occurring. It was hard for him, living under the constant barrage of Nazi propaganda and then having only rumors and third-party accounts to contradict what his father was telling him.

"Otto, I'm sorry, but we have to face facts," Howard said. "She wouldn't have risked the dangerous journey across occupied Europe to make it to Lisbon in the first place if her life wasn't in danger. Plus, she was meant for the earlier Kindertransport to Belfast anyway, but only her sister got on that flight before the Germans shut the program down. We need to get her up north so she can join her sister at the refugee farm outside of Belfast."

I watched Otto's face. He and I had had conversations like this many times. It always came down to who was going to win the war. Only a couple of months ago, Otto would have said, "But once the German army occupies Northern Ireland…" Now he wasn't so sure, both about which side was likely to win and which side he *wanted* to win.

But I knew I was the one Howard was *really* trying to convince.

"James." Howard turned his attention to me. "With the work you and Otto have done getting the IRA documents, we can get her here into Dublin. But we can't simply put her on a train to Belfast. She doesn't even speak English! If she's caught out as an illegal refugee by the Irish government, she'll be sent back to Germany."

And killed was left unsaid.

"She needs someone to accompany her on the train—to hand her off in Belfast. She'll have an Irish ID card for traveling across the border, and hopefully she won't be stopped. There's a lot of traffic between north and south still. But there's smuggling too. Housewives mostly, butter, tea, that sort of thing. Just to avoid rationing. But she needs to be traveling with someone who can speak for her. Two sisters traveling together, with one doing the talking if necessary, is *much* safer. Leah can't do this on her own."

We'd been over this. I *knew* she couldn't do it alone, and our options were limited. Otto was out, obviously. And Howard would look suspicious—an American minister taking an Irish girl over the border. "I'll do it," I argued once again. "There's no need to involve Bella."

"James, you're right," Howard agreed. "A brother and sister traveling together is nothing odd. But still. A man is more likely to be questioned, and the entire point here is to avoid anyone actually talking to Leah. Two girls together will be much less likely to attract any type of notice."

Dammit. "All three of us, then," I finally offered. "Me, Bella, and Leah."

Howard thought for a moment, then nodded.

"When?" Otto asked. "And what can I do?"

"I don't know yet. It's hard to get messages back and forth from the farm. Both the Irish and the English are intercepting everything, and they don't have a radio there. We'll need to send a messenger. It'll probably be a few weeks before everything is in place. And, Otto, just keep your ears open. Let us know if you hear anything about the border."

And that's how March of 1941—the best month of my life—came to a close. But life, I was to learn, has a way of turning on you.

Chapter Twenty-Five

APRIL 1941

We'd be taking Leah to Belfast on Easter Tuesday.

It was a good plan. A lot of people would be traveling home after family visits over the Easter weekend, so there would be crowds to blend into, and police and customs officials would be minimally staffed due to the holiday. Howard had exchanged messages with the refugee farm, and someone would be waiting to meet us in Belfast.

In early April, a week before the trip, Bella and Otto were conferring in the Werners' kitchen, heads together, whispering. Otto giggled at one point—never a good sign. I ignored them and went back to fixing the turf stove, refitting the flue sleeve to stop the smoke from seeping back into the kitchen. I heard Otto leave. Then I heard Bella pulling a chair over to the stove.

"I know you don't want me to do this," she said without preamble. There was no need to specify what *this* was. I pulled my head away from the stove and dusted off my hands but remained seated on the floor, looking up at her.

"That's not true." Even as I said it, I realized I meant it. "I'm proud of you. I just wish none of us had to do anything that puts us at risk."

"I'm glad you'll be with me," she said.

★

Midafternoon on Easter Tuesday, Bella, Leah, and I boarded the train for Belfast. Bella and I would be returning on an evening train. We each had our Irish identification cards with us. Bella and I were using our own, and Leah was identified as our sister, Elizabeth. We didn't expect to be stopped or questioned.

An hour or so into the trip, before we passed into Northern Ireland, the train slowly came to a halt. That wasn't too unusual, but when the engine was shut down, we knew something was wrong. All of the other passengers started murmuring, and Leah looked terrified. Bella put her arm around the girl, and we waited to see what had happened.

Eventually, a conductor came into our car, explaining that the coal had run out and they were waiting for a delivery of more. This wasn't a complete surprise to me. I knew better than most how short the nation's supply of coal was. It was entirely imported from England, and the British government was keeping the supply extraordinarily tight in order to put pressure on Ireland to abandon its neutrality and join the war. And the coal that was allowed in was of such poor quality that it sometimes wouldn't even burn. I wondered if that wasn't the real story with the train—coal in the bin, but unable to burn hot enough to power the engine.

Three hours later, we had been resupplied and the train began moving once more. I looked at my watch—a brand-new modern wristwatch—and tilted my arm so Bella could see. We would miss our return train, and it was the last of the evening. Neither of us had been to the North before, so an unexpected evening in Belfast could be turned into a treat. We had some money now. We could afford a room somewhere and a meal out.

When we arrived in Belfast, we found the station in a state of chaos. Late trains and missed connections had resulted in a massive crowd, and as we moved with everyone else from the Dublin train toward the exit, we realized there was another cause for the delay.

"Jimmy," my sister whispered, clutching my arm and nodding to the line of police officers moving up and down the crowd, waving certain passengers over to the customs booths. There didn't seem to be any system to it, but then I saw that all of the passenger groups with men were being sent over for questioning. It was too late to split up; that would just raise suspicion.

Some of the men in our group were passing information down the line. The gentleman in front of me turned and said, "Damn IRA. There's a rumor they're trying to sneak some of their lads in. All the men from the South are being singled out. As if the goddamned Germans weren't bad enough." He nodded to Leah. "Pardon the language, miss."

Bella gripped my arm harder. "It's okay," I told her. I had my business license and my ID. As long as they didn't want to actually talk to the girls, we should be fine.

Bella reached into her bag and pulled out a white dishcloth, plus a small bottle of some sort of liquid. Leah's eyes widened when she saw this. Bella patted her arm to calm her.

"What are you doing?" I whispered.

"Shh," she hissed back. But before I could press the issue, we'd made it to the front of line and found ourselves standing in front of two uniformed customs and immigration officials sitting behind a desk.

"IDs," one said. I placed our three travel cards on the table. The one on the left picked them up. "Name?" he asked.

"James Brennan," I said, "and my sisters Annabelle and Elizabeth."

"You first, miss"—he nodded to Leah—"if you could step—"

At some unseen signal from Bella, Leah let out a moan, gripped her belly, and bent over as if in pain. The two men looked up sharply.

"Officers!" Bella shouted in a panicked rush. "I need a towel, quickly, please!" Leah bent again with another moan. "My sister is on the cloth."

"She's…" one of them began, looking startled, then downright alarmed when he saw the rag Bella held up to show them, dripping with a red fluid of some sort. She held it toward them over the table.

"It's her monthlies. It came on bad on the train. Please, I need a towel!" Leah moaned again. "This one's sopping!" Bella thrust it toward them again, proving her point, splattering drops of red on the table.

Both men pushed back from her quickly, one only just catching himself from falling as he knocked his chair over behind him. "Go!" he yelled.

I reached forward and grabbed our documents.

"But I need a towel!" Bella insisted. "Look," she exclaimed, holding up the messy rag once again.

"Go! Go!" they both shouted, waving us away. I grabbed Bella's elbow and tried to direct her toward the exit. She leaned back in one more time, peering behind the men's desk. "Do you have a bin back there?" She waved the bloody cloth about. I thought one of them was going to vomit, he'd turned so white.

"Go!"

We did.

We exited the station and headed just a couple of blocks east to the River Lagan, where we were to look for a woman wearing a burning chalice pin. The chalice was the symbol for the Unitarian relief effort. My heart was still pounding from the close call, and I was dying to talk to Bella about how she'd managed it. Soon enough, as we strolled along the riverfront in the fading daylight, we were approached by a woman in a pale-pink spring coat and matching hat. It was an incongruously bright ensemble under the circumstances, but she wore the chalice pin and said, "Leah?"

I nodded to her. I was about to introduce myself when she held up a hand. "No. Don't."

She stooped down in front of Leah and whispered softly in halting German. I heard the name Ruth, which I knew was Leah's sister. Leah started to cry and hugged the woman, who held her in an embrace for a moment. Then she stood and faced me. "Thank you. I'll take over from here."

Later that evening, I was working on my third pint, and Bella was still nursing her first. We were sitting in a lovely warm pub not far from the hotel we'd found. A small group played music in the next room, and the familiar chatter of friends and family enjoying an evening out was comforting. "Not too different from home," Bella observed.

"No," I agreed. "Quite nice as long as no crazy lady starts waving around bloody rags." That started us laughing again. We'd been retelling the story to each other all evening.

"That was brilliant!" I'd told Bella when we first had a private moment to talk about it. "What prompted you to think of it?"

"It was all Otto's idea," she'd replied, much to my surprise. "He said Irishmen are really uptight about anything related to sex, especially 'female-related issues'! The three of us planned it out, with Otto translating."

Uptight about sex? Honestly, is that how Otto saw me?

"You could have included me in the planning." I took another healthy swallow from my pint, still mulling over the uptight comment.

"Otto said you'd give it away by your reaction. He said if you didn't know in advance, your response would be just as bad as theirs. And it was! You should have seen your face!" She wiped a tear from her eye and took a sip from her glass.

"Well," I spluttered. "A woman's monthlies, right there in public..."

"See!" she exclaimed.

I gave up. No use resisting both Otto and Bella plotting against me. It was nice to see her happy, though.

We were sitting in the corner, against a large window that would have offered an interesting street view, with an old stone church across the street, but for the fact that the window was covered in heavy black wool curtains. Unlike Dublin, Belfast was at war, and blackout curtains were required everywhere at night, making it difficult for strangers like us to navigate the dark sidewalks.

Those curtains saved my sister's life.

We had no warning of the blast, but others must have because an urgent shushing noise rippled through the crowded pub as people strained to hear…what was that? A siren?

A deafening explosion blew out the window and its framing behind my sister's head, the shattered glass mostly captured in the heavy folds of the black drapes. Across the room, the shelves on the backbar behind the counter dropped to the floor, and the door to the pub, a heavy oak slab, was blown off its hinges and thrown inside, slamming up against the back of a gentleman standing at the bar.

A series of nearby explosions followed the first, blowing out the remaining windows in the pub. In the other room I heard the ceiling collapse, and the air was suddenly filled with choking plaster dust. Before the screaming and calls for help took up in earnest, there was a brief, shocked silence. I heard the drone of planes overhead.

Then…pandemonium.

People were stumbling out through the hole in the wall where the door used to be; others were trying to tend to their friends in the darkness. Behind the bar, a torchlight switched on, its beam sweeping across the broken room, cutting through the thick gray air.

I was on the floor, half under the small round table, but I didn't recall how I got there. I was holding Bella against my side, and I felt a warm stickiness on my hand. I knew it was blood, but I didn't know whose. "Are you all right?" I asked Bella, not certain how loud I was. It felt like I was trying to speak underwater. I didn't hear Bella's response, if she made one, so I pulled her closer to me to repeat the question.

That's when I realized she was bleeding from the head.

Calls for help echoed through the night, both inside the pub and out, near and far.

I couldn't see and didn't want to leave Bella, but I needed to find a cloth to press to her head. A quick image of the fake bloody cloth Bella had waved about in the station flashed through my mind, and I stifled a giggle—realizing at that moment that shock was setting in. I couldn't let that happen. I steeled myself and tracked the bartender's torchlight as it moved about the space, but it never settled long enough for me to see anything useful.

More explosions shook the city, and the pub rocked violently as the blasts moved closer. There was a deep *whoomp*, unlike anything I'd heard before, and the smoke in the air seemed to be pulled all in one direction, then *boom*, the loudest yet, and the massive oak backbar lining the entire wall of the pub toppled and crashed onto the counter opposite.

"Over here," called the bartender from beneath the collapsed backbar. He waved the torchlight in our direction. "This is as secure a space as you'll find. Don't go outside!"

The backbar was sturdy and lay firmly against the solid counter. He was right. It would take a crane to lift it. Bella and I were only about five feet away. "Can you move?" I asked.

"Not my arm," she replied.

"I need to move you. We're going to take cover under the

bar."

"All right. Try not to jostle my left arm."

There was a loud crash outside. A wall collapsing, perhaps? A pained scream reinforced the bartender's warning that it wasn't safe out there. I gritted my teeth and gripped Bella around the waist. I raised myself into a squat, then slid and pulled us both across the short space. Bella grunted in pain as we went, but we made it.

Despite all the broken glass and puddles of alcohol, it seemed like a reasonably safe space. Next to us, on the open shelving under the counter, were a stack of clean bar wipes. I grabbed one. "Shine the light on her head," I instructed the bartender. He did. The wound was bad, but hopefully not *too* bad. It was bleeding steadily, but not gushing.

The bartender grabbed a bottle of gin that hadn't broken and held it over Bella's head. "Sorry, lass," he said, even as he sloshed the burning liquid onto the wound. That Bella only grunted told me just how badly she was hurt. I dabbed at the wound; then he rinsed it again with the gin. I took a clean cloth and kept it pressed against her head.

"Her arm's hurt too. Don't touch it." I took another pile of towels off the shelf and made a spot for Bella to lie down. "I'm James. She's my sister, Bella."

"George," the bartender said. "You sound like you're from the South."

"We are. We missed the last train back to Dublin."

"Bad luck that." He shined his torch into the ruined bar. A woman was helping a man limp toward the opening where the door used to be. "You'd be better off under here," he called. They turned and looked but continued on their way.

There was a fire nearby, and an orange glow flickered across the stone front of the church. An acrid smoky smell mixed with the thick plaster dust. Sirens began wailing, and over it all, the constant drone of planes.

The bombs kept falling, some nearby, some more distant. Pieces of the building continued to come down around us, but we remained safe underneath the barback. After a couple of hours, George's torch went out, and the only light was the glow of the flames seen through the breaks in the walls outside. By then, I'd determined that Bella's bleeding had slowed to a gentle seeping, and George and I took turns keeping a clean cloth pressed to her head. I had no way of assessing her other wounds, and Bella kept falling in and out of consciousness. I knew that could be a bad sign, but I had no options other than trying to keep her comfortable and warm.

Throughout the night, I clutched the claddagh pendant Otto had given me. I'd lifted it from beneath my shirt and let it dangle on top. I didn't care who saw it.

Sometime around dawn, the bombing finally stopped. We'd been lying in deep puddles of alcohol all night, so I couldn't be bothered to care that I'd pissed myself at some point. I imagined we each had, most likely.

When we deemed it safe to get up, George and I crawled out from under our cover and stood in the open wall at the front of the pub. The devastation stretched as far as the eye could see. He pointed out the train station, straight down the road a number of blocks, and then described where the nearest hospital was. "I'd stay to help, but I need to check on my family. If I see anyone who can help, I'll send them along. But…" He shrugged, indicating the destruction around us.

★

I was lucky. Well, Bella was, certainly.

I told her I was going for help and that if she heard rescuers, she should call out. I thought she understood because she nodded and managed to grip my hand.

I spent two hours looking for help. Everywhere I walked, stunned survivors were crawling out of basements and collapsed buildings. Everyone calling for my help. "My mother!" "My son!" "Trapped!" Trapped. Everyone was trapped. As I neared the hospital, the crowds were so dense I couldn't get through. I reversed course and headed for the train station. At one point I thought I'd gotten turned around.

More and more people with packages and bags were heading the other way, and I saw a sign indicating a train station in that direction. But it turned out that was toward the station serving most of the north counties, and that's where most people were fleeing, those in a state to evacuate the city, anyway.

I continued toward the station with trains serving Dublin. First, though, I planned on stopping in the pub and checking on Bella. Before reaching it, I came across a collapsed brick wall blocking the street entirely. It hadn't been there when I'd set off, and I looked up to make sure nothing else was about to come down. Directly on the opposite side of the rubble were three ambulances, sirens wailing.

I clambered around the pile of debris and waved frantically at one of the drivers, who was in the process of waiting for the ambulance behind him to back up away from the blockage. He rolled his window and leaned out. "Sorry, mate, we're full up with wounded. We'll come back this way after dropping them at the hospital."

That was a Dublin accent if I'd ever heard one.

"Even if you make it through, you won't get to the hospital," I told him, making sure my Dublin roots rang through in my voice. "The streets there are positively jammed with walking wounded." He looked uncertain and turned to the man in the passenger seat. I couldn't hear what they said.

It was then that I noticed the side of the ambulance. "Eire" was written on it in large white letters, and under that, "Dublin." I was thrilled my country would send emergency services support so soon after the attack. Neutrality be damned— we're all Irish, after all.

"Please," I called out. "My sister. She's right in there, hurt bad." I nodded to the pub and saw with horror that most of the top floor had collapsed. "We missed the last train home to Dublin last night."

There was another quick conference between the two men in the cab; then the driver said, "All right. Let's be quick." The two men jumped out and opened the back doors of the ambulance. It was packed with injured, lying and sitting. They pulled out a stretcher. "Lead the way."

I climbed through the hole in the wall and found Bella just as I'd left her. I explained about her injuries and what George and I had done to provide what first aid we could. The men gently pulled Bella out from under the bar, being careful of her arm, and got her strapped into the stretcher. She wasn't awake.

"We'll take it from here."

"Can I come with her?" I asked.

"Sorry, mate, injured only. We've no space as it is."

I saw that and understood. "Where is she going?" I called, following behind as they began carrying her out of the rubble.

"Don't know yet, do we? If it's as bad as it seems in the city, we may need to start taking people back into Ireland." Men from the other ambulance had come over by then and were trying to make room for one more stretcher in the back.

"Here's her ID card," I said, handing it to the driver. "She lives with her mother in Dublin. Please, if there's any way you could let her mother know..." He took the card but didn't make any promises.

Chapter Twenty-Six

APRIL 1941

It took me three days to make it back to Dublin.

The trains and buses were impossible. There were no schedules to speak of, and thousands of people crammed into the station, hoping for a ticket out. I spent the first night—along with what felt like most of the city—sleeping in the countryside, just in case the Germans came back. On day two, I caught a ride to the border in the back of a crowded military truck, and I spent the rest of the journey hitching rides and walking. The roads were jammed and traffic barely moved.

I learned later that nearly a thousand people died that night, and over half of the city's housing was damaged or destroyed. I was lucky to get out alive, and I worried about Bella the entire way home.

I went directly to my mother's flat when I reached Dublin that morning and found Howard waiting for me there. "Bella will be fine," he told me before saying anything else. "She'll be home from the hospital this afternoon."

My mother hugged me and cried. "But why?" she kept asking. "Why were you there?" I looked over her shoulder at

Howard, who simply shook his head. Meaning what? He hadn't told her? I shouldn't tell her?

"It's okay," I kept repeating instead of answering any of her questions.

"When can we go collect Bella?" I was still holding my mother but addressing Howard.

"We can leave now if you're ready," he responded.

As if I'd delay!

Once we were outside, Howard said, "We need to stop at your office first. Bella won't be released for hours yet, and we need to talk privately."

"Aye, that we do," I agreed.

We walked together quietly through the streets. It was a warm day for mid-April, but damp, so the smoke from peat and coal fires hung low in the air, like ground-level fog. It reminded me all too much of the acrid air in Belfast. Or maybe it was the smell coming off me. I hadn't had a chance to clean myself up since leaving Dublin four days earlier.

When we reached my office, I realized how much it had come to feel like home to me, familiar and safe. "I need a shower. Make tea, won't you?"

Although I was able to clean the grime and stench off my body, I knew it would be a long time before I could begin to wash away the trauma. Howard stood from his chair by the window when I came into the room and handed me a cup. "I've been keeping things moving here, but only just. I have a new appreciation for how much effort it is." My throat and lungs were still raw from all the plaster dust and smoke, and I took a soothing sip of tea before speaking. It was weak. Americans don't know how to make a simple cup of tea.

"I hated you for a while," I finally said. "I blamed you for having gotten Bella into that situation." He didn't respond. He simply nodded. He must have been expecting that. "All that work—all that *risk*—for one girl, when hundreds die every night in London, and now Belfast. What's the point?" I drank more of my tea.

"Did she—Leah, that is—make it?"

I realized Bella hadn't told him what had happened. And how could she have? She'd been too injured, and the hospital wouldn't have been the place to talk about it anyway.

"Yes. We handed her off right away. Hours before the bombing began."

He nodded again. He didn't say anything, and I was glad he didn't. I was not sure how I would have responded to a "that's good" or "at least there's that, then." My world had contracted to just my family.

"I had to spend a lot of time learning how to talk to bereaved people when I became a minister. Did they want comforting? Did they just want to let out their pain? Did they want an opportunity to rage? All that I could handle. The thing I could never do—still can't, really—is figure out how to deal with people who wanted answers. *Why* did this happen?" He took a sip from his cup. "This tea is shit," he said.

It was. I took our cups to the small sink in the WC and dumped them. I filled the electric kettle and began making a proper pot.

"The thing is, James, we just do what we can. If we could have stopped the bombing, we would have. But we couldn't. All we could do was try to save that one girl."

After the tea was ready, I filled our cups and brought them back. Now that I was safely home, I was beginning to ache from the injuries I had suffered. Cuts and bruises from the bombings, yes, but also sore muscles from all the walking and being crammed into the back of that damn truck. I handed Howard his tea and sat back down with a groan.

"I'm sure you're sore, but okay otherwise? Should we get you to a doctor?"

"I'll be fine," I told him. And it was true, physically at least. "And I don't hate you anymore. I realized quickly on that was…self-indulgent, I guess. None of this was your fault. And as you say, you're doing what you can. More than most." I glanced over at him and let that comment hang there. We both knew I was talking about Otto.

Howard was a smart man. "Go on, James, tell me the rest. You need to say it."

I took a deep breath. "I hated him too. I still might. I kept picturing him up there, flying those planes. That's who they are, you know—hundreds of Ottos dropping bombs on innocent people. Sure, maybe they're a few years older than him, but if he'd stayed there instead of coming here, who knows, in a couple of years he might be dropping bombs on Dublin."

"Oh, James! And here I thought you were going to tell me you were angry at God."

"God? Seriously, Howard? Do you *really* still think there's a God?"

"Great," Howard sighed. "Now you've managed to hit on the *other* thing I'm totally inept at talking to people about."

Despite my misery I felt a smile pull at my lips. I reached over and put my hand on his arm. "You're not a bad minister, Howard. You hear a good confession, and at least you don't lie to people."

We sat in a slightly more comfortable silence, drinking our tea.

"It's not Otto's fault either, James."

"No. I know he wasn't actually flying the planes. But it's his people, isn't it? It's his *father*. Who are they that they could do this? You can't tell me there's nothing else the Werners could have done to have stopped this."

Howard nodded. It was true.

"There's something else you should know," he said. "I considered letting him tell you this himself, but I think it's better you're forewarned."

The tea suddenly felt like an acid weight in my throat. "What?" I asked, bracing myself.

"Otto knew," Howard said.

I was sure I'd misheard. But no.

"He only found out after you left. He came to me in quite a state. He insisted we had to find a way to stop the train, to stop you from getting to Belfast. But we couldn't. He wanted to go to the train station to make sure you and Bella made it back before the raid—"

"Don't," I interrupted him. "Don't call it a raid. That makes it sound like a drill, or something quick and surgical. It wasn't. It was slaughter, hour after hour, with Bella bleeding out beside me, smoke thick in the air…" I began to shake. *God, is it going to be like this all the time?*

Howard stood, then pulled me up from my chair. "Come on," he said, guiding me to the couch across the office. We sat there, and Howard held me while I fell apart. I realized I was still in shock. The human body and mind aren't meant for the things I'd been through.

Finally, when I'd settled, Howard said, "I'll be right back. I'm going out for chips. You need to eat something."

He was right. I didn't feel hungry, but when he returned and I began eating, I realized how much I'd needed that. When I was ready, I asked him to tell me the rest.

"All right," he said. "Otto insisted on going to the station to wait for your train, but then we learned about the coal problem on the outward-bound train, and when the last Belfast train of the night arrived and you weren't on it…well. It was after nine. He knew the attack would start soon. James, he was devastated. I've never seen him like that."

Bella almost died, I thought. *We both might have.* It was just luck that we didn't. I was having a hard time finding sympathy for Otto being devastated. I didn't say any of that.

"I took him back to my place for the night. It got worse for him as we followed the news bulletins, and I had my radio, so I was hearing the truth of how bad it was. I'm not saying this to make you feel bad for Otto, but I think you should know how bad he was. I'm…well, I'm fairly certain he wanted to kill himself and may have if I hadn't been holding him captive all night."

That caught my attention and pulled me out of myself. There'd been so much death already. I had a flash of Otto and

Bella laughing and plotting in the kitchen before our trip to Belfast, and I realized now he'd been hatching the plan for the bloody rag. Someday, I was going to enjoy telling Howard that story.

"Let's bring Bella home," I said.

Chapter Twenty-Seven

APRIL 1941

That night, after Bella was safely tucked into her own bed and after promising Mother I'd explain at some point, I set off for the Werners'.

I'd never shown up at the Werners' at night before, at least not without planning beforehand with Otto. I had an excuse for explaining my presence—checking on the turf supplies—in case I needed one for Mr. Werner. The house looked dark from the front, but when I went around to the back alley, I noticed there was a light on in the kitchen. I let myself into the shed and knocked on the kitchen door.

To my surprise, it was Howard who answered.

"Oh, I'm glad you're here. I was hoping you'd show up, but I didn't know how long I should wait." He held the door open for me, inviting me into the kitchen. The light over the table was on, and Howard had a book open there, but other than that, there was no sign there had been a dinner prepared or a fire lit.

I didn't remove my coat. "Where's Otto?" I asked.

"I don't know. I arrived midafternoon for our lessons, and he wasn't here. His father showed up briefly a few hours ago, but when he saw there was no dinner to be had, he left again. Didn't even ask about Otto. I'm worried, James." Howard stood and picked up his book, then placed it in his satchel. He reached for his coat. "I've checked your shop already, and he wasn't there. Where should we look next?"

I was fairly sure I knew where Otto was.

"I think I know where to find him. Let me go alone. If there's a serious problem, I'll come get you at your place, all right?"

Howard looked like he might object. But he thought for a moment, then nodded. He didn't really have a choice.

A thick mist had settled in, alternating between a light rain and a stinging fog. As I got closer to the bay, it became even more dense, filling with a salty tang. I could barely see ahead of me and wished I had brought a torch. I reached the end of the walkway and carefully stepped down onto the sand, moving forward by feel more than sight.

The waters of the bay were choppy that night, and the crash of the breaking of waves filled the air around me, blocking out all other sound. City lights transformed the fog behind me into a bright glow, and I was reminded suddenly of making my way through the darkened streets of Belfast, laughing with Bella as we felt our way forward, avoiding curbs and grates.

I knew he was out there. I could sense him.

"Otto," I whispered. My voice melted into the mist.

I went forward until I felt a cold dampness soak into my shoes.

"Otto!" I called again. Louder that time, shouting his name into the sea.

There was an intake of breath quite near to me, and as I stared into the darkness, I saw a quick, soft orange flare illuminating his face.

I closed the small gap between us. "You've taken up smoking now?"

"It seemed like a good time." He held the cigarette out to me. I took it from his fingers and flicked it into a receding wave. We stood silently for a minute. Our shoulders weren't quite touching, but I could feel his presence next to me, the warmth, the smell of damp wool.

I broke the silence first. "Go ahead, say it." I told him.

"What?" he asked.

"Come on, we've rehearsed this a hundred times already. You're supposed to say, 'You came,' as if you thought I might not. Then I say, 'Of course I did.' So go ahead. Your move."

He sniffed. "No," he said. "I knew you'd come."

Of course he did. That's why he was here, where we met, where he comes to be alone, where he can see an unobstructed path across the ocean to his life, before.

He was wearing his Tyrolian hat rather than the sensible flat cap I'd given him. What was he thinking, walking through the streets of Dublin with a German hat on? That was a real risk, given how public opinion had turned since the Belfast bombing. Did he *want* to get attacked, or worse? The tide was coming in. A swell of water drifted across my shoes.

"Please tell me Annabelle will be all right."

"She will be." Part of me didn't want to give him that, but that was just mean. I didn't want to be cruel. "Maybe not right away, but eventually."

He let out a sigh. "Good," he said. "That's all I needed to hear." We didn't say anything for a few minutes. We fell back into silence. I looked out past the bay, into ocean, toward Dresden, where I tried to picture what Otto's life would be like if he'd stayed there.

He tilted his head toward me. "You don't need to stay here. I won't kill myself if that's what Howard's afraid of. I thought about it, but I'm not cut out for that. I know you must hate me. You don't need to find a way to tell me."

"Yeah, I do hate you a little bit." He sucked in a deep breath. "I guess that's not fair of me though, is it? I mean, it's not like you were piloting one of those planes."

He turned to face me then. The fog had settled into a light drizzle, and I could make out his damp face, a spectral white in the dimness, beads of water flashing gold on his eyebrows. "But that's just it," he said. "I could have been. They're no different than me. If I'd stayed in Dresden, I'd be in officer training by now; maybe I'd even become a pilot next month when I turn eighteen."

He was echoing the same thoughts I'd had. But Otto *was* different. "But you didn't stay in Dresden. You came here and now you've learned things the others haven't. You know more about the truth than they do."

"Yes. But does it matter? I mean, we're all…complicit, aren't we? Is that the right word, complicit? Meaning being responsible for something from the outside? Not the actual doing of the thing, but letting it happen."

"Yes, that's the right word." He was right too. It's why I'd been having such a hard time separating my feelings for Otto from the horror happening around me. He *was* German, after all. Wasn't that enough to shoulder some level of responsibility? "But, Otto, you couldn't have done anything to stop it."

"No. You're right. But if not me, who? Even my father couldn't have stopped it, and he's *certainly* complicit. He's a party member and supports the war. My whole country is complicit, James. We're the ones who are letting this happen, whether we're flying the planes or minding our business, looking the other way." I was glad we were in darkness, our emotions hidden from each other. He'd just managed to explain exactly what I'd been thinking, why I'd been angry at him, even though he wasn't at fault—not personally.

And at that moment, when Otto had provided me with a path to understanding my anger, it evaporated. I saw he was in pain, and I could only think of comforting him.

He lit another cigarette, cupping the flame from his lighter in his hands, breathing in the smoke.

He inhaled deeply, then let out a choking cough, spoiling the effect. "My point is," he continued once he could speak again, "I understand why you need to be rid of me. It was a beautiful fantasy—this idea that we could build a world where we could love each other. Where we'd be accepted, together. But this world won't allow that. My people have destroyed any possibility of that."

He was giving me an out, his blessing, as it were, to be done with him and the Germans and all the death and destruction they were bringing into the world. Otto always put me first. He had done so ever since we first met. And even as he tried to smoke a cigarette in the thick dampness, his silly

German hat wilting over his flattened curls, he was absurdly beautiful.

I took the cigarette from his lips and dropped it into the tide.

"Who's going to want to kiss you if your mouth tastes like ash?" I asked.

Even in the dark, I saw one golden eyebrow rise in surprise.

"Who—? Did you say—?"

I turned to face him, reached my hand behind his head, and pulled his lips to mine.

He deepened the kiss, but it felt involuntary, like a compulsion he couldn't avoid. He let out a soft gasp, then placed his hands on my shoulders and pushed me away, holding me at arm's length. He hung his head and muttered, "*Du bringst mich um.*"

It was never a good sign when Otto started speaking German.

"Um…?" I offered, confused that he'd pushed me away.

"You're killing me, James," he repeated in English. "You were supposed to walk away, and then I wouldn't have to do…this."

"What?" I asked. He wasn't making sense. I could tell by the way he kissed me that he didn't *really* want me to walk away. "Do what? What are you talking about?"

"I'm leaving, James. This was meant to be goodbye."

★

"Leaving?" *How could Otto be leaving? Where would he go?* "Do you mean you're leaving Dublin?"

"Yes, I'm leaving Dublin." He still had his hands on my shoulders, arms straight out, keeping me away.

"You're not...you're not going back to Germany, are you?"

He huffed. "That's the last thing I would do."

I tried to step closer, but he moved back. The mist had turned into a steadier light rain, and we were both getting soaked. The darkness and the rain dripping down my face were adding to my sense of confusion. "I don't understand. You can't go up north, you wouldn't be allowed into the UK, and I doubt you could sail anywhere with all the passenger restrictions. So you're staying in Ireland, then? Where are you going? I'll come with you."

"I can't tell you." He turned from me and faced the city, its lights glinting through the rain like sharp-edged gems, thick peat smoke swirling between the warehouses on the dock.

I grabbed his arm roughly and spun him around to face me. "This is bollocks, Otto! We *love* each other. God knows, it took me long enough to come to grips with that. I'm not letting you just walk away now."

"I'd hoped it wouldn't come to this," he said. He was whispering and looking down at my feet.

"Come to *what?*" I stamped my foot but only succeeded in splashing about the wet sand.

"There's something you don't know. Something I haven't told you."

"Argh!" I yelled. It was the only noise I could make. I grabbed him by the shoulders and *shook* him. Hard. His stupid hat fell off and landed with a plop into the damp. "No more secrets! Isn't that what we promised each other?!" I wished he'd light another cigarette so I could slap it out of his face. "*You're* the one who's killing *me*, Otto. What the devil is going on?"

He looked me right in the eye then and lifted his chin, as if daring me to deck him. "I'm going to become a Nazi."

★

"You're…you…after all the…" I trailed off. I'd heard him. I just couldn't make sense of it.

I didn't know what response he was hoping for, but he deflated a little when I simply stood silently, waiting for him to explain himself.

"If I stay, I mean." Otto took a deep breath. "I'll have to join the Nazi Party next month. When I turn eighteen." He let his breath out in a steamy puff, still faintly tinged with cigarette. "I didn't tell you," he continued, "because I wasn't sure it would even have to happen over here. I'd hoped maybe the rules were different. But no, there's going to be a big celebration at the legation, and I'll be presented with my Nazi uniform."

"Jesus" was all I could manage.

He took out another cigarette and lit it. His hands were shaking when he cupped the lighter, and he had to try several times before the flame took. I let him smoke it.

"Oh, and once I'm eighteen, I'll have to join the service. If I was home, I'd be conscripted into the Luftwaffe, but there's some discussion at the legation of whether or not I can stay in Ireland, legally, if I'm an active member of the armed forces. Or for that matter, if they'd even be able to transfer me home once I joined up." He inhaled deeply, triggering another coughing fit. He handed me the cigarette, and I took a small puff before tossing it into the waves. It was acrid and disgusting and the stench lingered around my nose.

"Jesus Christ," I said.

"The thinking is they'll just have me work for the legation for the remainder of the war. Which my father seems convinced will go quickly now that we've moved on to destroying the enemies' cities." He stooped and picked up his hat. He wrung it into a sopping wet lump, then threw it as far he could into a receding wave. "So you see, James, I can't stay. I can't let that happen. I won't become a Nazi."

I closed the gap between us, and he didn't resist. He was well and truly defeated. I pulled his head onto my shoulder. I ran my hands gently up and down his back. I meant it in a comforting way, but I imagined it was more annoying than anything else, what with the wet wool rubbing against his soaking waistcoat.

"Come on," I said. "We're going back to the shop. We're going to figure all this out." I threw my arm across his shoulders and began guiding him toward the street. "And we're figuring it out *together*."

★

We stopped for fish and chips on the way and received a few curious stares due to the state we were in. I was glad Otto had gotten rid of his hat—otherwise the stares would have been more hostile—and was pleased to see he'd stopped resisting coming along. At one point I cringed when my hip bumped a doorjamb; I'd hurt it at some point during the night of the bombing, and it was still sensitive to any sort of pressure. Otto instinctively reached out a hand to steady me and asked, "Are you okay?"

I hesitated before answering, and I saw Otto's guilty expression when he realized what had probably caused my pain. "I'll be fine," I replied.

When we got in, I put the tea on, and we both went upstairs to get out of our wet clothes. There was an unexpected shyness to our being naked together this time. It somehow felt more intimate than the lead up to sex or the relaxed moments afterward. We'd both been roughed up—me physically and Otto emotionally—and were exposed in front of each other in ways we'd never been before. Otto didn't comment on my many bruises or on the stiffness in my limbs as I bent to pull up clean drawers.

I rummaged in my dresser to find something for Otto to wear. An oversized work shirt of mine was suitable for him, but my trousers barely reached his ankles.

Otto sat in my desk chair, and I settled in on the bed, sitting up with my back against the wall and my cup of tea on the bedside table.

"Do you remember what we said in the very beginning?" I asked.

"In the beginning?" Otto repeated.

I nodded.

"Well, I remember thinking you were the most handsome sea monster I'd ever seen and that I needed to convince my father to call you over."

I blushed. "No, I didn't mean…wait…you thought I was handsome? Even scraped up and covered in seaweed?"

He sipped his tea. "Oh yes. From the very beginning. Even now, after I've damaged you so badly. All those bruises." He put his teacup down and ran his tongue along his lips, tucking a wet lock of golden curl behind his ear as he did so.

"Oh…um." I was distracted by his delicate fingers, and I was struck by a memory of them wrapped around my—"Stop!" I exclaimed. "You're just trying to distract me. And I'm trying to have a serious discussion about our future."

"Well that's new, but bad timing," Otto said. He got up and came to the bed. He climbed in and stretched out on his stomach, his feet dangling off the end. Then he propped himself up on an elbow to look at me. "I've been trying to tell you, James, there *is* no future for us. I need to…disappear, I guess."

"No. Remember what you said when we first started up together? Not the day we met, but later, when it was clear there was something between us."

Otto smiled at me, which was lovely to see, but it was his wicked smile, not his sunshine one. "Oh! You mean when I tricked you into committing sin—what did you call it? Self-abuse, yes, that's it—in the kitchen?" He sat up in the bed, facing me, legs crossed in front of him. I recalled walking into the kitchen that day and stopping dead in my tracks at the sight of Otto in the bathing tub.

"No! Not then. And I'm not going to have you keep guessing. Otherwise we'll never make it out of bed."

Otto looked down. "If I could stay here forever, I would." His smile had disappeared as quickly as it had come on.

"The first time you tried to talk about our future," I clarified. "When I told you there is no future that would allow for us to be together. Do you remember what you told me?"

"Yes. I do, James. I told you we needed to make our own future. To create a world where we can be together." He rubbed his hands along his exposed shins. "But you didn't believe me! You refused, time after time, to give any thought to a future for us!"

I could hear the pain in his voice. I hadn't realized until just then how much I'd hurt him by constantly turning away from his dreams. "And now it's too late," he continued. "I've taken everything from you! I've ruined your relationship with your family—all you offer them is lies now. My country has killed your countrymen for no reason, and poor Annabelle! And look at you, bruised from head to toe. I've brought nothing but ruin to you. You're betraying your brother for me. You've lost your faith. I could go on and on."

I was stunned he saw us that way. I leaned forward and took his hands in mine.

"I will *not* become a Nazi, James. I just can't."

"Otto, you haven't taken *anything* from me. In fact, you've given me everything I have! If it wasn't for you, I wouldn't have found my own way in the world. I'd still be stuck believing things I'd been told to believe rather than figuring them out myself. I would never have learned the truth about my heart. I wouldn't have found *love*! That's *everything*, Otto, and all because of you."

He looked up at me then, and I saw hope in his eyes.

"But, James, I just can't see a way forward."

I squeezed his hands. "Two months ago, when I turned eighteen, you told me you should be the older one because you're the one always taking charge."

"I know. I'm failing at that right now, I'm sorry."

"Don't be. It's my turn." I hadn't realized I intended to take charge until the moment I said it. But it felt true and right. Otto *had* always been leading us along our way. I wanted to take over now, at least for a while. "I'm going to take charge now. We're going to find a way. I'm not letting you disappear. I'll chain you to this bed if I have to."

Otto's eyes lit up, and he squeezed my hands, then scooted closer to me.

"So you think you know what's best? You think you can tell me what to do?"

"I do," I said.

"And you'd be willing to chain me to your bed? To take charge?"

I swallowed thickly. "I know what you need."

We were talking about more than the plans for our future.

Otto changed then; a weight lifted. I'd never seen him like this before, open, vulnerable. Waiting for direction.

I pulled him to me and showed him what we both needed.

Afterward, we started planning our future, creating the world we needed.

Chapter Twenty-Eight

MAY 1941

I sat at my desk with the contract in front of me. My father's cousin, Eamon, sat across from me. We'd reconciled, more or less, and he'd apologized for getting in my business and inflaming my father. He confessed that he'd felt manipulated by my father and that he hadn't realized how far lost in the drink he'd become until he witnessed him attacking me and tearing apart our home that night he'd been over. The night I'd left the house.

Ireland wasn't at war, but the world around us was, and we were all coming to grips with what was most important to us and questioning long-held assumptions that no longer seemed to apply. "I'm glad things have worked out for you, Jimmy." He picked at his grimy nails. He still worked at the port, but he'd also taken part-time work digging turf along with my father and other men from the parish. Each morning they'd pile into the truck and head into the countryside, armed with spades and shovels. It was dirty work for sure. "And sorry about the things I said about your German fellow. It wasn't my place."

"Water under the bridge, Eamon," I said although I didn't feel that way. Still, it was no time for alienating people who might be needed someday. I signed the contract. It was a commitment to supply turf to my business for distribution to all my new clients. Everyone was rushing to convert to turf burning as coal supplies continued to dwindle and the permitted hours for burning gas continued to narrow. "Send Michael around tomorrow and we'll talk." Michael was Eamon's fourteen-year-old son. I was going to give him a job working on the turf cart, unloading and stacking the rolls of sod at customer's homes.

"Your da says to say hello by the way."

I nodded to acknowledge I'd heard him. According to Eamon—and Liam and Father Flannery, through way of Bella—my father had turned himself around. I sensed even my mother was weakening, but I suspected that was more out of concern for her social standing than anything else. A woman alone, with a living husband willing to come back to her side, was not a common, or welcome, situation. Her new, near middle-class neighbors had begun hinting that she should take him back.

Bella was ready to forgive him. I knew that for sure. "Oh, come off your high horse, James," she'd said to me in the middle of an argument about Father. "You're hardly in a position to talk about other people's decisions in matters of the heart." I thought that was unfair and told her so.

"None of this is Otto's fault," I'd repeated for what felt like the hundredth time. "And he's not just looking the other way. He's actively trying to help the Irish people and even the refugees your own man is out trying to save." But, as usual, she and I had agreed to leave it unresolved. Our wounds were still too raw to pick at them.

Once the turf supply contract was signed and Eamon had left, Otto came down into the office from my living quarters.

"I'm surprised your father keeps paying Howard for the all the time you spend here rather than with him at your studies," I told him as he took a seat in one of the chairs by the window.

"Well, it's not coming out of his pocket. But I have thought the legation might stop paying once I'm eighteen and conscripted in some way. I don't like him, by the way." He nodded to the door, indicating he was talking about Eamon, not his father.

"He's okay," I said, although, really, I didn't like Eamon either. But Otto and I had had a major disagreement last night, and although I *thought* Otto was coming around to my way of thinking—there was no choice, after all—I didn't want to rile him this morning.

"I don't like him because he spied on you and interfered with your family. And because you told me he called me a molly boy." I didn't take the bait on any of that. Instead, I pulled open the filing drawer on my desk and tucked the new contract away. "I still don't know what molly boy means," he concluded. Then he let out a sigh when he realized I wasn't going to pick a fight on any of those fronts.

"You can probably guess," I replied.

I closed the file drawer and looked up and across the room to where Otto sat by the window. It was bright out for a change, and the midday foot traffic flowed past the glass in a constant stream. In the street, a horse pulled a cart loaded with milk jugs, and soft tendrils of bluish smoke swirled in front of the upper stories of the buildings across the street. I could almost imagine I'd gone back in time, before coal heat and petrol engines had taken over the city.

"So?" I asked him. "Are we agreed?"

He sighed again and plopped his feet on the table that sat in front of the chairs. He knew I didn't like that, and I sensed he was deliberately trying to agitate me, to prolong our argument to delay his eventual capitulation. I'd told him I was taking charge of our future, and I had, but this new, petulant Otto was an unwelcome side effect of his taking the back seat.

I pointedly looked at his shoes on top of the table.

"Right," he said, finally putting his feet back on the ground where they belonged. "I'm being a complete arse. You've been trying so hard to create a path forward for us, and all I do is complain. I just want to say I hate your plan. I loathe it. I think it's a horrible idea. Having said that, I can't think of a better one, and God knows I've tried. So, yes, we'll do it your way, and you have my gratitude for having thought of something that just *might* work."

I smiled. I knew how much that hurt him to say. I stood from my desk and walked across the room, then took the chair next to his. "Thank you, Otto. We can do this; we really can! And there's only one terribly horrible part to it."

"A fairly big part, I'd say," he replied, but he wasn't actually protesting, just noting what was, in fact, the truth.

"I know. I'm sorry. I wish there were another way—"

"No, no. You're quite right. There *is* no other way."

"Good." We'd been over the plan so many times last night, and each time Otto would balk at the bad part—well, the worst of the many bad parts. I felt for him though. I didn't blame him. Still, I needed to make sure we were on the same page.

"So," I said, "from the top. What's the main objective?"

Otto smiled. It *had* been funny—frustrating, but funny—coming up with this private little catechism. By now we could do this as easily as if we were an old vaudeville act.

"To stay together," he repeatedly dutifully, "and to stop all this silly bollocks about separating, even if James is being an arse and Otto is being…obsan…abtsan…*obstinate*." It was a new word for him, and he struggled with it, even though he admitted to being thrilled I thought of him that way.

"And why?" I prompted.

"So we can create the world we deserve, the one that lets us pursue our dreams and be together." I waited. He knew there was more to that answer. He rolled his eyes. "Really, James, this is ridiculous. I don't need—"

"Say it," I commanded, interrupting him.

"Fine." He continued reciting the agreement. "And a special reminder for Otto that James sometimes knows best, and Otto should always share whatever it is that's troubling him." We'd negotiated out the next part about James being handsome and strong. Even I had to admit it was excessive. I'd only included it to give Otto the win of having it removed. Because I knew the next part—the final part—was terribly hard.

We looked at each other. Otto's eyes were wet. I reached across the small table and took his hand but didn't say anything. I was waiting for a sign he was ready. He sniffed, then nodded.

I gave him the prompt. "And how are we going to accomplish that?"

I was proud of what he did next. I knew the price he paid. He lifted his head and looked me straight in the eyes.

"First," he responded, "I'm going to become a Nazi."

★

We ran through the rest of the plan, even the hazy part about me buying a cottage on the West Coast, as far away from civilization as possible. A place where Otto and I could disappear, *together*, when the disappearing time came. And it would come—that was the only thing we were certain of.

But we'd gone round and round in circles last night. Trying so hard to find a path that spared Otto from Nazi conscription. It just wasn't possible. Despite his earlier intention, he couldn't simply disappear now. He had nowhere to go and no way to hide the fact that he was German. He'd be found out within days and probably sent back to Germany at great risk to face an uncertain punishment.

And he couldn't defy his father. Mr. Werner was at just as much risk as Otto. He had to obey the party's directives even more than Otto did.

No. In just a couple of weeks, Otto would turn eighteen, and he would either happily join the Nazi Party or he would face that party's wrath. And we were learning more and more from Howard that was an outcome best avoided.

But once we got the past the *fact* of Otto becoming a Nazi, we could get to the *value* of Otto being on the inside. So we expanded our plan to create our future beyond simply accommodating our own happiness, but saving as many others as we could. With Otto working at the legation office, which seemed to be what his father and the rest of the delegation wanted, he'd have access to more information we could use to misdirect the IRA and to feed false IRA intelligence to the Germans that would perhaps delay bombing campaigns and save additional lives.

And then there was Howard. He'd told us the refugee crisis was beyond desperate now, and if we could manage to smuggle even a handful of Jews into Ireland, where they could remain hidden amongst the Jewish community until the war was over, we'd have accomplished something worthwhile.

The ability to fight the Nazis and our commitment to make that an important part of our plan was what finally got Otto on board. I swore to myself I wouldn't disappoint him.

Chapter Twenty-Nine

MAY 1941

It was near the end of May, just days before Otto's birthday, and I was having another staff meeting in the office. It was crowded! Bella and I were there, and so was Clara, and three other girls as well. Now that I knew what it meant to flirt and to want someone in that way, I saw all the signs I'd missed with Clara back when we had lived in the same building. The smiles, the quick touches, the attention. I knew I was seen as an extremely desirable catch, so I was careful that my returned friendliness didn't imply an interest in anything more. Bella just rolled her eyes.

Eamon's son, Michael, was there, as well as two other boys who managed the turf cart and the associated labor. We were discussing hiring out another cart, as well a donkey to pull it, and bringing on three more boys. There seemed to be no end to the turf business.

Clara and the other girls, who were much closer to the hand-to-mouth existence that Bella and I had left behind, were perfectly fine cooking and cleaning for the Germans. It was light work consisting mostly of small households of men stationed here alone, and as long as two girls worked together at all times, they seemed to avoid any unwanted attention. Bella kept busy working for the Americans and, increasingly, wealthy Irish families who valued the international connections of shared service providers.

We could triple the size of our business if we'd wanted to.

But that was tricky. Otto and I knew what we'd planned was dangerous, playing one side against the other. It was only of matter of time before the game would be up, and although we could *hope* to make it through the war without being found out, it wasn't at all likely.

Far more likely would be a sudden need to disappear, and my plans to make that possible would take months, and money too. I needed enough to buy a small cottage holding with room for farming of some sort, sheep probably. And I also needed to amass enough cash to get me and Otto through until we were back on our feet again.

Therefore, I had to carefully balance keeping the business as a going concern while pulling out just enough cash that it didn't die prematurely. Increased capital expenditures for long-term growth just weren't a part of the plan any longer. I hadn't told Bella about our plans yet, and I asked her to stay behind after the others left.

"Tea?" I offered once we were alone.

"Yes, thank you," she replied as she arranged herself on the narrow couch along the wall. She looked smart in her new shorter-hemmed skirt and jacket with padded shoulders. No matter what future Otto and I managed to create for ourselves, Bella was the one I thought would really change the world.

"I need to tell you something," I said as I handed her the tea and took a spot perched on the other end of the couch.

"Of course you do. My brother never makes me tea unless he has something on his mind." She smiled to take the sting out of that. "Go ahead."

"I need to know what Howard's intentions are." She stiffened at that.

"Oh, not *again*—" she began.

I held up my hand. "No, not like that. Honestly, you've convinced me you're entitled to your own life without my oafish and entirely unnecessary interference. You should live however you like." I picked up my tea and sipped while I let Bella consider my words.

"Well, thank you, James. I agree. But I'm thrilled to hear you say so." She waited for me to continue.

I studied her face, intentionally not looking at the new scar that ran from her hairline down to her cheek. I hadn't even noticed the cut the night of the bombing, and there'd been so much bleeding anyway, it was easy to overlook in the darkness. It hadn't been stitched for two days, and the results weren't neat or pretty. To her credit, she didn't go to great lengths to hide it or cover it over in thick makeup. It was what it was, and she was who she was, and thank God, Howard was who he was.

"I ask because I need to know if you'll be moving to America with him or if you need to make your own way here."

It was her turn to study me. I could tell she realized this was important to me and could see her decide I deserved a straight answer. "I don't know, honestly," she responded. I must have let my disappointment that Howard hadn't moved things along show on my face because Bella quickly explained further. "He's asked me to marry him, and I've said yes." I beamed at her. I couldn't be happier for both of them, and I said so, reaching over and giving her a hug about the shoulders.

"But," she continued after I'd released her, "we haven't told anyone yet. It's so hard to make plans right now with the war. But he won't want to stay here forever. So, yes, I suppose someday I'll be heading to America." She stopped and made a face like she'd bitten into a lime. "To be a minster's wife! Imagine that!"

We had a good laugh at the idea, but it was more a nod to our old selves than any real sense of our futures being somehow limited.

"That's a relief, then. I need to tell you my plans, but it involves closing the business, and before doing that, I wanted to make sure I didn't need to find a way to transfer it to you."

I'd caught her mid-sip and she nearly spit out a mouthful of tea. "Close the business? But, James, it's a gold mine! Why on earth would you give that up?" She managed to get her cup placed in its saucer on the table without further mishap.

"Bella, please listen to me. I know you don't understand how Otto and I can have the relationship that we do. But you saw the truth of it before I did. We *do* love each other, and I'm going to make this work for us."

She looked down at the floor. But I continued.

"And I know your feelings about Otto and the Germans…changed…after what happened in Belfast. Understandably. Mine did too. Why, if I didn't love him so much, I might have been permanently turned against him too. But I *do* love him that much, and now both he and I need to turn our worlds upside down in order to stay together. We're going to have to disappear."

I told her the rest of the plan. From Otto joining the Nazis to my buying a remote cottage. I explained how we'd devote ourselves to resisting the Nazis, saving as many refugees as we could and falsifying intelligence to prevent as many attacks on civilians as possible. She was listening to me at least, nodding occasionally, no longer avoiding my gaze. Finally, I told her I was pretty certain it would end badly, and Otto and I would need to flee without much, if any, advance warning.

"But it will be worth it, Bella, if we can make a difference. You saved that girl. Doesn't that make you feel good?"

"You're brave, Jimmy, to face all that. When we were in Belfast…well, I knew it was all serious…but I never thought the war would come so close to me. Personally, I mean. I was so frightened," she whispered. "I never want to feel that way again."

"I know, Bella. I was scared too. I still am. But we can't hide away from it. Last summer Howard told me he thought things would get really bad and that the evil would come closer and closer to home. Well, it's here now. The question is, what are we going to do to confront it?"

Bella gave me a searching a look. She picked up her cooling cup of tea and downed the rest of it in a single gulp, as if it were a fortifying shot of whiskey. "How did my little brother get to be so smart?" She stood and walked behind my desk, studying the map of the city on the wall above it. "We were so *poor*…" she whispered, her finger tracing the North Strand street where we had grown up. The street that had contained the entirety of our lives until two years ago.

"But I know evil when I see it," she continued after turning back to face me. "And you're right: regardless of what Father Flannery says, what you and Otto have is *not* evil. What *is* evil is what the Nazis are doing to the world. I can't go through life grasping tightly onto everything I've managed to gain. That's a sure way to lose it."

Relief flooded through me as I realized Bella was going to be all right. She was coming back to herself after the brutal attack that had nearly killed her. It would still take time, but I knew then she'd be stronger than ever.

"See?" I said. "You're already a good minister's wife."

"Careful, Jimmy, you don't want me changing my mind." She walked around to the front of the desk and leaned back against it, stretching her legs out in front of her. "So, how I can help?"

Otto's birthday arrived on a warm and bright late-spring day.

I had intentionally scheduled an ice delivery at the Werners' that day so I could check in with Otto and make sure he was coping with that evening's ceremony, when he'd be inducted into the Nazi Party. He was a wreck.

"Otto, I know this is hard. I wish I could be there with you."

"I'm glad you won't be. I'd hate for you to see me in my uniform."

For some reason I hadn't thought of that. I knew it was an important ceremony, but I was thinking it would be more about swearing oaths or signing papers. An actual uniform wasn't something I'd considered. There would undoubtedly be photographs, too, capturing Otto's humiliation forever.

"Is it here? Can I see it?" I wasn't sure why I asked that; I just knew I didn't want Otto to shoulder this burden alone.

"It's upstairs. Do you really *want* to see it? I'd rather I never saw it again."

I did want to see it. It was hard for me to imagine Otto in this other world—a world I wasn't a part of at all. We went up to his bedroom.

The uniform's jacket, a deep, mossy green, was carefully laid out on his bed. Ropes of braided silver attached at the shoulders, and each tall triangular collar was etched in matching trim. Brilliantly shined black shoes sat neatly on the floor, and a thick silver belt hung over a chair. A pair of dress trousers, pressed and folded, rested next to the jacket.

"Wow" was all I could think to say. I'd never seen anything so fine.

"It's called a waffenrock," Otto told me. "The belt and the braiding mean it's meant to be an officer's dress uniform, but I'm not an officer—not yet anyway. But all of the legation staff thought it was appropriate, so here we are."

I fingered the silver belt hanging over the chair. "Wow," I said again.

A wash of shame rolled through me as I realized my first thought was that Otto would look spectacular in the uniform. With his height and athletic frame, he would be the perfect model for the Nazi vision of the master race. I remembered the first time I'd seen him on the pier, glowing in a sudden shaft of sunlight.

Fortunately, I caught myself before I suggested he put it on for me.

"And there's this," Otto said. He walked to his dresser and took something off the top. When he threw it on the bed, I saw that it was a bright-red armband with a large black swastika.

That extinguished the fantasy. And just in time too.

"I'm sorry you have to do this, Otto."

"Me too," he said.

After that, Otto told me he had a lot to do to prepare and needed time to be alone. I left reluctantly after begging him to come to my office after the ceremony. He declined though, insisting he'd want to be alone and promising to check in with me the next day. I pretended to accept that.

Later that night, as I was skulking about in a small park down the block from the Werners' residence, waiting for Otto to return home, I had a vivid experience of what my grandmother called "the second sight." I was sitting on a bench near a thicket of bushes when it happened. I'd been in the park for over an hour, alternately strolling its small square perimeter, then sitting, with increasing impatience, on the one bench with a view down the street to the front of the Werners' house.

An older gentleman had circled by me several times, boldly looking me in the eye each time, slowing as he passed by, as if I'd invite him to take a seat. It took me an embarrassingly long time to figure out what was happening, at which point I scowled at him and drove him off.

But my second-sight experience involved Otto, and it left me truly rattled. There was no real warning or any trigger that I could determine. One moment I was gazing down the street, and the next I was looking at the landscape transformed, broken and smoking, as Belfast had been the night of the bombing. From the wreckage of one of the buildings, I saw Otto, crawling out, blood-soaked arms holding…something. He was dressed in civilian clothes, not his Nazi uniform, and somewhere along the way he'd lost one of his boots. He looked up and saw me, and then the wall of the building collapsed on top of him.

The image dissolved as the legation car pulled up in front of the Werner residence. I shook my head to clear it. My grandmother claimed the second sight could be a tricky thing, possibly presaging the future, but also perhaps not, or rather, only one of a series of possibilities. It was up to the person graced with the vision to take care and be vigilant.

From my hiding place in the shadows, I watched the car doors open and the Werner men step out. I'd been right. Otto was striking in his uniform. He tugged on the thick braided belt, settling it on his waist, and, turning away from his father without a word, headed for the door. His father leaned into the window to speak with the driver, then followed his son into their home.

I hoped Otto would go straight to bed. It was late—nearly midnight—and I was certain the evening had been an ordeal for him. But I was afraid he'd head for the bay instead, where he could truly be alone in his own head and think the dark thoughts that so often got him in trouble. The thoughts that time and again pulled him away from me.

I decided to give him an hour. If he hadn't reappeared by then, I'd know it was safe for me to head home. But hardly ten minutes had passed when I saw Otto slip around the corner. He must have gone out the back, perhaps to hide his departure from his father. I didn't want to make him nervous by trailing him late at night, so I took my time before setting off to the harbor.

Chapter Thirty

MAY 1941

A thick slice of moon illuminated the water that night. The clouds were wispy and thin, so even from the walkway I could clearly make out Otto's figure standing knee-deep in the bay. I stepped onto the sand and noted that he left his boots and socks neatly arranged far from the tide line. That was a good sign. He'd had the sense to take them off before venturing into the water. And he had his sensible flat cap on too. In fact, he looked like a proper Irishman, in his heavy cable-knit jumper and plain brown trousers rolled up to the knee.

I stopped at the tide line, about twenty feet away from where Otto stood. I was contemplating taking off my own shoes and continuing out to meet him, when he spoke. "I know you're there, James," he said, still facing away from me. "Even though I told you not to come, that I wanted to be alone tonight."

"You may have wanted to be alone, but *I* don't want you to be alone," I called back. "And I'm in charge now, remember?"

"How could I forget?" he responded as he turned and began walking back to me. "And I knew you'd come. We drove by the park on the way home, and I saw you pretending not to be there." When he reached me, he took his cap off, then ran his hands through his slicked curls, causing his hair to stick up at odd angles. "Now who's the kraken?" he asked.

I was glad to see he was in good spirits. I knew we'd gone over our plan again and again, and I didn't *really* fear that he would have been tempted, again, to abandon me, but I let out the tense breath I'd been holding anyway. He turned back to the sea for a minute. "I was just telling my mother about tonight and asking her to forgive me for what you and I are doing." That could encompass a lot of things, but I chose to interpret it to mean his betrayal of his country.

"Was it terribly bad?" I asked.

"Yes." He put his cap back on. "But something possibly useful happened too. It turns out my job will be listening to the radio transmissions we're intercepting across the British Isles. None of the legation staff can understand the accents here, especially you Irish blokes."

I smiled at that. Even Howard occasionally expressed dismay at the Irish accent.

"I'm good at it though, thanks to you," Otto continued. "Just think about all the misinformation I'll be able to provide!" That did open up a lot of possibilities, and maybe Liam's IRA pals could even provide code words.

"So the night wasn't a complete loss, then?" I asked.

"No." Then he gave me a suspiciously evil grin. "And since it was a celebration of my birthday as well as my joining the Nazi Party, I got to meet several nice Irish lasses, all from the best Nazi-sympathizing Dublin families. And I danced with them too." A hot ball of jealousy formed in my gut when I pictured Otto in his uniform, his hand around some silly girl's waist while they moved gracefully across the floor, her hand on his shoulder, maybe brushing his curls. "I'm quite a good dancer," he told me. Then he leaned in and whispered in my ear, "I thought of you throughout each dance, though."

I felt myself turning red and was grateful Otto couldn't see in the dark. He put his hand on my hip and pulled me closer, then took my other hand in his and began humming something—a waltz, I thought, although I wasn't much of a dancer and didn't know much about music. Whatever it was, it was mesmerizing, and I let Otto lead me in a tight swaying circle. We danced there for the first time, on the sand of Dublin Bay where we'd met, both of us becoming aroused by the contact and the motion, neither of us quite sure what to do next.

I was trying to decide just what we *could* do, here in public, or if we shouldn't rather make our way back to my office when I heard the plane.

We both froze, listening intently in the dark. *Had* that been a plane? The sound faded as soon as it had registered, leaving only the gentle swooshing of the waves. Then we heard it again.

"That's a plane," Otto and I both said.

I couldn't see anything in the night sky but was trying to orient where the plane might be by the sound of its engine. "There's two, I think," Otto said. Sure enough, when I listened for it, I could hear at least two—maybe three—separate engines, the drone rising and falling as the planes circled overhead. I was immediately brought back to my nightmare in Belfast. Otto gripped my shoulder. "I won't let anything happen to you," he said.

A bright searchlight lit the sky over Dublin, nearly blinding me, as my eyes had adjusted to the dark. Two more searchlights switched on in short order, painting the night sky a misty white.

"There!" Otto said, pointing toward where one of the lights had picked out a plane making a long arcing curve high above the city. Three more searchlights switched on, and at least two more planes could be seen. They weren't flying in formation but instead were meandering about, swooping low and then climbing.

A flare shot high into the sky, burning a bright green. It hung in the air and was quickly joined by two additional flares—one white and one orange. "Smart," Otto said. "It's the Irish flag. The pilots will know they're over neutral territory." But the planes kept circling.

"Why aren't they leaving?" I asked. Otto didn't respond.

A red flare went up. "*Scheisse,*" Otto muttered. "That's a warning. It means they're going to start firing on the planes if they don't vacate the airspace."

The planes continued to circle above the city, moving in and out of the shifting spotlight beams. The flares faded away; their tangy, chemical smell drifted across the bay. One plane flew directly over our heads, and we craned our necks to follow its passage.

"Are they English or German? Can you tell?" I asked.

"German," Otto said. "Those are Junkers."

He looked down and I followed his gaze. A small wave just reached his toes before seeping back into the sea. The tide was coming in.

"Come on," I said as I tugged his arm. "We'll be able to see what's going on better from on top of the dock." He let me lead him off the sand, collecting his socks and boots on the way. We climbed up onto the pier. We were standing where Otto had been when I first caught sight of him, his mother fussing with his tie, when we were startled by the sudden burst of antiaircraft fire. All at once, the night was filled with the rattling mechanical sounds of the guns, and the sky bloomed with puffs of smoke.

Underneath all the noise, I heard a soft *boom* from far away. Otto heard it too. We looked at each other. We both knew what it was.

"James," Otto began. "I'm—"

"If you apologize for that bomb, I'm going to slug you." And I meant it. We were beyond his taking ownership of the atrocities committed by his country. He wisely closed his mouth.

There was a louder *boom*, much nearer, just on the other side of the city center. I scanned the skyline and saw smoke rising not far to the north. I mentally superimposed the map of the city from my office on what I saw in front of me.

"That's the North Strand."

Chapter Thirty-One

MAY 1941

I was nearly paralyzed with fear. My night spent huddled in the rubble of the Belfast pub with Bella near death next to me came roaring back. The memory of acrid, gritty smoke, the sounds of collapsing walls, the pain. I couldn't relive that.

But Otto had already rushed to the edge of the dock, where he sat and struggled to tug his thick woolen socks over his muddy feet. *What is he planning?*

"Otto, we're safe here in the open. We need to stay here until it's over." I felt like a coward even as I said it. But he didn't know what it was like, the shattering glass and all the stones and bricks raining down from above. He looked at me, then looked away. He was still fighting one sock, trying to tug the heel into place. "No," he said. "I *have* to go. I might be able to help."

I wanted to say how much more help he could be if he stayed and followed our plan. How many lives we could save with his support from inside the legation office. But anything I might have said fled from my mind when I saw what happened next.

He'd gotten his socks on, finally, and was reaching for his boots. He grabbed the nearest one and pulled it toward him. One of its laces snagged on a board, and Otto gave the boot a harsh tug. The lace snapped, and momentum sent the boot sailing over the edge of the pier and into the bay. I rushed to the edge, hoping to find the boot floating on the surface.

But it was gone.

"We have to get your boot. We *have* to!"

By then, Otto had joined me and was also peering over the side. "But I don't see it," he said. "I think it's gone."

"But…" I couldn't explain my second-sight vision to him. He'd think I'd gone completely mad.

Another explosion—a smaller one, I thought—from the same northerly direction.

Otto looked up at the city. "Don't worry about it. They weren't expensive boots." He put the remaining one on and stood, wobbling unevenly.

"Take that one off too, then." I tried to make it sound like a reasonable suggestion, but I knew it came across as more of a desperate plea. I was convinced if I could change what had been in my vision, where he was wearing only *one* boot, I could change the outcome. He looked at me, then looked down at his boot. He tested walking a few feet.

"Those are thick socks," I added.

"Fine," he said with an air of resignation. "If it keeps you from trying to stop me from going…"

"I'm coming too."

★

By the time we reached the North Strand, the planes were gone and the antiaircraft guns had ceased their firing. Two ambulances raced by us with sirens wailing and a thick smoke hung in the air. People were out on the streets with torchlights, most heading in the same direction that we were—toward the site of the nearest bombing.

We were about three blocks away from where I'd grown up and lived my entire life when we heard one of the planes return. It flew right over our heads, sending people scattering for doorways. Moments later, a deep *whoomp* and *boom* filled the air. We were close enough to be quickly enveloped in a cloud of gritty dust. A woman next to us was hit in the arm by a small piece of masonry, and a girl next to her pulled her aside to tend to the bleeding wound.

We continued forward, in the direction of the blast. Or Otto did anyway; I simply trailed after him, my mind growing numb with each step I took, heading closer and closer to home.

"Jimmy!" I heard my name being called from down the block. "Jimmy!"

It was Clara, stumbling out of the chalky dust, along with a half dozen or so others, some with bleeding wounds. They were all heading away from my former home. We were nearly in front of it now, a partially collapsed building on the edge of the greater devastation closer to the center of the bomb blast. Clara and the others must have just escaped.

"Jimmy," she cried again as she reached me. She was in her bedclothes, but other than the grit in her hair and a long scrape on her arm, she seemed unharmed. She looked back at the tenement. "Mrs. Gleason," she said, turning to me again. "I was on my way upstairs to get her. We were all heading into the basement to shelter—just in case—but I knew she wasn't good with the stairs so I—" She cut off abruptly then, her eyes going wide as she realized she hadn't mentioned my father, who presumably still lived below Mrs. Gleason.

"Oh, Jimmy, I didn't think about your da. I just…" She trailed off. There wasn't anything to say.

"*That's* where you lived?" Otto asked. "That's where your father lives *now*?" he demanded.

Clara turned to Otto, only then realizing who he was. She'd seen him while she was working at the Werners and, based on the fact that she and Bella were friends, probably knew that Otto and I were friends as well. But still. He was a German, here, now. "Oh," she said. "Mr. Werner." She didn't seem to know how to respond, seeing him in the midst of the carnage. And she was probably in shock. Others had reached us by then and were stopping there at the edge of the destruction, where it seemed safe. I heard the word *German* somewhere in the crowd.

A wall collapsed nearby, and in addition to the cloud of dust, smoke from a fire began to fill the air around us. "Maggie?" someone yelled, and Clara looked around.

"I didn't see her come out," someone else shouted back.

"What about the baby?" another called. "Where are the others?"

But it was all becoming indistinct. The collapsing wall had triggered a severe shock in me. I'd dropped in a heap, shaking. I was overwhelmed with memories of Belfast.

Distantly, I heard Otto demanding to know if others were still in the building and where they'd be. When I realized what he planned, I reached up to him. "No," I called out. "You can't. The wall." In my mind everything was jumbled—the collapsing pub in Belfast, the collapsing wall of my father's home in front of me, the wall that collapsed—or *will* collapse—on Otto in my vision.

There were flames now on the upper floors of the buildings near us. I was sure that was real and not something I was imagining. "I have to go in," Otto said as something crashed deep inside the tenement.

"I'll come," I insisted, but my voice was weak, and I wasn't really sure which city I was in anymore.

"James Brennan. You will stay right there. If you so much as move a muscle, I swear to God I will deck you so hard you won't get up for week." And he meant it. I could tell by the way he held his body and pleaded with me with his eyes. I knew what he was doing, even if he didn't. I'd done it myself.

He was serving his penance.

He spoke quickly to Clara, who looked uncertain but nodded. Then he disappeared into my boyhood home.

I didn't know how long he was gone. It couldn't have been long, but I was experiencing time in a strange way. When the fire brigade trucks arrived, I was sure I was back in Belfast, where I'd last seen them. But when Eamon came up to me, I knew I was in Dublin.

"They told me you were here," my father's cousin said. "Were you visiting your da? Is he all right?"

"Otto," I managed to say.

"What? Your German fellow?" Eamon looked confused. "Is he here?"

Clara pointed to the door of the building. Smoke was wisping out of it, and the flames had spread significantly since I'd last looked.

Otto was stooping through the opening, which was when I realized a beam had fallen and partially blocked the opening. This was it. This was my vision. But he wasn't wearing boots at all, just his socks, and his arms weren't bloody, and he was carrying…a baby? Yes. A baby. He rushed forward and handed the screaming infant to Clara. A cheer went up around us.

"Eamon," he said as soon as he noticed him. "I need your torchlight. There're others stuck downstairs, but I need to re-move debris to get them out. The smoke is getting thick."

Eamon flicked on his light. "Come on, then," he said and headed for the doorway, Otto right behind him.

"You there! Stop!" one of the fire brigade called out. He was unrolling a flat hose attached to the truck. "You can't go in there. It's not safe." But Eamon and Otto disappeared into the darkness, the light of Eamon's torch visible for just a sec-ond or two before it faded into the smoke.

Clara sat next to me, holding Maggie's baby. Neither of us spoke.

Minutes later, first one, then two, then at least a half dozen people scrambled through the doorway, followed by Eamon and, lastly, Otto, who made it as far as my side before collaps-ing and passing out.

★

The bodies of Mrs. Gleason and my father were found in the rubble the next morning.

In all, twenty-eight people were killed in the raid, with a hundred others seriously wounded. Dozens of houses were destroyed. The German Minister leading the Dublin Legation apologized to the Irish people the next day, claiming the attack was an accident, and the Irish press dutifully repeated that assertion. Most people didn't believe it.

Nearly two hundred people needed to be rehoused, and Clara, Maggie, and Maggie's baby had all been taken in by Mother. There was no room for me there after that, so I'd permanently made the move to the quarters above my shop. I preferred the privacy there anyway.

Otto was hospitalized with smoke damage to his lungs. No one was sure what to make of him. If accounts from the scene were to be credited, he was a hero—rushing into a burning and collapsing tenement, saving multiple lives. But he was a German and, according to the rumors, a Nazi. That was all just too complicated for the gossip mill, so Eamon became the celebrated hero of the day.

Three days after the bombing, I was still mostly bedridden from…whatever it was that happened to me in the North Strand. I remembered being confused about where I was and being, well…terrified, honestly. I couldn't have moved if I'd wanted to, so Otto's threats to beat me if I tried to follow him into the building hadn't been at all necessary. I remembered watching him collapse onto the ground next to me, and then…nothing.

Howard was sitting next to my bed. He and Bella had taken turns checking in on me, and I was embarrassed by that. There was nothing *wrong* with me, not exactly. So why was it so hard for me to get out of bed?

"It's shock, James. I keep telling you that. And not just shock in the moment, but a severe reaction from your time in Belfast." Howard was patiently explaining, *again*, what was going on with me. I blocked out what he was saying because it sounded like I was crazy or something. "It's a known phenomenon. Soldiers returning from war suffer from it all the time. They call it shell shock."

I'd heard of that. I'd even seen it in older men—veterans of the *last* war—who would jump a mile if a car backfired on the street. I didn't want to be like that.

I remembered my paralysis. "I was useless."

"You were in *shock*. You weren't *useless*. Don't forget you saved Annabelle's life in Belfast."

I knew that. I didn't want to lie around feeling sorry for myself. I needed to pull myself together.

"Your father's funeral is in two days," Howard said softly. What he didn't say, what he didn't *need* to say, was that I had to be there. For my mother, if for no other reason.

A large public funeral for over a dozen of the victims was planned, which was good because each death didn't have to be personalized. Many of these poor souls would have had no one to mourn for them. Father Flannery would say the Mass, and everyone would gather at the cemetery for the burials before a wake at the parish hall afterward.

"Otto will be released from the hospital tomorrow. He doesn't believe me when I tell him you'll be fine. He's convinced you've been left for dead somewhere and we're just not telling him."

That did it. I swung my legs over the edge of the bed and committed myself to finding a way through my mess. "Give me

ten minutes to take a shower?" I asked Howard. "With everything that's been happening, I haven't been able to fill you in
on our plan. We need to talk."

Chapter Thirty-Two

AUGUST 1941

There were no further bombing attacks on Ireland.

In fact, even the bombing campaign of London ended that month, too late for the 36,000 Londoners killed during the Blitz. Otto told me it was because Hitler had turned his attention to Russia, and the staff at the legation office were worried about what it could mean for the war against Britain.

As the summer progressed, Otto and I had settled into a new rhythm. He worked long hours every day and sometimes at night, depending on radio traffic. If the circumstances hadn't been so serious, it would have been comical to watch the Germans struggling to translate the Irish banter they intercepted over the radio. Until I had to try to explain it all to Otto, I hadn't fully appreciated just how vulgar we Irishmen were with one another.

But Otto gained a wealth of information. He intercepted IRA communications, which we were able to use to help misdirect Liam when it came to interfering with IRA bombing campaigns in the North, but we also used the information—sparingly—to establish legitimacy with Liam's local IRA unit, demonstrating that we knew things only the IRA command would know. And Otto also intercepted British communications detailing operational plans. Those we were able to use to misdirect the Germans, having them deploy resources to protect against attacks that didn't happen or having them plan assaults on troop formations that weren't where they'd thought they would be.

We saved lives. I know we did.

But we were playing both sides against the other, and we knew the game was coming to a head.

Liam came by my office one morning. I had just sent the turf delivery crew off on their rounds and was alone when he came in.

"Jimmy," he said as he took off his hat. "Nice to see business doing so well for you." I offered him tea, and he accepted as if we were two reasonable adults and not brothers who'd been squabbling and scrapping our entire lives.

"Ma misses you," he said. "She told me you haven't been around so much."

He was right. I hadn't been back often enough. Seeing Clara and Maggie and her baby—it brought me right back to that night in the North Strand. I'd been meeting with an American bloke once or twice a week—another minister Howard had recommended I talk to—and he'd been good at helping me figure out how to deal with my…shock issues. He'd dealt with a lot of service members from the last war back in the States. But it was slow going.

"She's doing great," Liam said. He was walking about my office slowly, studying everything in the room, running his hands along the furniture as he went. He always had the air of a man who was searching for something to steal.

I handed him his tea. "It's a lot of women in one flat though, and that's the God's honest truth," he said.

I was glad my mother was doing well. Once Father had died, she'd morphed overnight from a slightly questionable older woman living apart from her husband to the highest pinnacle of respectability for Irish women—widowhood. It suited her. And caring for a young mother with a baby too! Why, hers was now the most popular apartment for lady's tea in all of the Galway Arches.

And the delicate new tea set Bella and I had acquired for her cemented her reputation as a gracious hostess.

Liam took his cup over to the wing chair by the window and sat. He nodded to the other chair, which I took as an invitation to join him. Evidently, he had something he wanted to say.

"The lads are all talking about your German fellow." By "the lads" he meant the IRA. And "your German fellow" was how everyone in my orbit had begun referring to Otto, with varying degrees of knowledge regarding the depth behind the label. "He's quite a hero, risking his life like that. Eamon says the rescue was all led by him, even though Eamon himself is getting most of the credit."

I was happy to see Otto's bravery recognized, but I wasn't sure I liked the idea of people talking about him.

"The thing is, Jimmy, he's a Nazi now."

That caught me off guard. I hadn't realized that Otto's joining the party was known outside of the legation office.

"That doesn't matter to me or my boys, of course," Liam continued. "The 'enemy of my enemy is my friend' and all that—" He paused there, to look out the window, as if he was expecting someone. "—but be careful, Jimmy. The government spies are watching the Germans, where they go, who they spend time with. Now that your German fellow is working at the legation office, he's in the mix too."

"That's good to know," I said. My mind was racing with the ramifications of people knowing Otto and I spent so much time together, frequently here at my office. Often late at night.

"We appreciate all the work you two do getting information to us and sharing our intelligence on the English with the Germans; just…be discreet, won't you? I'd hate to see my little brother get hurt."

I felt a twinge of guilt that I'd been betraying him the entire time. But I liked to think that if he knew everything Otto and I knew about the Nazis, he'd feel the same way. I wasn't sure enough about that to come clean though.

Otto spent entire nights with me by then. Although our time together was more limited, we made the most of it. We still called our time in bed wichsen time, but it was really much more than that. We were in love, and we expressed that through intimacy, sometimes tender and sweet, sometimes more athletic. But never what could be called adventurous. Otto had been right when he told Bella that we Irishmen were squeamish about certain things.

He tried to raise it with me once. We'd spent the evening constructing a particularly elaborate ruse misdirecting a German bombing campaign in the North and had celebrated our creativity with a robust bout of wichsen. When we were spent and lying next to each other, trying to decide if we should wash or simply fall asleep, Otto said, "You know, there's more we can do. In bed together, I mean."

His left leg was hooked over my right, and he gave it a shake, sending a vibration up my side. He tilted his head toward mine so he could see my face. I continued to stare at the ceiling, thinking about whether or not I could convincingly pretend I didn't know what he was talking about. I decided Otto wouldn't let me get away with that.

"I *like* what we do," I said. "And judging from the state of my sheets, I'd say you do too." I laughed at my own joke and hoped Otto would take the hint and dismiss the entire idea of more. He didn't.

"*Of course* I do," he insisted, giving his leg another shake. "Sometimes I'm just curious," he added. He left that opening for me, probably hoping I'd say, "Curious about what?"

I didn't take the bait.

But he wasn't giving up. "You know, curious about why homosexual men seem to like having—"

"No!" I interrupted him before he could actually *say* it. "I mean, no, I'm not curious about…that. Sorry I screamed. Can we *please* change the subject?"

"Saints in heaven!" he exclaimed. It was a phrase he'd picked up from Bella, and one that was totally inappropriate coming from a young man. But I found it endearing and never had the heart to tell him it made him sound girly. "You're acting like I set off a bomb next to the bed. Calm down."

Ouch. Making fun of my shell shock seemed like a low blow, but he dropped the idea of *more* after that, so it was a small price to pay.

Chapter Thirty-Three

OCTOBER 1941

After Liam's warning, Otto didn't spend the night at my place nearly as often, and when he did, we went through a lot of effort to make sure he hadn't been followed. It was unnerving to know we might be under surveillance.

The business continued to grow. By October we had over a dozen girls working for us. Since the Belfast and Dublin bombings, none of the Germans felt comfortable in public, so they relied more and more on my company for shopping and other domestic tasks. I spent less time at the Werners' because Otto was always working. But Bella came to me one day to tell me that the gas had been shut off there.

She said the Glimmer Man showed up for an inspection and claimed that the Werners had been using the gas stove off-hours, even though it hadn't been turned on in days. It was clearly just retribution and intimidation, but who could we complain to? Otto told me afterward it had happened to all the German households. Good news for my turf business, at least.

Otto and I had developed a Saturday night routine. We would meet late in the evening along the river. I usually arrived first and would sit on the bench we'd shared the day Otto first tried to talk to me about a future together after the war, the day we learned Germany had invaded Belgium. It seemed like a lifetime ago, although it was only a year and a half. And it seemed I had known Otto all my life, even though it was just over two years.

Once Otto joined me at the bench, we would take a leisurely, roundabout walk back to my office. We always did our best to make sure no one was following us.

One Saturday night, at the end of October, I was uneasy as we walked through the city. I didn't dare tell Otto about Samhain, the ancient Irish celebration of the harvest, which, according to my grandmother, marked the time of the year when the veil between the worlds was at its thinnest. He mocked the pagan influences that lay not too far under the surface of our Christianity, but that was the reason I was on edge.

I had a profound sense of ending, of things rushing to conclusion.

Otto was uneasy as well, but that was because he had "things to tell me" that would have to wait until we were home. My apprehension increased when he stopped to purchase a bottle of whiskey on our way. That night, our wichsen time was of the sweet and slow variety. Twice, actually, before Otto got around to speaking what was on his mind.

"Do you ever feel like things are just rushing forward faster than we can keep up?" he asked.

Yes! It was what I was feeling too. "It's the veil between the worlds," I said. "It's at its thinnest this night. The other world is sending us a message."

"Your pagan heathenism is strangely erotic, James." He gave me a look that promised more to come, but neither of us was quite ready for a third go just yet.

He leaned over the bed to pour two more glasses from the bottle on the bedside table. His hair had been cut short, and his curls were gone, but the golden stubble on the back of his head had its own appeal. I ran my hand through it as he poured. He handed me a glass and sat up in the bed. I did the same.

My claddagh pendant hung in the center of my chest. Otto reached out a finger and gave it a tap. "You have so much hair here now this never touches your skin!"

"It touches my heart every day," I said.

"A pagan heathen romantic! How did I get to be so lucky?"

I smiled and sipped my whiskey. I wasn't going to ask Otto what was on his mind. I knew he'd get to it in his own time, which he promptly did.

"Howard has been dismissed," he said.

It shouldn't have, but the news came as a surprise.

"My father said I don't need a private instructor anymore now that I'm eighteen and a party member with a job at the legation. Plus, there's rumors that the Americans are going to be drawn into the war, and it won't be on our side."

Liam had said the same, and he'd told me the IRA was worried that America joining up with Britain could possibly prompt Ireland to do the same thing.

"Can't they bring in a new instructor for you? A German? I mean, you should be doing university-level work now, not just intercepting radio transmissions."

"No. Ireland isn't issuing visas for Germans any longer. When we want to bring spies in, we airdrop them by parachute! Or land them on a beach from a U-boat. Can you imagine such a thing? But I can't see them sending me a college professor like that!"

I had no idea about the spies. Otto was learning so much through his new job. I was about to ask more about that when the news about Howard hit me in the gut. He'd have no reason to stay on in Ireland. He'd be taking Bella away soon.

Otto was studying my face, waiting for the moment I realized about Bella. He sighed when I did. "I'm sorry, James. I know you love your sister. I miss my sister too." I sometimes forgot about the fact that Otto hadn't seen his own mother or sister for over two years. I should be more thankful for the good fortune I had.

"Anyway," Otto continued. "Howard told me he's not in a hurry to leave. He's finding our…arrangement…extremely helpful in his work, and he's going to try to stay on. But we'll have to think of a way for the three of us to get together outside of my home."

"I suppose if we're careful about it, we can all meet here," I said. But it didn't seem right to put the business at risk that way, which was an odd reaction for me to have since I planned on abandoning it as soon as Otto and I had to go to ground. Yes, things were starting to move quickly.

"But I have even worse news," Otto said, finishing his glass in one swallow.

I finished my glass too.

"Do you know how many Jews there are in Ireland, James?"

I hadn't ever thought about it. Not too many, I supposed. You'd see them occasionally, especially around their holidays. "I don't know. A hundred or so, maybe?"

"Four thousand," Otto said.

Wow. That was far more than I would have thought. "Huh. But why—?" I stopped then. It was my night for being two beats behind apparently. "Shite!"

"Exactly." Otto poured two more glasses. "There's going to be a big conference in December to discuss the 'Jewish Problem.' They're collecting data on how many Jews there are in each country. I'm afraid Howard's worst fears were justified. The Nazis plan on removing all the Jews in Europe. And by removing, I mean killing. They're planning a genocide."

Chapter Thirty-Four

NOVEMBER 1941

One morning in November, Howard showed up quite early at my office with a cannister of coffee and a milk bottle.

Otto and I were upstairs. More to the point, we were still in bed, and Otto had just begun making those German guttural sounds I loved so much, right before he climaxed.

But Howard had a key, so he was able to let himself in.

"Good morning!" Howard called out, far too cheerily for anyone at this hour of the day. "You won't believe what I found!"

"Down in a moment," I called back. And, rather than leaving Otto hanging, I clamped my left hand tightly over his mouth and started working him faster with my right. Otto's eyes widened in surprise. It was quite daring to do this with Howard downstairs, and I saw that the element of risk excited Otto. I filed that bit of knowledge away for later. I tightened the pressure over his mouth, maybe even being a little bit rougher than I needed, and it was over in seconds.

I cleaned up in the bathroom, threw on some clothes, and went down to meet Howard.

He shook the cannister at me. "Look, James, coffee!" He held it aloft like it was the Holy Grail. He'd been complaining incessantly about not being able to find coffee in Ireland, and I was alarmed he already had the kettle plugged in and two mugs out on the table. I had no interest in trying it. I'd smelled coffee and thought it was vile.

He was scooping spoonfuls of what looked exactly like dirt into both cups. "Come on, James, there's more to life than just tea! You have to try new things once in a while." *Right*, I thought, *and there's more to sex than just wanking, and I have too many men in my life trying to break me out of my comfort zone.*

"Hmm," I offered.

The shower turned on upstairs.

"Oh," said Howard. He paused, then reached into a cabinet for a third cup. "Does his father know he's here?" Buried in that question was another: Does his father know about the two of you?

Luckily, I could answer both questions the same way. "I don't think his father knows anything he doesn't want to know."

Howard nodded. "Good skill for a Nazi to have." He scooped more of the dirt into the third cup as the kettle started whistling. He removed it from the hot plate and began pouring the steaming water into the piles of brown grit, creating a thick, hot mud in each cup. "I don't suppose there's any point in my trying to provide moral guidance to the lad, is there? It *was* part of my duties as his private instructor, after all." Then he laughed. "Oh wait, no! I don't have to worry about that anymore, do I?"

I sniffed the coffee and made a face that answered his question.

"Milk?" he asked.

"Yes! Thank you." I poured myself a glass and left the coffee untouched.

Otto joined us eventually, his hair wet, a smirk on his face. He basically screamed wichsen time. I colored in embarrassment. Howard offered him coffee.

"Oh, coffee!" Otto exclaimed. "I haven't had coffee since Father and I were in France." He eagerly grabbed his mug and took a sip. He scrunched up his face. "This is that dried stuff, isn't it?" He reached for the milk bottle.

"I'm afraid so," Howard replied. "We live in a land of barbarians."

I ignored them both. Otto looked pointedly at my glass of milk. "Honestly, James, you're not even going to try the coffee? How do you know you wouldn't like it if you aren't even willing to give it a try?" His smirk was growing wider.

I knew what he was *really* talking about, damn him.

"Humans aren't meant to drink ground-up dirt. It's not natural. I don't need to try it to know it would hurt...um, I mean, taste bad."

Otto laughed, and Howard looked back and forth between us, obviously aware that there was a subtext but, hopefully, not figuring out the specifics. My color must have gone up another notch or two because they both tried to give me some space.

"Right..." said Howard.

"So..." said Otto.

We all sipped our drinks.

"Actually," Howard began, "I'm glad I caught both of you here." At Otto's raised eyebrow, he rushed on. "What I mean is, I have a dilemma. Or, we do, assuming you're both still up for this type of thing."

Otto and I both nodded. I assumed Howard meant helping him in his efforts to save refugees.

He pulled an envelope out of his satchel, and from that he withdrew a photo and a few pages of paper. "I need to get this man into Ireland, and quickly, but I don't know how to go about it."

I peered at the photograph. I was surprised Howard had said "man." The photo looked like that of a boy, or even a young woman, with delicate facial features and wispy white hair. He looked German, and that impression was confirmed when I saw the identification papers. I couldn't read the details, but I could make out that his name was Hans Schmidt.

"He doesn't *look* Jewish," Otto said.

I knew Howard well enough by then to know he was struggling between correcting Otto on his assumptions about how people look and getting on with the conversation. Expediency won.

"He's not. He's one of you." Howard looked back and forth between us. At first I didn't understand; then I heard Otto suck in his breath.

Oh, Hans was a homosexual.

Otto and I looked at each other, and I turned back to the table and studied Hans's features more closely. He looked to be about fourteen or fifteen. "How old is he?" I asked Howard.

"I'm told he's twenty-four."

"Yes," Otto said. He tapped a section of the identification card in front of us. "Here's his date of birth, 1917."

I looked up at Howard. "But why Ireland? Why bring him here?"

"Because no one will take him. In most countries there are safe houses for Jews if we can smuggle them out. But nobody is simply taking refugees, especially not ones convicted of moral offenses. Technically, he's a criminal."

Otto looked angry. "But, Ireland won't take him either, will they?"

"No," said Howard with a sigh. "That's my predicament. I just feel that if I could only get him here, I could keep him...hidden...somehow, until things"—he glanced at Otto—"are resolved." Otto flinched but didn't say anything. More and more we were talking openly about the possibility that Germany might *not* win the war, but Otto and I hadn't even begun to think about what that might mean for him. Or for us.

"Where is he now?" Otto asked.

"Lisbon. He worked at a university in Berlin, and there's still an underground network throughout academia trying to smuggle people out. By some miracle he made his way across France and Spain to Portugal. But he can't stay there. He's holed away in my contact's basement, but she needs to move every week or so, and every time she does, it risks exposing him. He'll be sent back to Germany if he's found out." Howard looked at Otto again. Left unsaid was Howard's implied assessment that would be a death sentence for Hans.

"Would it work if we got him fake Irish documents like we did for the Jewish girl?" I asked.

"I don't think so," Howard responded. "I don't think that would be enough. First off, she was a girl traveling with an adult woman. That was Elsa, my contact in Portugal, by the way, and she can't make the trip too frequently without it becoming suspicious. Plus, Hans is an adult male; he'll be subject to much greater scrutiny. So it probably wouldn't help if he was traveling with Elsa anyway. And, well…" Howard paused and gave Otto a meaningful look. I noticed Otto braced himself for what came next. "We think they're searching for him. The Nazis, that is. We believe Hans escaped from one of their detention camps. He'd have a lot of useful intelligence he could provide the British."

So the Nazis would have their eyes glued to the ports, looking for him. That wasn't good.

"I'm not even sure how we can manage to get him onto a boat in Lisbon, let alone figure out a way to get him into the country here." Howard looked tired. He'd been doing this work for two years. It was beginning to take a toll.

"Can't you send him to America?" I asked.

"Wouldn't that be nice!" Howard said in an exasperated tone. "There's virtually no passenger traffic across the Atlantic now, and the few American-flagged ships making the route are dedicated to repatriating Americans still trying to get out of Europe. Hopefully we can get that to change. Maybe if the US ends up entering the war it will be different, but right now we're worse than the damn Irish about the whole neutrality thing." Howard looked at me. "No offense, James."

"Saints in heaven," said Otto.

Howard glanced at me and raised an eyebrow. I looked at Otto. "We need to talk about that later," I told him.

"It could work too. Even though the US wouldn't take him as a refugee, I imagine I could convince my church to sponsor him. But right now that's just not a path open to us."

We all looked at Hans's picture again. There had to be something we could do. I reached across the table and pulled my coffee mug toward me. I lifted it, sniffed, and took a cautious sip. Disgusting. "Interesting," I said. I looked at Otto to show him I was making an effort about trying new things.

"Give us this afternoon to think, Howard," Otto said. "James and I have become quite good at plotting."

Chapter Thirty-Five

NOVEMBER 1941

"No, Otto. Absolutely not. It's too dangerous."

"And your idea is…?"

"You're right; I don't have one," I acknowledged. "But I won't have you risking yourself that way. We'll think of something else."

Otto was sitting at my desk. After Howard left, we'd been moving about my office all afternoon in a complicated dance, coming together to work cooperatively and then pulling apart to argue. From couch to chair to desk and back. He banged a fist on the desktop.

"But, James! We've been over this. Again and again. There *is* no other way."

"We can't save everyone, Otto." Even as I said that I realized it was selfish and weak. It's just that we'd worked so hard to achieve what we had! To risk it all…then I remembered having that exact conversation with Bella only months ago.

"I know we can't, James. But we can save *him*. I think."

Maybe. But maybe not.

"This could trigger the endgame, you know. We'd have to run." I didn't feel like we'd ever be ready for that. But we were as ready as we could be. I'd bought the cottage last month, a tiny stone thing with holes in the walls for windows and dirt floors, sitting high on a bluff over the Atlantic Ocean on the West Coast. It was private, isolated even, and I'd squirreled away enough dried food there that we could lay low for a while. I had money put aside, and when things blew over, I could afford a flock of sheep.

It wasn't much of a plan, and it had more holes in it than the cottage itself, but it would give us somewhere to go if we had to run. *When* we had to run.

"Yes, I know that. But that was our deal, James. I wouldn't disappear alone, but we would both disappear together once we'd done everything we could do."

And we'd accomplished a lot. For months now we'd been blocking the Nazis—and the IRA's bombing campaign—at every turn.

"If they catch you—" I began.

"Stop," he said. "I know that. That's why we have to be ready to run. I don't want both Hans and me to be sent back to Germany to face…whatever we'd face."

We'd come full circle again. And Otto was right. His was the only plan either of us had come up with that could…*possibly*…work. If I'd been alone, I was fairly sure I would have taken the safe way out and turned a blind eye to Hans's plight. But Otto and I were good together that way. We completed each other, and he gave me the moral courage to support him in his plan. Our plan, now.

"Fine," I said finally. Otto's face lit up. "I'll talk to Liam, and you talk to Howard. But let's be open to what they have to say in case there's something we're missing." I fingered the claddagh pendant hanging beneath my shirt. I was worried for Otto. This was no small crime he'd be committing.

He came around the desk and embraced me in a tight hug.

Bella rubbed the bridge of her nose when I'd finished explaining our plan.

I'd stopped for a Sunday visit with my mother, and after dinner Bella and I had gone for a walk in the complex's courtyard, where we could speak privately. If I had Bella's blessing, I planned on approaching Liam while we were both still at my mother's.

"I need to sit," she said. We took the bench in front of the rose bushes. "I need to think a minute."

I gave her the space she needed and tried to focus on the late-season blooms. Most of the petals had dropped, and the leaves on the bushes were yellowing. But there was still a heady scent of flowers in the air, and a few bees lazily circled behind us.

"It's insane," she concluded. I nodded in agreement. I knew that already.

"But...well...it just *might* work." That's what I thought too.

"You'll come visit us in our little cottage, won't you? Before Howard whisks you off to America?" This suddenly felt like a goodbye to me.

"But what about Ma?" Bella asked. "You can't just abandon her. She relies on us."

"She'll be fine. I'm going to make sure Eamon knows that the business proceeds support her first. She'll be taken care of; I promise."

I could see Bella struggling for a reason to object. But in the end, she found none.

"Oh, Jimmy!" She turned to me and flung her arms around me. "How did our world come to this?" She was crying, and I felt like I might do the same at any moment.

"Shush now," I whispered into her ear. "Aren't you the one always telling me the world is changing? We just need to get through this little rough patch before we can make the world we both deserve."

She choked on a laugh. "I hate it when you throw my words back at me." She offered me a genuine smile as she wiped tears from her cheeks.

Then it was my turn to laugh. "But you know, Annabelle. You were way ahead of me on that. We really *are* remaking the world to suit us. I'm proud of us."

Back upstairs in my mother's flat, I asked Liam if I could stand him a pint at the pub. He agreed.

Two pints later, I was beginning to wear him down.

"But a visa! It's impossible, James. Ireland just isn't issuing visas to German nationals. Even if we could manage to forge one, anyone checking it would know it doesn't make sense."

Otto and I had concocted a background story as to why it just *might* make sense. And it was the part of the plan that could get Otto into the most serious trouble. But I couldn't tell Liam any of that, because my brother had to believe we were smuggling in a German spy.

I pulled out the envelope I'd prepared for him. It included a passport photo, a blank German passport Otto had obtained from the legation office, a few biographic details—height, weight, hair and eye color, hometown—that sort of thing. "We're working on that part. You don't need to be concerned about it. All we need is the completed passport with the visa stamp."

He looked at the documents. "Well, I can try," he said, frowning. "But I don't want to do anything where you guys get caught, and this seems too risky."

It *was* risky. And was that a sense of brotherly concern I was hearing from Liam?

"I mean, we've got a really good setup here. I'm rising in the ranks because of the information you provide me. I'd hate to risk that."

So, no, not brotherly concern at all.

Chapter Thirty-Six

DECEMBER 1941

By early December we were ready to execute our plan.

"But, Howard, are you *sure*? It's just so…risky." Elsa's voice faded in and out over Howard's radio. He and I were in his tiny apartment above the garage, which Howard had kept as a base of operations even after he lost his job as Otto's instructor. He and the other members of his Unitarian Service Committee had decided he shouldn't leave Ireland until he was no longer able to get the intelligence Otto kept feeding him. I knew that time would come, and probably soon.

Howard looked at me. It was the same sentiment he had shared when I first explained Otto's plan. I nodded.

"Yes, Elsa. We've been through it over and over on this end and just can't think of any other options. Unless you can keep him safely there?" That would be best outcome—not to move him at all. To have him wait out the war in Lisbon, like so many refugees seemed to be doing—or trying to do, anyway.

"I wish we could," she said. "But something is going on with this young man, Howard. Not only are the Germans looking for him, but even the Portuguese officials are asking around—they must have come under heavy pressure from the Germans to find him because they usually stay out of this type of thing. He *needs* to leave, and soon."

"Then we'll do it as I described. You'll have the documents he needs by Friday. If you could get him equipped with appropriate travel gear, he could sail on Saturday with a Sunday arrival in Dublin. We think getting him here on a Sunday would improve our chances."

"Right," said Elsa. "I'll do my best to explain the situation to him."

"There's a letter for him from Otto in the package too. We thought seeing it laid out in German might be helpful for Hans."

"Otto sounds like an amazing person," Elsa said. Howard looked at me and nodded. I felt myself tearing up. "I hope to meet him someday."

"You will," said Howard with a certainty I didn't feel at all.

★

Eamon was the final piece of the puzzle I needed to fit into place. We were sitting in my office's wing chairs, with mugs of tea between us. Eamon had wisely turned down my offer of coffee. There was a cold rain falling outside, which threatened to turn into one of the city's rare, sleety snows.

"That's an amazing offer, Jimmy," Eamon said again.

"Well, Michael has been doing a great job, and he's a hard worker. I want to encourage him to stick around."

Eamon nodded. I could see him considering his options. I was offering him and his family a ticket into the middle class, but he'd been around long enough to know to question the source of good fortune. "Just how illegal is it, this thing that you're asking me to do?"

"It's not exactly *illegal*, Eamon. It's just...looking the other way. And only if you have to."

He sighed. I was concerned that I wasn't convincing him, and having him against us would be worse than simply keeping him in the dark and hoping for the best.

"Look," I said. "I know it seems dodgy, and frankly, it is...a little. But you *know* me, Eamon, and you saw firsthand how Otto risked his life to save those people in the North Strand. You know we wouldn't do anything to put Ireland or her people at risk. Just the opposite, in fact."

He nodded. I thought he saw the truth of that.

"But the business, Jimmy. Why would you walk away from that?"

That was a good question. I didn't *want* to walk away. But there was no way to explain it without explaining *everything*. And maybe Eamon could be trusted with the truth, but maybe he couldn't. "It's just for a short time. I might need to go away for a while. I'd appreciate your help in keeping the business going, and I'm happy to share my good fortune with you. You've been good to my family for as long as I can remember." *But Otto doesn't like you*, I thought and didn't say.

"And, Eamon, no matter how long I'm gone, this business takes care of my mother, yeah? She gets paid first, no matter what." I looked him straight in the eye. This part was important.

I let him sit quietly for a minute while he finished his tea. When he put his empty cup on the table, he stood and offered me his hand. As we shook, he said, "I've got your back, Jimmy."

★

Sunday was terrifying.

The ship from Lisbon was due in at ten in the morning, but by evening it still hadn't arrived. It could have been torpedoed or simply delayed. We had no way of knowing. Bella was our lookout. Otto and I didn't want to be seen waiting around the port in case our presence brought unwanted attention. I was waiting in a nearby pub for word from my sister. When she spotted the ship, she would come alert me and then go and collect Otto.

At least it was a clear evening, and we would have plenty of advance warning of the ship's approach. Assuming it arrived at all.

And it did, finally, nearly twelve hours late.

By the time the passengers began disembarking, Otto and Bella and I were waiting by the harbormaster's office. Eamon and another man were seated behind a desk waiting to check documentation.

There were far fewer passengers than I had been expecting. Less than a dozen. I'd been counting on a crowd to help move things along.

But it was easy to pick out Hans.

"There she is!" Otto called out, waving excitedly to the lone young woman in the line. She waved back and smiled. Even knowing what I knew, the subterfuge was so well done it was hard for me to see Hans as anything other than a young lady.

Bella had stepped up next to Eamon, and I was just a foot or two behind.

"That's her," Bella said to Eamon. "The one I told you about. Otto's sister, Ada. I'm so glad the ship finally made it. She must be exhausted." The man next to Eamon frowned, looked first at Bella, then at Eamon, and then back to the young woman next in line.

"Ada!" Otto called out as he stepped toward her, his arms open for a hug.

"Sir!" called the man next to Eamon. "Stand back, please, until everyone has been cleared through."

"Oh, right," Otto apologized. "It's just that I haven't seen her in over two years since she left Dublin with the other families when war broke out."

"Easy, Frank," Eamon said to the man sitting next to him. "She's just a girl."

"A German girl," Frank replied.

Frank and Eamon busied themselves studying the documentation of a man directly ahead of Hans in line. After a moment, Frank ran his finger down a list of names on a paper next to him. He must have found what he was looking for or, more likely, not found his name on a list of prohibited people. "All set," he said and waved the man around the table.

"Papers, please," Eamon said to Hans, who stepped up to the table, placed the small valise he was carrying on the ground, and handed over a package of documents.

"What's all this, then?" Frank asked as he took a letter from Hans.

"My sister is coming to live with my father and—" Otto began.

"I didn't ask you," Frank barked at Otto. He turned and glared at the three of us. "You lot," he said, "back up; give us some space to do our work." We all took a few steps back. "And you," he said, looking at Hans. "Put that bag up here on the table and open it. We'll need to search it."

Hans lifted the small bag onto the table and undid the latches. He turned it toward Frank and opened the top. It looked to me like it contained just a few items of clothing.

I was getting concerned. This wasn't off to a good start. Eamon refused to look at me. Instead, he pointed back toward Otto. "That's the German bloke who saved all those people in the North Stand a few months back," he told Frank.

"I don't care if he's Hitler himself. They shouldn't be crowding us like that." Frank shook the papers in his hand and settled his glasses more firmly on the bridge of his nose. He studied them a moment, then turned to Eamon. "Let me see the passport," he demanded.

"She's just a girl, Frank, and after a long journey at that. Everything seems in order; let's just turn her over to her brother." *Oh no*, I thought. Eamon seemed too eager. Frank must have thought so too.

"You don't say, Eamon? Passport, please." He held his hand out, and Eamon placed the passport in it.

Frank opened it and his eyes widened. He let out a soft whistle. "Would you take a look at this?" He turned it so Eamon could see the open page. "It looks like an actual visa, from our legation office in Berlin! I haven't seen one of these in over a year." He waited to see if Eamon would say anything, but Eamon was at a loss.

Frank turned back to Hans, and his eyes hardened. "What's your story, then, lass?" He poked through the nearly empty valise. "What's going on here?"

"You see, sir—" Otto began.

Frank whipped around. "Last warning, Nazi! Shut your gob."

He couldn't possibly know Otto actually was a Nazi. I pulled back on Otto's arm when I sensed he was about to continue. I heard Bella swallow.

"Good evening, sirs." Hans's voice was soft and convincingly feminine. I wondered how much of that was an act. "I'm Ada Werner," he continued in halting, stilted English. "Please forgive my brother." Hans nodded toward Otto. "My father works at the legation office here, and my mother and I left Dublin when war started with Britain. We're just so excited to see each other again. We didn't think we'd be separated for so long."

"Should've thought of that before you started the shooting, then, right?"

Hans looked down. Eamon said, "Frank."

Frank seemed to realize he'd overstepped. "Go on, then," he said to Hans.

"My mother died last month, and I've come back to live with my father and brother until the war ends."

Frank didn't offer any sympathy, but his tone softened slightly.

"And you managed to get a visa stamp out of the Irish legation? That's highly unlikely, lass."

"Yes, sir, they called it a"—Hans looked up as he sought the words he needed—"a 'compassion exception,' I think. That is a letter from the German legation office explaining the circumstances. I am Mr. Werner's daughter."

Frank picked up the letter again and read it over. I held my breath. This was where it could all fall apart. Otto had written the letter and had made most of it up. We had no idea if there was such a thing as a compassion exception. I was afraid Frank would see through the whole ruse. But I was sure he'd never seen a letter from the legation office before, let alone one trying to explain someone's presence in the country.

Frank didn't look completely suspicious, but he also didn't look convinced. "Well," he said, reaching for the phone on the desk. "Let's just call the legation and let them know you've arrived." I pulled harder on Otto's arm.

"Well, Frank, her brother's right here to collect her and bring her home," Eamon said. "It's late on a Sunday; I don't know that there's a need to bother the diplomats over such a small thing." Frank's hand was resting on the telephone, and he frowned at Eamon. I think Frank *did* become suspicious then.

I nearly jumped out of my skin when the phone rang under Frank's hand, startling all of us. "Who on earth would be calling down here at this hour?" Frank asked.

He picked up the handpiece. "Harbormaster," he shouted into it. His eyes widened as he listened. "Right away," he said. He held the phone away from his face and turned toward the remaining group of men behind Hans awaiting entry clearance. "Any of you blokes American?" he asked.

They all shook their heads no.

Frank turned back to the phone. "Not on the Lisbon run, no." He listened longer, nodding occasionally. "Right," he said.

"This *does* change everything." Then he hung up. He looked at Eamon. "The Japanese just launched a massive attack against the Americans in the Pacific. The Yanks will be in the war now."

Chapter Thirty-Seven

DECEMBER 1941

I was still holding Otto back when Frank explained about the Japanese attack on the Americans. Then, suddenly, I felt him sink, and I found myself holding him up. He knew as well as I did what this meant for the course of the war.

Eamon and Frank looked at each other. "Good God," Eamon said. This was momentous news. The men behind Hans started murmuring. "I imagine they have their hands full at the legation this evening," Eamon said.

Frank blinked, as if he'd forgotten what they'd been doing before the phone call. "What? Oh, right." He looked at Hans and the men in line behind him and reached a quick decision. "Right then, off you go, lass." Hans closed the valise and lifted it off the table. My hands were shaking, but Hans's seemed under control.

Eamon took the documents from Frank and handed them back to Hans, who came around the table and embraced Otto like a long-lost sister would.

★

By then we were acutely aware that we might be under surveillance, and we'd planned the next stage carefully. Otto would accompany Hans back to the Werner residence as he would if Hans actually were his sister. If Irish government spies were tracking Otto and they asked about the young woman, both Eamon and Frank would say that it was one of the diplomat's daughters, coming to live in Dublin after the death of her mother back in Germany. Unfortunately, they'd probably also mention a visa that was never issued and an official legation letter that was never sent. The good news was that Eamon had pulled through there at the end by masterfully slipping the incriminating documents back to Hans.

No, the real problem was that the ship was late. The plan had been for Otto and Hans to return to the Werners' in the daytime, when Mr. Werner would be safely at work, so that anyone watching would see exactly what they would expect—Otto and his sister going home, settling in, awaiting their father's return from the office. But now it was nearing midnight, and Otto and Hans couldn't simply walk in the front door if Mr. Werner was home.

I couldn't be of any help in that, though. If we were being watched, there was no reason for me or Bella to accompany Otto and Ada to their home that late at night. So, as we'd agreed, Bella and I peeled off and headed home. Except instead of accompanying Bella back to the Galway Arches, I set off to find Howard, hoping he was still awake and that he'd heard the news about the Japanese.

As I climbed the stairs to Howard's flat over the garage, I heard him on his radio.

At the top of the steps, I stood outside his door and listened.

"Yes, Werner, first name Ada. If you hear *anything*, please let me know." There was an indistinct, garbled response, then nothing further from Howard.

I knocked softly on the door, and Howard opened it at once. His hair was a mess, sticking out in all directions, and his clothes were disheveled.

"Good *God*, James. It's about time! What's happened? Has he made it safely?" Howard looked over my shoulder, as if there might be German spies climbing the stairs behind me, pulled me all the way into the room, and swiftly shut—and locked—the door.

"Yes, he did," I said, removing my hat and unwrapping my muffler. "But only just. It was a close call. Thank God for the Japanese. It's so late now, though. I don't know how Otto is going to slip him past his father."

Howard had a puzzled look on his face. "Wait. Back up. The Japanese?"

"Oh! You haven't heard, then." And, even though the topic was serious and the stakes were high, I was embarrassingly pleased to have news I could reveal to Howard instead of the other way around for a change. "Right. Seems like your lot are entering the war now. The Japanese attacked an American fleet in the Pacific."

"What?" Howard pointed at the bed. "Sit." He pointed to the open bottle on his desk. "Drink." He picked up the oversized black headphones. "Keep quiet," he said finally and slipped them over his ears.

I sat and drank quietly.

He went to his radio and began sending out calls. Eventually, he connected with whoever he wanted to speak to and, after five or ten minutes, learned what he needed. He signed off and removed his headphones.

"Jesus Christ. What a night!" he exclaimed.

Howard grabbed the bottle and took a huge gulp. "Why are you so late?"

"Well don't go yelling at me. It wasn't my fault the ship was late. I've had buckets of tea, waiting and waiting. Speaking of…" I got up from the bed and stepped behind the curtain in the corner to use his WC. It was a primitive setup, and I remembered thinking the first time I saw it how luxurious it was to have an indoor private toilet.

"Ugh," I called over the stream of my urine gushing into the bowl. "It's like you live in a tenement."

"Could you at least *try* for humility at times, James?"

After I'd returned, I took the bottle from Howard and had another sip.

"But he made it through?" Howard asked again, almost as if he couldn't believe it.

"So far. I don't know how long the stories will stand up if people start asking questions though."

"And did he seem…convincing?"

"Yes!" I replied. And he certainly had. "It was extraordinary. Almost as if he really was a girl. I'd have a hard time picturing what he'd look like as a man. He makes a bonny lass; that's for sure."

"When did you learn about the Japanese?"

"Right there! I thought we were sunk for sure. Frank—the guy checking the documents—had his hand on the phone to call the legation and check on our story. That's when the call came in. Maybe that God of yours does exist after all."

"He certainly works in mysterious ways," agreed Howard. "And Otto? How did he take the news about the Japanese?"

"I don't know. I was holding him back from lashing out at Frank, who'd just called him a Nazi. But then everything started happening really fast." I thought for a moment. "This means the war's all but over, doesn't it?"

"Not at all," Howard replied. "Nothing's ever certain in war. We don't know how it's going to go in Russia or how successful the Japanese will be. But I do think this takes the heat off England for a while, anyway.

"Things will move fast now," Howard said. He walked back to his desk and flipped through one of his notebooks there. "You probably don't know this, but there's already over a thousand US troops in Northern Ireland. They've been building military camps since this summer. It's all very hush-hush since we're not supposed to be there at all. But the US has been reading the tea leaves, and we've been preparing. I imagine US troops will start coming over by the boatload within the month." He paused then and looked up at the ceiling. I could tell he was trying to figure something out. "I wonder..."

"What?" I asked.

Howard pulled his attention back to me.

"Nothing right now. Let me think on it some more."

Chapter Thirty-Eight

DECEMBER 1941

I'd arranged to have my company's linen service show up at the Werners' the next morning, which gave both me and Bella a chance to be there first thing, before Otto left for the legation.

The girls were clearing the bedsheets and gathering up towels, so Otto and I waited in the kitchen. We didn't want to speak too openly while others were in the house.

"Father was away at the legation all night. They were all called in to deal with the Japanese attacks on the Americans. I wasn't around, so I missed the call to work. Thank God." He smiled, but it was a soft, sad one. "I think they mostly hoped the Japanese wouldn't have dragged the Americans into it."

I nodded toward the shed and raised a questioning eyebrow. Otto nodded. So that's where Hans was—in my hideaway. Good. Although I wondered what Howard's plan was for him.

"When can I see you?" I whispered to him.

"I don't know," he whispered back. "Late tonight, maybe? I need to leave for work after everyone leaves. I think things are going to be busy there for me, what with the news about

America. And now there's the question about Howard. Since our two countries will be at war with each other, he can't possibly come here again."

I hadn't thought of that. Howard would be the enemy now as far as the Germans were concerned. I imagined that would complicate whatever his plans were for Hans.

"I'll talk to Howard today and find out what he's thinking," I told Otto. "If you can manage it, come by my office after you're free tonight. Just make sure you're not followed."

"I'll try, but I can't make any promises," Otto said.

Finally, the girls left with the laundry, and Otto locked the shed door behind them. I noticed he'd installed a wooden dead bolt on the outer door as well, and although it wouldn't stop someone from kicking their way in, it would buy time if anyone arrived with a key.

Otto went to the fake wall and rapped softly on it. He said something in German at the same time, and in a moment I saw the wall start to move. Otto helped from our side and soon the wall slid to the side, exposing the narrow space where I'd spent so much time and where Otto and I had perfected our wichsen techniques.

Hans was sitting on the foot of the bed, still dressed as he'd been last night. The room smelled—both of human sweat and of urine. A chamber pot sat on the floor and Otto stepped into the space and picked up. "Be right back," he said and turned to take the pot into the kitchen.

Hans looked up at me. I wasn't sure why I was surprised to see him dressed as a woman still—he obviously wouldn't have had men's clothes in his travel bag. He stood and stepped out of the room. We'd have to buy him clothes. He wouldn't fit in anything of Otto's, or mine for that matter. He was short. Shorter than me even, and slight. He might be able to get away with wearing my trousers if we rolled up the cuffs and pulled a tight belt around him, but my shirts would just puddle on him.

"Thank you," he said. He was quite pretty. There was no other word for it with him dressed as a girl. Even dirty as he was after days of fear and travel, there was something compelling about him. We heard water running in the kitchen. "I was dead," he said. I thought that wasn't just an English language issue; he meant that.

While we waited for Otto, he talked about his trip. His ship had been directed to a British port for a search, which explained the long delay. His English was actually quite bad, and I realized the story he told Frank and Eamon must have been written down for him by Otto, and he'd memorized it before arriving.

Otto came in with a jug of water and a plate of cold food salvaged from the icebox. He took both into the hideaway and placed them on the small dresser there. "I can't be delayed this morning. They're expecting me already." He turned to Hans and started speaking to him in German.

"English, please," he interrupted. "I need to learn." I was struck by the tone of his voice, how feminine it still sounded.

"I'm sorry we don't have time to let you get cleaned up or anything. I have books on learning English I'll leave with you, and the torchlight should last all day. But you need to stay hidden in here. We can't risk you being seen until we know what Howard's plans are." He turned to me. "James, you can't be here either, not alone."

Both Hans and I nodded.

"I'll get the books and the chamber pot."

Otto left, and Hans held out his hand to me. "Thank you, James. I'm Hans."

I took his hand in mine. It felt delicate and small, too vulnerable to actually grasp, so I just held it for a moment, then let it drop.

★

I went back to my office. The streets were filled with an electric buzz; everyone was buying newspapers and telling each other what they knew about the attack on Pearl Harbor—a pretty name for all the devastation wrought there yesterday. I planned on taking care of the day's business and then heading directly to Howard's, but I found him waiting for me in the office when I arrived. The room smelled of his awful coffee.

"I didn't make you coffee," he said.

"Thank you," I replied and set about making a cup of tea.

"Everything okay over there?" he asked. That's how paranoid we'd become. He didn't even want to say "at the Werners'" or ask about Hans specifically. I didn't blame him. The enormity of what we'd done, the fraud we'd committed, on both governments—it was sinking in.

"Everyone's fine. Not very comfortable, though. What's the plan?"

The water was still hot, and the kettle took no time before it began whistling. I poured my tea, then took a seat in the wing chair opposite Howard.

"Well," Howard said, "I was originally thinking we might be able to tuck him away here. But I'm not so sure now. I think I may have been trailed coming here."

"Why would they follow you? *Who* would follow you?" This was all getting to be far too confusing.

"I don't know," he said. "Maybe the IRA or maybe the Irish government. Maybe all Americans are being watched— just to see what happens with the US entering the war." He took a deep drink of his coffee and grimaced. "Or maybe I wasn't followed at all. I jump at shadows now."

I knew the feeling. "Well, we can't leave him where he is." I looked out the window. Any of those men could be watching us.

"I suppose not," Howard conceded. "Though there is a certain poetry to hiding him away from the Nazis right under their noses."

I wasn't in the mood for poetry. "Howard," I warned. "Otto would kill you."

"I know," he agreed. "Could we get him here quietly? I was thinking maybe blended in with the girls as they leave. Maybe Bella could stay behind so if anyone was watching, they'd just see the same number of girls coming and going."

It was clever, but too risky. "That would require Clara or Maggie or one of the others to be in on it. I don't know if we can trust them that far." I thought about it more. "What if it was just me and Bella, though? She could wear a bulky winter coat and a big hat. The two of them are close enough in size that anyone watching probably wouldn't notice. After all, we have no reason to believe anyone even knows Otto's sister is supposed to be there. Eamon won't say anything unless questioned, and Frank doesn't have any reason to tell anyone." I thought that would probably work, but then what? "Would it be safe for him here?"

"It's not safe for him anywhere. At least here he could stay upstairs and not be seen by anyone." Howard had a point, and it was probably the best alternative. A small, petty part of me resented further reducing the time I'd have alone with Otto though.

"I guess that's the best path," I said. "Not today though. Otto was adamant no one should go there if neither of the Werners were home."

"That's smart," agreed Howard. "It would be too risky in case people are watching the house."

"I'm hoping to see Otto tonight. If I do, I'll see if I can arrange for Bella to bring groceries and cook a few meals tomorrow first thing. I'll go, too, so I can accept a turf delivery. Hans and I will leave together and Bella will stay behind. Hopefully no one will notice when she slips out alone. Or if they do, maybe they'll just think they missed her coming back."

Howard finished his coffee. He stood and took his coat from the peg on the wall. "Everything is changing now, James, with the Americans entering the war. We need to be ready to act when we have an opportunity."

I wasn't sure what he meant, but I didn't ask any questions. I had a lot to do and was eager to put my mind to my job and not think about the war or Hans for a while.

Otto did manage to make it that night. He'd stopped at home first to take care of Hans, empty his chamber pot, bring him more food and water. Otto was stressed because he only had fifteen minutes to do all that, having rushed from the office just minutes before his father.

Earlier in the afternoon, I'd bought a secondhand chair for my upstairs quarters. It looked like there might be need for that now. When Otto arrived, I brought him right up, just so no one would see him from outside, although again he swore he hadn't been followed.

Neither of used the chair though. Instead, we both collapsed on the bed, anxious and on edge. "What were we thinking?" Otto complained.

"We did the right thing. *You* did the right thing. We just have to get through this part." He was lying facedown, and I rubbed my hand up and down his back.

He grunted but didn't say anything.

"And we can leave whenever you want. If it gets too much, I mean. The cottage is ready." I hoped we wouldn't have to leave too soon. I wasn't ready to say goodbye to Bella, and Howard, and my mother. Although I supposed I never would be, not entirely.

"We can't exactly flee to the coast and leave Hans hiding in our shed."

I explained about the plan Howard and I had come up with that afternoon, and Otto seemed relieved that he'd have Hans out of the house soon.

"He's an odd bloke," I said, not quite sure how to express what I was thinking. "He's seems comfortable being a girl. I mean, it suits him somehow." I sighed and stopped rubbing Otto's back. I sat up in the bed, crossing my legs in front of me. "That doesn't make any sense. I don't know what I'm saying."

Otto rolled over and propped himself up on an elbow, facing me. "It makes perfect sense, James. I was actually wondering if you'd notice."

"So it isn't me?" I asked. "There really is something off about him?"

Otto raised himself and settled into his own sitting position, mirroring me. He reached forward and took my hands. "Not *off*, James. Just different." He tapped his fingers against my palm. "Do you remember, back when you still weren't willing to think about our future, when I told you about a man I knew back home, older than me?"

I nodded. "The one who told you about men dancing with men in Berlin?"

Otto smiled brightly. "So you *were* paying attention to me! Sometimes I think you don't hear a word I say."

"I always hear you, Otto. I just ignore you sometimes; that's all."

He slapped my arm lightly. "Anyway, he was like that too. Sometimes he wore women's clothes. He liked it."

"He was a molly boy?" I asked.

"Ah," said Otto. I realized I had never told him what that term meant.

"I don't think Eamon thought of you that way, Otto. I think he was just reacting to your being all refined and stuff."

"Oh, James, of *course* he thought of me that way. Thinks of me that way, I should say. I mean, I *am* that way." At my startled look, he added, "No, I don't wear women's clothes, or want to either, but I'm not nearly so obsessed with the whole manliness thing you Irish boys seem so stuck on. I can enjoy being…lighter…than that."

I'd turned deep red again as I thought about the new things Otto wanted us to consider doing in bed. "You'd think after more than two years you wouldn't be able to make me feel so uncomfortable," I stammered.

Otto laughed and fluttered his hands about in an exaggerated way. "Saints in heavens, James! Lighten up a little."

Chapter Thirty-Nine

DECEMBER 1941

The next morning went smoothly. Right up until it didn't.

I'd managed to extract Hans from the Werners' without incident. He and I were walking back to my office. Hans looked perfectly natural in Bella's coat and hat, and he walked in a way that was almost *too* feminine, though even I wasn't sure what I meant by that. I was having a hard time figuring out how I was supposed to think of Hans. At one point, as we crossed a broken curb and made our way around a puddle, he rested his hand on my arm for support, just as a woman would.

When we were safely across the street, he let go, but not before giving an appreciative squeeze of my bicep and saying, "Thank you," in a high, breathy voice. I blushed. *If Clara had been half this skilled, I'd be married by now.*

Why men are so vulnerable to a woman's attentions will always be a mystery to me. But I was enjoying myself and enjoying the flirtation, forgetting momentarily who Hans really was. My high spirits came crashing down, however, when I spotted Liam waiting for me by the door of my shop. And he spotted me too. Spotted us.

"Well, hello, brother," he greeted me, but his eyes were glued to Hans, traveling up and down his length. "And who do we have here?"

Hans stood, shy and demure now, eyes cast slightly down. I took the keys from my pocket. "Liam, this is Ada. Please wait here a moment. I'll be right with you." And without a further word I unlocked the door and escorted Hans inside. I shut the door behind us and noticed Liam craning his neck to get a better look. "That's my brother," I told Hans. "I'm not sure what he wants, but I'll get rid of him as quickly as possible. Go upstairs"—I nodded to the hallway in the back—"and try to be quiet." Once Hans disappeared down the hallway, I waited a minute, then opened the door.

Liam leaned against the doorjamb with a wide grin on his face.

"Come in," I told him. He stepped past me and peered around the room.

"Oh. You sent her away? I wanted to meet her!" He walked to the kettle and picked it up, holding it out to me. "Tea?" he asked.

"Not this morning, no. What do you need, Liam?"

He put the kettle back. "No, no tea, then. I'm proud of you though, Jimmy. I was getting worried about you. I never believed the rumors about your German fellow, but you never did seem to be much of one for the ladies. Even though you've got your fair share of the Brennan good looks."

"What can I do for you, Liam?"

"You *did* read that book I gave you, right? I'd hate to see you doing it all wrong?"

"Right, that's it, then. Don't take your coat off, Liam. You're not staying. Out you go." I walked to the door and began opening it.

"All right! All right!" he said. "You're in a hurry. I get it. She's a looker; that one is. I'd be in a hurry too."

I turned the doorknob.

"But," he continued, "I do need just five minutes of your time. It's about"—he lowered his voice—"our business arrangement."

"Fine," I said. "Sit." I pointed to the wing chair.

"No tea?" he asked again.

"No tea," I confirmed.

He sighed. "Fine. So here's the thing. The Americans joining the war on the British side changes things. Lots of things. Most importantly though, the lads think there's no way Germany can beat England now. The Irish people, damn us all to hell, are going to go full-blown pro-Britain now, and it's been decided that we need to cool off on cozying up to the Germans. They're afraid it'll turn people off to our cause if we're found out."

That made sense. At that stage of the war, after the Belfast Blitz and the "accidental" bombing in Dublin, Irish sentiment had solidified against the Germans. It wouldn't do for the IRA to be seen as Nazi sympathizers.

"What are you saying?" I asked.

"I'm saying our arrangement has to end," said Liam. "We can't be providing you and your German fellow with information anymore or taking more from you, for that matter. We're pausing the campaign against the English for the duration of the war."

"So that's it, then? We're done?"

"Exactly so, like it never happened, yeah?"

"Sure, fine," I said. It was more than fine. I was glad to be done with it. Otto and I might just decide we'd done what we could and head for the countryside sooner rather than later now.

Liam pulled his coat tight around him. "And read that book. You won't be wanting any babies any time soon." And with that, he was gone.

I went up to check on Hans.

He was sitting on the chair I'd brought up, waiting. I imagined he'd been doing a lot of that lately. Before I left that morning, I had laid out some men's clothes Bella had picked up. It was just a couple pairs of drawers, trousers, a shirt and waistcoat, and socks and shoes.

I looked at Hans and remembered what Otto had told me last night. "If you'd prefer to keep the ladies' clothes, we could do that too." I offered.

He smiled at me. "Thank you for asking that. But those on the bed will be fine."

Now that he wasn't wearing Bella's overcoat, it was obvious that he smelled. God knows when he'd last had the opportunity to bathe properly. "There's a shower down the hallway. Do you need anything?"

He stood. "No, I don't need anything," he said as he uncinched the dress's waist, then slid it over his shoulders and down past his hips. It pooled on the floor and Hans stepped out of it. He was wearing a heavy pair of men's drawers underneath, but that's not what caught my eye. I sucked in my breath as I scanned the bruises and cuts covering his limbs and back. He took off the rest of his underclothing, the stockings and drawers and some sort of band that narrowed his waist even further.

He stood before me naked. His buttocks were the worst of it. How he must have been—well, tortured, there could be no other word for it—for the bruises to still be evident weeks afterward, for the cuts to still seem raw.

He turned in a slow circle in front of me. I was speechless and discovered to my surprise I was softly crying.

"I don't want to talk about it. But I needed you to see it, to make it real for someone else too. I'm going to clean myself now. Please, wait downstairs?"

I nodded and left to make tea.

Chapter Forty

DECEMBER 1941

Several weeks passed, and for the first time my mother was able to have a Christmas Day open house, inviting friends, neighbors, and family to share in my family's good fortune. She was the height of respectability now: a widow, whose children had solid jobs and supported her generously, and who was big-hearted enough to open her home to a young woman in need. She even had a phone now! It was sitting on top of a small end table taking pride of place in the parlor. Bella would call me at my office occasionally—I think because I was the only other person we knew who had a telephone.

I chipped in extravagantly to support the day, and my mother set out a lovely spread that would be the talk of the Galway Arches for weeks.

Liam pulled me aside after Christmas dinner.

"I still hear things, Jimmy," he said after inviting me for a walk in the courtyard. He pulled a flask from his waistcoat pocket and took a quick swallow. "And I've heard something you should know."

I braced myself.

"The government boys have their eye on you for sure now." I had a sinking feeling in my stomach, the black pudding I'd had earlier suddenly feeling heavy and thick. "They know you spend a lot of time with your German fellow. A lot of time." He took another sip. "That's all right though. You can a have a friend, can't you? Don't let your guilty conscience reveal too much. But, well, he does seem to spend a lot of time *over-night* at your office. They think that's suspicious."

Sweat broke out on my forehead, immediately chilling my skin in the damp December air. Otto hadn't spent the night with me since Hans took over my bedroom, but we had managed to meet a few times at his father's house. And it was unnerving to know I was under surveillance.

"Now, some say the poor sod just needs a bloke to spend time with. That he needs to get away from that Nazi father of his. And who could blame him?"

Liam looked at me then and squinted at me, like he was trying to study me, to see who I was. "But," he continued, "and here's the worst of it, Jimmy, they've learned something about a run-down cottage you might have bought way out at the end of County Mayo. 'A perfect place to hide,' they called it." He waited for me to say something.

When I remained silent, he asked, "Do you know anything about that, Jimmy?"

I was frozen in place.

"Nah," said Liam. "I didn't think so. But thought you should know anyway, being the good brother I am."

"Thank you," I managed.

"It's nothing." He paused for a moment, then looked me in the eye. "I came up a bit short this month; you wouldn't happen to have an extra ten pounds you could spare, would you?"

★

Shite. Shite, shite, shite. Now what?

They knew about the cottage, so our plans for making a clean escape were ruined. And I knew Otto was near his breaking point, immersed as he was in the daily details of the war.

I met Howard for a pint shortly after New Year's Day. I wanted to unload my own problems on him, but he had a few more to add to my load instead.

"I need to take a detailed statement from Hans. The US government and my church's refugee group both need to know what's going on in Germany. I think my church can help, especially now that the US is in the war."

Poor Hans. I knew this would be difficult for him. And I didn't know if his English was up to the task of providing a detailed statement. I told Howard that.

"That's why we also need Otto. To translate and make sure we have it all correct."

We were in the same pub—the Croaking Frog—where I'd first "confessed" to Howard a couple of years ago. We came back occasionally. It was nice to maintain a routine and enjoy something familiar when all the world was changing around us. We were at the same slick table, and I liked to slide my pint glass toward Howard, watch it surf across the tabletop, watch Howard shrink back as it got close to the edge. I never let it spill on him, though.

"Isn't it dangerous to try to get the four of us together?" I asked. Although, really, *everything* was dangerous now. I couldn't see how any of this could end in anything but disaster.

"Yes, it is," he agreed. I'd told Howard about what Liam had said, so he knew there was nothing Otto and I could do that wasn't at least *possibly* being observed. "But don't forget, there's nothing wrong or illegal about you and Otto spending time together. You've known each other for a couple of years now. You're allowed to have friends, even German ones."

I *did* keep forgetting that. We'd been hiding so much— our relationship, our work with the IRA, our work with the Germans, our work with Howard and the refugees—I'd gotten used to hiding everything. To just *hiding*, all the time.

"Here's my plan. You and me and Otto are going to have a poker night at your place. We'll have the curtains open and the lights on and lots of beer. After several boring hours of card play, Otto will have had too much to drink, and we'll put him to bed on the couch. I'll be stumbling about, too, and in no shape to make my way home, so you and I will close up the shop and head upstairs to crash."

I nodded. That made sense. We were already connected with each other. We knew we were under surveillance. There was nothing wrong with the three of us playing cards. Although it was odd that Otto would meet with his former instructor, especially as their two countries were at war. Still, our options were limited.

"After a bit," Howard continued, "we'll all reconvene upstairs, with the curtains tightly closed, and we'll take Hans's statement. Otto and I will stumble home the next morning."

It was a good plan, and we executed it the following Saturday. It was well after midnight by the time the four of us settled in a rough circle around the bed upstairs. Chairs had been brought up, and Howard placed a stack of notebooks and pens on the bedside table. Howard would be asking the questions, and Otto would be helping with translation, so I became the primary notetaker.

"All right, let's begin," said Howard.

★

We sat in stunned silence.

Otto and Hans were sitting on the side of the bed, embracing and crying softly, mourning what had become of their country.

Hans's testimony had taken three hours, and I was certain there was more he could have added. Every time we went back over something, he was able to reveal some new horror. But Howard said he had more than enough to "put things in motion," whatever that meant.

Hans had even showed us the scars on his back and buttocks. The ones left by the camp guard, the cruel one who liked rough sex with unwilling boys but didn't want anyone to know. The one who removed Hans from the camp some nights and sexually abused him, returning him broken and bruised.

"I killed him," Hans told us. He had a look of wonder on his face, as if he couldn't believe he had it in him. "With my bare hands."

After what the guard had done, I could only be proud of Hans. There was no conflicted morality involved at all.

The story took a long time to tell, with Otto asking for clarification in German, then repeating back to us in English what Hans had said.

The cafés frequented by homosexuals had been closed years earlier, Hans told us, but through intimidation, threats, and torture, one by the one, the names of the patrons had been disclosed. Hans had been one of the last caught up, perhaps because he had a good job at a university. Or maybe it was just luck.

He'd been brought to the prison in a police van, along with a few other men, but he described the crowded livestock cars that arrived frequently, filled with Jewish families. There was an immediate culling of prisoners unable to work upon arrival. "They were sent into big buildings," Hans said, "and then we would smell some sort of chemical, and they would all be dead. Some of us had to remove the bodies. Never me, thank God."

Howard got up and went into the bathroom. We could hear him retching. I didn't think even he knew it had gotten that bad there.

After that, it got harder to tell the story because we were all crying. I was watching Otto and could see him coming to grips with the fact that this was his future, too, if he was ever found out, if he was sent back. Even if Germany won the war, he'd be tortured and killed if they knew he was a homosexual.

After killing the guard outside of the camp one night, Hans made his way to a nearby university where a colleague he knew sheltered him. The next months were a harrowing story of close calls as he was smuggled out of Germany, through occupied France, through Spain, and into Portugal.

I was shocked and more afraid than I'd ever been. We had no escape plan now. The Irish government was suspicious of me; maybe the Germans were too. I felt trapped and was beginning to panic.

I watched Otto and Hans on the bed and began to feel like I was intruding into a private, personal grief. They whispered softly in German; then Otto turned to me. "Hans and I are going to stay up here tonight, if that's all right?"

Howard and I retreated downstairs, where we sat up the rest of the night, trying to plan a future for all of us.

Chapter Forty-One

JANUARY 1942

As hard as it was for Hans to relive his time in the prison camp, I think it helped for him to be able to share the experience with others.

He continued to recover physically and to improve his English. I spent as much time as I could helping with that. Neither of us saw much of Otto. With no information from the IRA and no false intelligence to be created for them to use, Otto and I had little to do. And we were afraid of spending too much time together anyway. We never knew when someone might be watching.

One late afternoon I oversaw an ice delivery to the Werners, and I waited for Otto to come home from the legation. He was surprised but pleased to see me.

"This is perfect," he said, pulling me into an embrace and giving my arse a tight squeeze. "Father will be at the office all evening. It seems like forever since we've been alone."

It had been a long while since we'd enjoyed wichsen time, and I suspected we might be good for two rounds tonight.

Otto nodded at the icebox. "Have something to eat while I take a bath."

I took a long sniff at his neck and flicked him there with my tongue. "Doesn't seem like you need a bath to me," I said.

"Indulge me," he replied as he began stripping off his clothes. "I have a plan." He wriggled his bright gold eyebrows. When he was down to his drawers, he carried the pile of clothes upstairs and returned wearing a blue robe.

I had no idea what that meant about a plan, but I wasn't displeased to eat a cold chicken thigh while watching a naked Otto fill the tub with hot water, then climb in. I remembered the first time I'd seen him in that tub and what had happened afterward. I hoped he didn't plan on taking too long.

He didn't.

"Hans likes you," Otto said after he'd climbed out of the tub and begun to dry off. He had his head bent forward, and all I could see was the towel he was using to rigorously rub his hair. Well, that and the full glory of a wet, glistening Otto.

"What was that?" I asked, thoroughly distracted.

"Hans," Otto repeated. He finished drying his hair and was giving his belly a final swipe with the towel. "He likes you. We talked about you a lot that night." He bent over to dry his calves. "He said he was impressed with how much you were doing for others when you could just be minding your own business. And he was pleased that you could love a German, even after everything. He also thinks you're adorable."

I blushed. "He said that?"

"Well, no," admitted Otto. "*I'm* the one who thinks you're adorable. He called you a *kuschelbar*."

"Do I want to know?"

Otto laughed and slipped on his robe. "Roughly, it means a cuddly bear." He walked over to me. "We talked about a lot of things that night. I told him all about us."

Otto took my hand and pulled me from my chair. The chicken thigh bone clattered onto the plate. "Come on," he said.

"Are we going upstairs?"

"No," Otto replied as he led me toward the shed. "I wasn't sure when we'd be able to do this, and I wanted to be ready in advance."

Well that was…strange. After watching Otto bathe, I was more than ready for round one of wichsen time. But I always got a little nervous when Otto was being cryptic.

We went through the shed, and I removed the false wall to my hiding spot. Otto stepped in first and turned on the torchlight, setting it back on top of the dresser. "I put new batteries in." He sounded nervous for some reason, which was unlike him and unnecessary. This was second nature for us now. There was nothing to worry about.

That's when I saw the other items on top of the dresser. Two stoppered bottles of something liquid. A small hand towel. Oh.

"Do you remember the first time we were together in here?" Otto asked. I sure did. I'd never forget it. "When I showed you new things we could do? With our mouths?" I nodded. "I want to show you something else now," he said.

"Oh, Otto. I don't know. I don't think—"

"You think too much, James. Hans told me all about it. How to do it. How to make sure it doesn't hurt. Or not too much anyway. How to make it feel good."

"Too much?" I squeaked. "I'm not— I don't—"

"Relax, James. You don't have to do anything. It's my bum we're talking about."

"Oh, er…well…"

Otto took my hand. "Listen, James. I really want to do this. And you need to get better about trying new things. So, would you rather have coffee or stick your cock up my bum?"

That was an easy one. "Cock up your bum it is, then."

"I knew you'd see it my way." Otto smiled.

I'd lost a little bit of my enthusiasm, but it was out of nervousness, not lack of interest. We took our time getting ready, and Otto showed me the fluids in the bottles. "Hans told me what to ask for at the chemist's. This smells nice and is good for your skin too." He waved the bottle under my nose. It did have a pleasant aroma, not floral, more like an Indian tea.

Once we were both fully naked, he slicked his fingers with the oil and dribbled some on mine too. It was unexpectedly slippery and thick.

I was on my back in the middle of the tiny mattress, and Otto was using his slick fingers to stroke me, getting ready. "Stop!" I exclaimed. I grabbed his wrist to stop his movements. "Jesus, that feels good. Why haven't we been using that all along? Christ. That was close." We waited a moment until I was under control again.

Otto had been lying on his side, but then he swung one leg across my belly and straddled my chest. If I leaned my head forward, I could have taken him in my mouth, something we'd done often enough, but I resisted the temptation, even though it was *right there*, bobbing in front of my face. I knew he had other plans.

His fingers were busy beneath him, and I didn't want to think too much about what he might be doing. But whatever it was involved *a lot* of oil. It dribbled freely from him onto my belly.

"All right," he whispered. "I'm ready. I think." He started lowering himself. He missed on his first attempt. "Ouch," we both said.

He made it on the second approach, and—sweet Jesus!— it was like a vise! But the slippery oil was doing its job, and suddenly I knew I shouldn't move. One twitch was going to send me over the edge. I gripped the sides of bed and grimaced. Above me, Otto was grimacing for a different reason. His eyes were scrunched closed, and he let out little pained grunts as he lowered himself farther. He stopped once and froze. "I need to breathe," he said. "Don't move."

I grunted to acknowledge him.

He cracked open an eye and looked down at me. "Oh, Jesus Christ, James." He was panting, and a little annoyed too, I thought. "I'm the one who's being skewered. No reason to look like I'm killing you."

He had that part wrong; that was for sure. I clenched my teeth. "Feels…too good. Can't hold back…long."

Otto opened both eyes, and there was a lovely gleam in them I'd never tire of seeing.

"Oh!" he said brightly. He lifted up a fraction, then inched all the way down. "Oh…" he said again. "Don't move."

Right. We both froze in place, breathing heavily.

"Oh," he said again, this time with a note of pleasant surprise. Then he began cautiously moving up and down, the oil providing the necessary lubrication.

"Oh, sweet Jesus!" I said, moving my hips just a little, creating the friction I was suddenly craving.

Otto reached down and grabbed the chain of my claddagh, cinching it tightly around my neck. Very tightly. "Don't you *dare* move! Not yet," he commanded. Then he began to raise and lower himself more freely, developing a rhythm.

I bit my tongue. In my head I repeated the catechism and the stations of the cross. I tried to remember as many saint's days as I could. But it was no use; my release was soon upon me like a freight train. But Otto was writhing above me, too, and shouting unintelligible German words. He exploded right before I did—without even touching himself. I'd never seen anything like it. I heard something splat against the wall behind my head.

Eventually, Otto slid off me and collapsed against my side. We were both gasping for air.

My only thought was *I'll have to thank Hans when I get back.*

"Saints in heaven," Otto said.

Chapter Forty-Two

JANUARY 1942

I *did* thank Hans.

He smiled. "Otto is a persistent man, yes? He gets what he wants?"

"Always," I said.

"That's good." Hans sighed. "I hope you find a future together."

"We will," I insisted. "We just have to build the world we need first. But we're almost there. There's room for you in it too."

"Me? No. I will grow old and die right here above your shop. But it's a nice place. I'm content."

Not if I can help it, I thought. The plan Howard and I had hatched that night when Hans told us his story was hardly foolproof. But I was an expert now at shifting gears after a plan falls through, and I had high hopes that Howard could pull this one off.

For the next few weeks, Otto and I spent as much time as we could together. Sometimes we even shamefully asked Hans to wait in the bathroom while Otto and I explored our new favorite pastime. If I'd had any idea I could make Otto come undone like that, I would have acquiesced to trying it much earlier.

He enjoyed it so much I was almost—*almost*—tempted to try being on the receiving side of things myself. Someday, maybe. But not anytime soon. Maybe I'd try coffee again first.

★

One morning, Howard woke me by knocking on the office door. I had taken to sleeping downstairs on the couch and leaving the bed for Hans. We'd tried sharing—after all, I'd slept in the same bed with my father and Liam for most of my life—but somehow it just seemed…odd. Like sleeping with my sister, although I knew that made no sense.

I stumbled to the door and let Howard in. He looked wild.

"I need cash, James! How much do you have?"

Quite a bit actually; every week I'd tucked more aside in preparation for fleeing to the cottage. Even though the cottage was no longer an option, I was ready to go. If only there was some place *to* go. I didn't want to wait any longer for an emergency to push us out.

"Probably enough. What do you need? *Why* do you need it?"

"I need to bribe a priest. Annabelle and I need to get married today!"

"What! You haven't gotten her in trouble, have you?"

Howard patted my cheek. "It is so *cute* when you get all brotherly like that," he said as he moved into the room toward the kettle and the hot plate. "But you should have some tea before you try to make sense in the morning."

I thought that was a good idea.

"But why today?" I asked once I had my tea in hand and I'd had a chance to think about things.

"Well, tomorrow or the next day would work too, I guess. But the priest she talked to doesn't want to marry us because I'm not Catholic, even though I told her she could raise the children any way she wanted."

"But...married right now! Does Mother know? How about Liam?"

"Oh," Howard said. "Right. I guess tomorrow would be better. Give people some time to prepare."

"Jesus, does *Bella* know?" I exclaimed.

"Of course she does. Although maybe not that we should do it *today*..." He trailed off. "I have more work to do, don't I?" he asked.

"Yes," I agreed. I went to the cabinet and brought down a coffee tin.

"Oh, no thank you. I can't stay."

"Uh...right," I said. "This was one of your empties." I opened the lid and took out a wad of bills. "No self-respecting Irishman would ever steal a coffee tin." I handed him a fair number of bills. "This, and a bottle of whiskey, should be more than enough for any priest."

He snatched it from my hands. "Thanks!" He turned abruptly for the door.

"Howard, wait. You didn't answer my question. Why the rush?"

He was already halfway out the door when he turned his head to answer.

"The troop ships!" he called over his shoulder.

★

Bella and Howard were married the next day in Saint Agatha's by Father Flannery. It was a simple, small family service, and we all gathered afterward in Mother's sitting room at the Galway Arches. Liam was there, as well as Clara and Maggie, but not my German fellow and certainly not the refugee from the Nazi prison camp.

Bella wore a smart, rich green dress with pink trim and a matching broad-brimmed pink hat. She carried white lilies. Pink flowers filled my mother's flat.

After we'd all had a drink or four, Howard asked me if Father Flannery was the one who'd filled my head with "all that wanking nonsense."

When I told him he was, Howard said, "That bastard," and went off for a private word with the priest. The two "men of God" had a heated, whispered confrontation in the corner of the kitchen. Father Flannery turned a bright red, from anger, I assumed, not shame. Bella noticed and came up to me.

"What's that all about?" she asked.

"Sorry," I replied, because it was all my fault at its heart.

"No worries," she said. "He's served his purpose. I don't mind burning some bridges there." She looked at our mother, sitting like a queen in her parlor. Her new tea set gleamed in the light from the window, and tiny cakes sat on delicate plates here and there throughout the room. She couldn't have been happier, I thought.

"You know." Bella turned back to me and lowered her voice into a conspiratorial tone. "We lied to Father Flannery, Howard and I. We have no intention of raising a brood of Catholics in our home." She took my hand. "You and whoever you love will always be most welcome with us."

Chapter Forty-Three

JANUARY 1942

Otto and I spent the night of Bella's wedding at my place. I wondered where Bella and Howard were; crammed into his tiny flat above the garage, I supposed. I realized belatedly I should have offered to rent a room in a nice little hotel for them.

"This is intolerable," Hans complained. His English was improving rapidly. Otto and I had brought back toast and sausages for breakfast. Hans was picking at his, sitting cross-legged on my bed, while Otto and I balanced plates on our knees. "I can't keep spending hours in the bathroom," he continued, "listening to you two carrying on out here. It's...disturbing...and arousing...all at the same time."

"Well," I mumbled as a hot burst of sausage grease exploded in my mouth, reminding me immediately of something else. "It's your fault, after all. If you hadn't told Otto about..." I trailed off. As much as I enjoyed bringing that pleasure to Otto, I still had difficulty *speaking* about it. Naming it.

Otto snickered at my evident discomfort.

"I'm just glad I never told you about the prostate gland," Hans muttered.

"What's that?" Otto perked up. "What gland did you say?"

We were saved from further explanation by the phone ringing in the office downstairs. I left them alone to go answer it, but I heard Otto pressing Hans to elaborate.

I picked up the receiver. "James Brennan Property Management," I said.

"It's me," Howard said.

"Huh. Shouldn't you be in bed with my sister?"

"No time for your witty banter now, my boy. Today's the day. Be ready by five this evening. Meet me at my place then."

So soon. I knew it was coming. And every day we were stuck in this holding pattern increased the risks for Otto and Hans. Still. The enormity of it.

"Put Bella on, would you?"

There was a shuffling noise.

"Good morning!" Bella exclaimed with far too much cheer and contentment for my comfort.

"Right," I said. "Can you and Clara come over here? And maybe bring some clothes too, yeah?" We'd decided earlier there was a small chance that the operators were listening to my calls. We agreed not to be explicit about our plans.

"Clothes? Oh…" she said.

"Right. Traveling clothes, please. And you might want to fill Clara in on the way."

"All right. What time?"

I'd tried to plan all this out already, but I hadn't known the time we'd be leaving. I worked the logistics in my head. "Three," I said.

"We'll be there." Bella hung up.

I looked around my office, but then decided I had no time for nostalgia. I went upstairs to tell the others what we needed to do.

"James!" Otto said when I walked back into the bedroom. They'd cleared the plates away and were both now stretched out on the bed. "I've just learned the most extraordinary thing from Hans. I can't wait to show you—"

"Sorry, Otto," I interrupted. "It's moving day."

I had kept one final secret from Otto. I shouldn't have. God knows we'd done enough damage by keeping things from each other. But I just hadn't been able to bring myself to tell Otto that our plans for the cottage had fallen through. I needed him to remain hopeful. And when Howard and I hatched our new plan, Howard was insistent, for good reason, that I not share it with Otto or Hans. The fewer people who knew our plans the better.

And having learned Hans's story, Howard and I both thought it would be best that Otto not know anything in case he was "questioned" by his Nazi colleagues.

"We're going to the cottage today?" Otto asked, both excitement and fear evident in his voice. Hans was looking back and forth between us. He hadn't been apprised of any plans, only that Howard was working on a better solution for him.

"No. We can't do that right now. It's been compromised."
I didn't look Otto in the eye when I said that, but I saw his
reaction. Anger. Disappointment that I hadn't been honest.

"James—" he began.

"Please," I said. "There's a plan. Trust me." I did look him
in the eye, silently pleading with him. Hans looked uncomfortable.

Otto looked away and sighed. "Fine. But we'll talk about
this later."

Much later, I hoped.

Bella and Clara arrived on time.

"There are some suspicious-looking characters lurking in
a doorway across the street," Bella said by way of greeting.

"Yes, Mrs. Fulman, I know. Ignore them," I said. Bella
blushed and Clara giggled at my use of her married name.

"That's the first time anyone has called me that," Bella
said, a sense of wonder in her voice.

"How does it feel?" I asked.

"Glorious," she responded.

Otto had left about an hour earlier. I told him only that
he'd need to pack a rucksack, nothing suspiciously large, and
meet me at Howard's at four.

Clara was carrying a wrapped bundle. The clothes, I assumed. "Your sister told me what you're doing, Jimmy. I'm
proud of you."

"Thank you, Clara. You'll need to stay here, hidden upstairs for a few hours. Bella told you that, yes?"

"Yes, I've got my sewing with me."

"Good. Lock up tight when you leave. First thing tomorrow, go find Eamon and tell him he's running the show for now, all right? He'll take good care of you and the other girls."

She nodded and reached over to grab Bella's hand.

Less than an hour later Bella, Hans, and I stood in my office. Ready to leave.

Hans had been thrilled to see the dress, even though it was a working maid's outfit, and he blossomed when he put it on. Bella helped with his hair and pinned a delicate, flowered hat in place. He looked lovely. I hoped when we walked out the door, the men across the street wouldn't notice that he was even prettier than the girl who had gone in.

We looked at each other, and Bella cast one final look around the space. "Ready?" I asked.

The door opened and someone stepped in. I turned to see who it was.

"Brennan," said Mr. Werner.

"Miss," he added, nodding to my sister. He cocked an eyebrow at Hans. Then his eyes widened. "Oh," he said. He turned back to me. "Is Otto here?" he asked me.

"No," I answered truthfully but offered nothing further. My heart was pounding. I thought surely everyone could hear it.

"Ladies, could you please step outside for a moment?" Mr. Werner asked. "I need to speak with Mr. Brennan privately." He was carrying a bag, which could easily accommodate a gun. Bella looked at me, silently asking a question. There was nothing we could do at this point. "Go ahead," I said to Bella and Hans. "I'll be out in a moment."

When we were alone, Mr. Werner said, "That's amazing. You wouldn't even know if you didn't…know." So he knew. He looked up at the ceiling as if he could see through it and into my bedroom. "I was hoping Otto would be here."

"He's not, sir."

He nodded. "I've failed my son," he said. "I know that. They're waiting to arrest him at our house." He paused. There was nothing I could say. "The Germans, not the Irish," he clarified. "You know what that would mean now, I take it? If Otto was brought into custody and sent back to Germany?"

I didn't trust myself to speak. I nodded.

"I was hoping to catch him here. But I'm too late. I can only hope he spotted them in time and didn't go in." He ran a hand through his hair, a gesture I'd seen Otto use many times when he was frustrated. "I don't know what your plans are." He held up a hand to forestall my saying anything. "I don't *want* to know."

He held out the bag to me. "Just…give him these, please."

I took the bag. It wasn't sealed, and I looked inside. I notice the framed photographs of Otto's mother and sister that Otto had placed next to the Christmas tree that first year. There was also a small wrapped bundle in the bottom of the bag.

"It's his mother's gold jewelry and her diamonds. We all thought she'd be back by now." He fixed his eyes on the map hanging over my desk. He took several deep breaths. "This all should have been over long ago," he said, more to himself, I thought, than to me.

"This might be enough to help him if it proves necessary," he said.

"I'll leave now," he told me. "Those men outside are your guys, not ours." That was good to know. As far as I knew the Irish were just watching us, but the Germans would pick me up right off the street. He tightened his coat. "Oh, and we know the American is involved somehow. Our men are watching his flat."

Oh no. Otto was going to meet us there in an hour.

"Would it help if I told our people that my son was coming back here to meet you later in the evening?" he asked.

"Yes. Enormously," I replied.

"I will, then," Mr. Werner said as he grabbed the doorknob. Before he opened the door, he turned to me one last time. "I know I don't have the right to ask this of you. But, if you can, take care of my son, Brennan. You're a good man, and Otto needs someone to look out for him." Then he turned and left.

As soon as he did, Bella and Hans stepped back in.

"Are you all right?" Bella asked. Hans was shaking.

"Yes. He's…not all bad." I tucked the bag Mr. Werner had given me into my own rucksack. "Change of plans," I told them. "Go to Howard. Tell him to meet us at Dublin Bay as soon as possible."

Chapter Forty-Four

JANUARY 1942

Of course he was there.

Thank God.

"Otto," I said, coming up next to him. "They're looking for you."

He'd kept his shoes on this time and hadn't gone far into the wet sand. It was low tide, and the salty tang of the bay wrapped around us. I pulled a breath deep into my lungs, infusing myself with my birthplace, not knowing when I might be here again.

Otto did the same. "Every important thing in my life has happened right here," he said.

We stood for a while, looking out at the darkening sea. I silently sent a thank-you to Mrs. Werner for her jewelry and diamonds. And I thanked her for Otto too.

"They were waiting for me," he said. "The entire way home I was developing a list of things I wanted to take, just in case I didn't make it back." He looked down at the sand. "But I couldn't go in. I have nothing."

I put my arms around him. "You have me," I told him. "Always."

We stood like that. All we were doing was waiting now, waiting for Howard, waiting to see if the plan would work.

"Where are we going, James?"

I owed him the truth; I knew I did. But there was still so much risk. The Germans were looking for him. If we were caught, they might let me go, but Otto would be taken away. They'd call it questioning, but I'd seen Hans's scars. I knew what they were capable of.

I could tell him part of the truth, anyway. "We're going to Belfast."

Otto sucked in a breath. "James! No. We can't." He turned to me and grabbed my hands. "I'm German. I can't cross the border. If I did, I'd be treated as an enemy soldier. I'd be sent to a prison camp."

I didn't mention that was probably better than what waited for him here. But he knew that. He was just expressing the hopelessness of the whole situation.

"No, Otto, you *can* go to Belfast. Howard has papers."

"Howard? Why is Howard involved? What's going on?" I couldn't stand it anymore. He sounded so confused and lost.

"Otto, we're war heroes! Howard talked to his church and his government, and he said the work we've done saving refugees, helping Hans escape a death camp, our efforts to sabotage the Nazis, you sacrificing—"

We were interrupted by a car pulling to a stop at the end of the pier. I half expected it to be the Germans, and if it was, I was prepared to make a run for it. We could disappear into the countryside if we had to.

But it was Howard. He leaned out the window and called to us. "Hurry!"

Epilogue

JANUARY 1942

The cold ocean mist clung to me, but the air had stilled, and it wasn't as cold as it had been. It was dark, but there was a half-moon to light our surroundings, and it brightened the ocean waves as the low clouds began to break apart.

I could hear a foghorn in the distance and, perhaps, the rumble of a boat engine. Otto and I looked at each other excitedly. Howard held Bella and pulled the blanket closer around her shoulders. We were crazy to be out here in the cold, waiting as we'd been for hours now.

I felt like we were the only people on earth. It was so empty—this enormous ship. It had been filled with thousands of American soldiers just days ago. Now it held only a few dozen souls.

"There!" I shouted, pointing. And for some reason I took off my cap and started waving it wildly in a circle over my head. Otto did the same, his golden hair, just starting to grow back into curls by then, reflecting the light of the moon.

"Saints in heaven," muttered Hans, who was huddled a few feet behind us in the shelter of a covered hatchway. Otto looked at me and rolled his eyes.

More horns sounded, and a tugboat pulled up alongside us.

Out of the darkness she appeared, solidifying as we got closer. She loomed above us, her torch—a beacon of freedom—was extinguished, as it would be for the remainder of the war. But she welcomed us nonetheless, to a land of freedom and opportunity.

A place for new beginnings.

A place to create a future.

About John Patrick

John Patrick lives in the Berkshire Hills of Massachusetts, where he is supported in his writing by his husband and their terrier, who is convinced he could do battle with the bears that come through the woods on occasion (the terrier, that is, not the husband). John believes that queer characters in fiction should reflect the diversity of their lives—not just their identities, but all of their struggles, challenges, hopes, and loves. Nonetheless, despite all the conflict and drama John imposes on his characters (spoiler alert!), love will always find a way.

Email
John@JohnPatrickAuthor.com

Facebook
www.facebook.com/JohnPatrickAuthor

Website
www.JohnPatrickAuthor.com

Other NineStar books by this author

Paradise Series
Franklin in Paradise

Also from NineStar Press

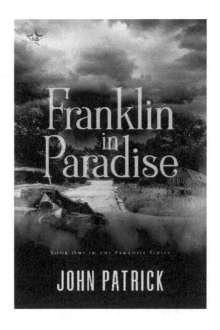

Franklin in Paradise by John Patrick

Life is good for eighteen-year-old Franklin. He lives on the spectrum, structuring and organizing his days, avoiding messy situations and ambiguity. But what he really wants is a boyfriend.

Twenty-one-year-old Patrick has a past he can't seem to shake, and a sexual identity that's hard to describe—or maybe it's just evolving.

When a manmade virus sweeps the globe, killing nearly everyone, the two young men find themselves thrust together, dependent on each other for survival. As they begin to rebuild their world, their feelings for each other deepen. But Franklin needs definition and clarity, and Patrick's identity as asexual—or demisexual, or grey ace?—isn't helping.

These two men will need to look beyond their labels if they are going to find love at the end of the world.

Connect with NineStar Press

www.ninestarpress.com

www.facebook.com/ninestarpress

www.facebook.com/groups/NineStarNiche

www.twitter.com/ninestarpress

www.instagram.com/ninestarpress